Lucretius
Poet and Epicurean

Philip de May

CAMBRIDGE
UNIVERSITY PRESS

CAMBRIDGE UNIVERSITY PRESS
Cambridge, New York, Melbourne, Madrid, Cape Town, Singapore, São Paulo, Delhi

Cambridge University Press
The Edinburgh Building, Cambridge CB2 8RU, UK

www.cambridge.org
Information on this title: www.cambridge.org/9780521721561

First published 2009

Printed in the United Kingdom at the University Press, Cambridge

A catalogue record for this publication is available from the British Library

ISBN 978-0-521-72156-1 paperback

ACKNOWLEDGEMENTS

We are grateful to the following for permission to reproduce copyright photographs:

akg-images/Electa: p. 89; akg-images/Erich Lessing: pp. 23, 75, 110, 135; © Peter Horree/
Alamy: p. 10; The Art Archive/Gianni Dagli Orti: p. 56; The Art Archive/Museo del
Prado Madrid/Gianni Dagli Orti: p. 78; Galleria degli Uffizi, Florence, Italy/Giraudon/
The Bridgeman Art Library: p. 8; Museo Archaeologico. Florence, Italy/The Bridgeman
Art Library: p. 45; © The Trustees of the British Museum: pp. 15 & 112; Reproduction
by permission of the Syndics of the Fitzwilliam Museum, Cambridge: p. 9; Getty Images:
p. 60; HBO/RGA: p. 61; The Metropolitan Museum of Art, Gift of Henry G. Marquand,
1897 (97.22.24). Image © The Metropolitan Museum of Art: p. 41; The Metropolitan
Museum of Art, Rogers Fund, 1903 (03.14.13a-g). Image © The Metropolitan Museum of
Art: p. 93; Foto: Lutz Braun, © 2009/Photo Scala, Florence/BPK, Bildagentur für Kunst
und Geschichte, Berlin: p. 52.

Cover picture: *The Wanderer above the Sea of Fog*, 1818 (oil on canvas) by Caspar David
Friedrich (1774–1840). Hamburger Kunsthalle, Hamburg, Germany/The Bridgeman
Art Library.

Picture Research by Sandie Huskinson-Rolfe of PHOTOSEEKERS.

Contents

Preface

Philosophy is coming back into fashion, even if the cause is the pseudo-religious cults so favoured by Hollywood celebrities. Go to most bookstores and there will be a shelf or two of self-help books, promising you the secret to happiness and offering ten simple steps on the road to contentment. Yet if you want a more rational guide to achieving contentment and not just the latest fad, you need look no further than Lucretius. He set out to explain life and to explain it in a rational and scientific way, but he was not only interested in such knowledge for its own sake: he also wanted it to inform our own lives, to give us some ethical framework for the decisions we all have to make.

What Lucretius was advocating, however, was somewhat out of tune with his time and his message was never going to appeal to many Romans. In the first place, only a minority would have had enough education to be able to understand and appreciate his poem, and that minority consisted of the very men who held political power in Rome and who were unlikely to heed Lucretius' advice to relinquish it. In addition, Romans placed great value on participation in government and on proper respect for the gods, yet Lucretius advocates withdrawal from public life and argues that the gods have nothing to do with our world. As he was writing, Rome was on a mission of global expansion and was accumulating vast wealth in the process, yet he demonstrates that basic human needs are few and cheap and, once those are satisfied, there is little more pleasure to be had in life, even if one has a great deal of money.

Lucretius is also pulled in two directions: his philosophical guru Epicurus had advised against writing in verse, as he felt poetry complicated or obscured what needed to be simple and clear advice about life, but Lucretius himself had a talent for poetry and was also endowed with remarkable powers of observation. In terms of Roman epic poets Lucretius is read much less often than Virgil and Ovid and it is easy to explain why: in his poem there are no heroes or heroines, no villains or monsters, no adventures or romances. The value of his poem lies in his poetic skill, not in the drama or the action of the stories he is telling, for he does not tell any. There is, however, plenty of other action in the poem, plenty of drama of a different kind.

All poetry is notoriously hard to translate. It is always better to read a poem in its original language, but for many students nowadays there is little or no opportunity to learn Latin. Just as Lucretius translated the Greek of Epicurus into Latin because he wanted to introduce the teachings of Epicurus to a wider audience, so I hope that, by translating the Latin of Lucretius into English, I will introduce the work of Lucretius to a wider readership. Of course, Lucretius added his own poetic elegance and artistry to the Epicurean original, whereas

I necessarily detract from the Lucretian original when I render it into English prose, but even so I hope that those who read this volume gain both insight into the content of the poem and some appreciation of Lucretius' artistry. However, I have picked passages representative of the poem as a whole, not just passages which have since become famous.

I would like to acknowledge the great debt I owe to my series editor, Eric Dugdale, whose numerous and helpful suggestions improved my various drafts enormously.

Introduction

Lucretius' goal is simple: he wants to show his readers a way to achieve happiness. By helping them understand how the world works, he will also help them understand how best to live life; this in turn will allow them to achieve contentment and inner peace. Thus the title of his work, *On the Nature of Things* (Latin *De Rerum Natura*), indicates its impressively broad scope, for he chooses as his subject-matter: everything. As if that were not a great enough challenge, he sets it all to verse, for he appreciates the intrinsic attraction of poetry and understands that his readers will be more likely to keep reading if they are enthralled by the artistry of the material.

Lucretius' subject-matter

Lucretius divides his poem into six books. In Book 1, he establishes that the entire universe, infinite though it is, consists of just two fundamental components: atoms and void; in Book 2, he gives more details about the behaviour and properties of those atoms. Taken together, Books 1 and 2 thus look at the world in terms of atoms and their compounds, and show how the world works according to the laws of nature and independently of the gods. In Book 3, he discusses the atomic nature of the mind and the spirit; the book ends with the conclusion that death is nothing to be feared. In Book 4, he treats the processes of thought and sensation: since both are atomic, neither can take place after death. Thus together Books 3 and 4 look at the world in terms of its human inhabitants. In Book 5, he gives an account of how our world was formed and how life on it began, and also how civilization developed: he explains that our earth was formed by chance and was not created for us by a divine being, and that change and progress do not necessarily bring increased happiness. In Book 6, he explains various natural phenomena of the sky, the earth and below ground, and thereby shows that they are not caused by the gods. Books 5 and 6 thus look at the world in terms of earth, planets and sky.

Lucretius' times

Lucretius lived through an age of political upheaval in Rome, upheaval which may well have led him to shun public office and seek a recipe for happiness and inner peace. He lived in a period of Roman history we call the Late Republic: 'Republic' because Rome was ruled by a senate of noblemen but 'Late' because the Republic soon became an empire governed by a single man, the emperor, whose Latin title was *princeps* ('first person') and whose period of power is therefore known as the principate.

Rome, traditionally founded in 753 BC, gradually defeated her neighbours and then the other towns in Italy over a period of several centuries to become the dominant power on the Italian mainland by the middle of the third century BC. This dominance brought her to the attention of the other major Mediterranean power at that time, Carthage, and the two nations clashed. Rome defeated Carthage in a series of wars (known as the Punic wars), and in the process acquired her first province, the island of Sicily. This success led Rome to continue to expand her dominion during the second century BC and she conquered numerous lands around the eastern end of the Mediterranean; these newly acquired territories, in particular the cities of Asia Minor (modern Turkey), brought her great wealth. However, many of the troops involved in these campaigns were levied from subject-towns throughout Italy and these towns did not feel that the fruits of the campaigns were being properly shared out or that they enjoyed equal rights, so they revolted in what is known today as the Social War (91–89 BC). Rome only put down the revolt by granting citizenship to her allies. It was about this time that Lucretius was born.

Rome's political system – based on authority (Latin *imperium*) by election to political office – struggled to cope with administering her ever-increasing empire. The very generals who conquered these wealthy territories turned much of that wealth to their own ends, paying out bonuses to troops who officially owed allegiance to Rome but who often felt stronger ties to their commanders, who themselves then began to claim political power in Rome on the back of that loyalty. Rival generals vied with each other for political supremacy in Rome and the first century BC witnessed major political upheaval during the sometimes bloody transition from Republic to Empire. There were four major civil conflicts in which Roman killed Roman: in the 80s Marius fought Sulla, in the early 40s Caesar fought Pompey, in the late 40s Brutus and Cassius fought Antony and Octavian, in the 30s Octavian fought Antony. When he was a child or possibly in his teens, Lucretius witnessed both the civil war between Marius and Sulla and the political turmoil which followed; he may also have lived to witness the political tension before the civil war between Pompey and Caesar, if not the onset of civil war itself. There are no references to specific contemporary events in the poem, but it is against such a backdrop that Lucretius advocates the idea that the most effective way to achieve inner peace is to withdraw from public affairs.

Lucretius' biography

The poet of the *De Rerum Natura* is a mystery to us, for there is almost no independent evidence about his life. We can be confident that Titus Lucretius Carus lived during the first half of the first century BC, though we do not know the exact dates of his birth or death. The only reliable dated reference is found in a letter from the great orator and politician, Marcus Tullius Cicero, to his brother Quintus (2.10.3), dating to February 54, in which he praises Lucretius' poem for its genius and artistry. Virgil almost certainly alludes to him in *Georgics* 2.490–2 and Ovid (*Amores* 3.15) mentions him by name, while other poets seem to allude to *De Rerum Natura* in their own works by quoting or adapting lines or phrases from the poem. All of this together provides a measure of his influence on his peers and successors.

About Lucretius' social status we must make assumptions based on the poem itself. He appears to know one Gaius Memmius, in all likelihood the senator whose career flourished in the 50s. Lucretius addresses him in the opening lines and states he hopes to claim him as a friend. From the many literary and scientific allusions in the poem, it is fair to assume that Lucretius was one of the educated elite: formal education in general, and poetry in particular, were the preserve of the upper classes, for though many Romans were schooled to read and write, only the well-born and the wealthy continued their education beyond those basic skills and on to rhetoric, philosophy and literature, as well as the learning of Greek.

Literary influences

As part of the expansion of her eastern territories, in 146 BC Rome conquered Greece (which became the province of Achaea). She quickly fell under the spell of Greek culture, learning and art: near the end of the century the poet Horace remarks (*Epistles* 2.1.156) that uncultured Rome, having conquered Greece, was herself conquered by Greek culture. The sons of wealthy Romans began to be sent to Athens to complete their education under the tutelage of the Greek philosophers and rhetoricians, as Cicero himself was, while Greek culture and language became fashionable among the Roman educated elite and some Romans with a strong interest in literature and philosophy began to build up their own collections of the works of the great Greek writers. In 85 Cicero's great friend Pomponius Atticus withdrew from Roman public life and chose Greece as his new home, where he lived a life of commerce and culture, free from the stresses and hazards of Roman politics.

The two epics of Homer, the *Iliad* and *Odyssey*, were so well known and revered that almost all ancient literature seems to have been influenced by them in some way; the *De Rerum Natura* is no different. Lucretius writes in the same hexameter that Homer first used, he echoes Homer's elevated epic diction and he adopts his frequent use of simile. He differs, though, in his world-view and in his approach to the gods: Homer depicts them as interfering in human affairs and displaying human emotions and behaviour, whereas Lucretius rejects such a picture out of hand.

Composing poetry at around the same time as Homer was Hesiod: he too wrote in hexameters, but one of his surviving poems, *Works and Days*, is didactic rather than narrative, giving its audience practical advice on how to run a farm successfully, as well as advice on how to live life, and so Hesiod can be regarded as the founder of a didactic tradition into which the *De Rerum Natura* falls. The ancients did not see philosophy and poetry as mutually exclusive, and in the next few hundred years several philosophers set out their ideas in verse, including Empedocles and Parmenides, both of whose works influenced Lucretius' poem greatly. In the third and second centuries didactic poetry experienced a revival, though poets of that era enjoyed the challenge of setting technical subject-matter to verse more than the chance to offer philosophical guidance. To judge from the *De Rerum Natura*, Lucretius seems to be familiar with both those early didactic poets and their later successors. Romans took up the didactic tradition: Cicero translated a Greek didactic poem on the movement of the stars and the causes of the weather (Aratus' *Phaenomena*) and later in the 30s Virgil himself in his *Georgics* would offer instruction on agriculture, horticulture and other farm-related activities.

It is easy to see from his poem that Lucretius was also well-read in other Greek writing: the tragic and comic dramatists of fifth-century Athens, the fifth-century Athenian historian Thucydides, the epigrams of third-century Greek-speaking Alexandria. In addition, Lucretius was familiar with the earliest works of Latin literature, which was still in its infancy in his own time (especially when compared to the long and rich tradition of the Greeks): the comedies of Plautus and Terence, the epic historical poem of Ennius, the love poetry of Lucretius' own contemporary, Catullus. In all cases Lucretius may echo their style and language but he will pointedly reject their philosophical, religious or mythological content.

Philosophical influences

In the seventh century BC Greeks living in Ionia (in modern Turkey) began to explore natural philosophy and ask questions such as 'What is the world made of?' They came to be known as philosophers – though to modern eyes the question might seem more one of science – and men like Thales and Pythagoras, and later Empedocles and Heraclitus (both mentioned by name in Lucretius' poem), answered that the world is made up of individual elements: some suggested earth, others air or water or fire, or a mixture of these. In the fifth century Leucippus and Democritus suggested the existence of a fundamental unit of matter which could not be divided, the atom. All these philosophers are known by the general term pre-Socratics, for in the fifth century BC Socrates shifted the focus of philosophy from questions of natural philosophy to ethics. He asked about man's place in the world, how we should consequently behave and what the ultimate purpose of life might be. The philosopher Plato recorded and developed many of Socrates' ideas, particularly his thoughts about the immortality of the soul and the nature of justice and good, and Plato's pupil Aristotle did likewise, though he wrote more widely on logic, ethics, physics, metaphysics and biology. However, the philosopher Epicurus (341–270 BC) felt that philosophy should above all provide a guide to life and he founded a school to teach his ideas: it is on Epicurus' teachings that the content of Lucretius' poem is based, though much of the poem's subject-matter had been addressed by those earlier philosophers.

Epicurus was born on the Greek island of Samos, but after some travelling around the Greek-speaking world he moved back to the birthplace of his parents, Athens, where he bought a house and set up a philosophical school, which became known as the 'Garden' because that is where he did his teaching. He also wrote a great deal, but very little has survived down to modern times. Our main source for his work is the biographer Diogenes Laertius (third? century AD), who wrote about the lives and doctrines of the famous philosophers from Thales to Epicurus. Diogenes quotes in full several letters written by Epicurus in response to students who had asked for summaries of the main points of his various works. These are the *Letter to Herodotus*, which summarizes his natural philosophy, the *Letter to Pythocles*, summarizing his ideas on astronomy and meteorology, and his *Letter to Menoecus*, summarizing his moral doctrines. Diogenes also includes a list of philosophical maxims or *Principal Doctrines*. Parts of Epicurus' major work *On Nature* have also survived on charred scrolls salvaged from the excavations at Herculaneum, after being buried in the eruption of Mount Vesuvius in AD 79.

Epicurus held that the purpose of philosophy is to offer a guide to life that will enable people to live a contented and peaceful life. His moral philosophy had the most important role to play in this, but Lucretius bases much of his poem on Epicurus' theories of physics and epistemology (what we can know and how we can know it). For Epicurus' atomic theory formed the starting-point for his moral philosophy: if we are composed of a mixture of atoms and void, then the aim of life or its highest good is to avoid disturbance to those atoms, disturbance which we call pain. He therefore held that the highest good is absence of pain, an absence which he called pleasure. It is from this belief that Epicureanism gained its reputation for luxury and indulgence, though they are far from what Epicurus himself advocated. Not only can pain affect the body but it can also affect the mind, which is itself composed of atoms: according to Epicurus two sources of pain to the mind are fear of what the gods may do to us and fear of punishment after death (and perhaps of death itself). He set out to dispel these fears by two means: first, to persuade his followers that the gods neither have any interest in human affairs nor can they affect them anyway and secondly, that at death the spirit, the mind and the body all break down into their constituent atoms, which then disperse far and wide.

Epicurus' ideas did not die with him. After his death his school in Athens continued to attract students from each new generation in turn. With the influx of Greek culture and learning into Rome, Epicureanism found a new audience. In his poem Lucretius regularly and vociferously acknowledges that he owes the entire philosophical content of the poem to the teachings of Epicurus, whom he worships like a god (see p. 109) and whose teaching he never fails to praise, while at the same time dismissing explicitly or implicitly the teaching of all other philosophers, most particularly the Stoics, adherents of the one philosophical school to rival Epicureanism for popularity at the time Lucretius is writing. He begins each of the poem's six books with praise of Epicurus himself and the brilliance of his teachings.

Poet and Epicurean

Lucretius seems to have been the first to write any philosophical poem in Latin and the first to bring Epicureanism to a Roman audience in poetry; though the philosophy contained in the poem belongs to Epicurus (who himself borrowed ideas from previous Greek philosophers), its expression belongs wholeheartedly to Lucretius, as we can observe if we compare the *Letters* recorded by Diogenes to Lucretius' reworking of the same material. His are the elegance and artistry of the poetry, the teacher's intuitive use of analogy, the smorgasbord of literary allusions, the passionate commitment to the Epicurean cause. By way of comparison, while praising Lucretius' poetry, Cicero also mentions in his letter to Quintus (see pp. 2–3) a poem by one Sallustius based on Empedocles' teaching and says that Quintus is more hero than ordinary mortal if he has read it all the way through. Indeed at times Lucretius seems to contravene Epicurus' recommendation that all philosophy be expressed in simple and unadorned language: one critic called this contradiction 'anti-Lucretius within Lucretius' (French '*anti-Lucrèce chez Lucrèce*', H. Patin *Etudes sur la poésie latine*, 1868). Epicurus devised an all-encompassing philosophical system, but Lucretius' achievement was to coat it all in the 'honey' of the Muses (**1.947**; references to the text in bold refer to passages contained in this volume).

1 The existence of atoms and void

Invocation to Venus

1.1–43   Mother of **Aeneas' line**, pleasure of men and gods, life-giving **Venus**, who beneath the wheeling stars of the sky fills with life both **ship-carrying sea and fruit-bearing land**, through you every species of living creature is conceived and emerges to see the light of the sun. **You, goddess**, it is you the winds flee, the clouds in the sky 5 run from you and your coming. The earth in her artistry sends forth sweet flowers for you, the waters of ocean smile for you and the sky is becalmed and shines resplendent all around. No sooner does the first day of spring show its face and the 10

Aeneas' line   Aeneas, the son of the goddess Venus and the Trojan hero Anchises, was the mythical founder of the Roman people; he escaped Troy's destruction and led a band of survivors to found a new city in Italy. Julius Caesar himself claimed descent from Venus, adopted her as his protectress and invoked her as *Venus Genetrix* (Venus the Mother), a title which Lucretius uses here.

Venus   the Roman goddess of beauty and love here represents the life-force present in the world, the force which urges procreation and so gives life to all creatures. The Greek philosopher Parmenides (*c.* 510–450 BC) opened his philosophical poem with a similar allegory.

ship-carrying sea and fruit-bearing land   though such compound adjectives can sound awkward in English and are not common in Latin either, Greek lends itself to their coining; compare the frequency of compound nouns in German with their infrequency in French and other Romance languages. Sedley suggests that to find two such Greek-sounding compound adjectives in the same line is an indication that Lucretius is imitating an original by the Greek philosophical poet Empedocles (*c.* 492–432 BC), and he goes on to remark (p. 87) that 'Lucretius is the servant of two masters. Epicurus is the founder of his philosophy while Empedocles is the father of his genre. It is the task of Epicurus' first poet to combine the two loyalties.'

You, goddess   both the *Iliad* (1.1–7) and *Odyssey* (1.1–10) open with a short invocation to the Muse of Epic, as does the *Aeneid* (1.1–11); each then provides the briefest of overviews of the action of the poem. Lucretius' extended invocation to a goddess is unique in extant hexameter verse, both for its length and for its direct address of an Olympian goddess rather than one of the Muses, the goddesses who inspired poets. This invocation contains some of the formulaic elements of an ancient prayer: the address to a god, compliments and praise, a list of his or her spheres of influence and a request for favour or help.

The Birth of Venus, c. *1482, by Sandro Botticelli. Compare this to Lucretius' portrayal of Venus: the flowers appearing, the Zephyr blowing, the hint of eroticism.*

life-giving breeze of the **zephyr** blow strong upon its release, than straightway the birds in the sky proclaim you and your arrival, goddess, their hearts invigorated by your power. Then the beasts, both wild and tame, frisk in the rich pastures and ford the fast-flowing streams; so captivated are they by your spell that they follow 15 you eagerly wherever you proceed to lead them. In short, across mountain, rapid river and sea, in luxuriant meadow and bird's leafy home, you drive the allure of love into all hearts and cause each generation eagerly to propagate the next. Only 20 you govern the nature of things: without you nothing springs up into the bright realm of day and nothing can be happy or lovely. So I desire you, goddess, as my companion as I write a poem attempting to set forth **the nature of things** for my 25

---

zephyr the wind from the west that disperses the clouds and brings warmth after winter; it has been released by Aeolus, god of the winds, from its imprisonment in its cave during the winter months.

the nature of things this phrase (Latin *de rerum natura*) provides our name for the poem. Epicurus had written a work with the title *About Natural Science* (Greek *peri physeōs*), on which Lucretius draws heavily for his subject-matter.

A coin minted by Lucius Memmius in 106 BC; the obverse shows the head of Saturn crowned with a laurel wreath; the reverse shows Venus driving a biga *(two-horse chariot) and reads L MEMMI GAL = Lucius Memmius Galeria.*

Memmius, whom you wish to excel in all things and to be honoured at every opportunity. For that reason too, grant my words everlasting appeal, divine one.

Meanwhile, make the **brute business of war** come quietly to rest across all land 30 and sea. For only you can bestow serene peace on mankind, now that warlike

---

Memmius Gaius Memmius (c. 90–c. 48 BC), a contemporary of Lucretius: the only one mentioned in the poem. He is a typical example of a Roman with political ambition: he made important political connections by marrying the daughter of the dictator Sulla (138–78 BC) and then embarked upon a career in politics. In its early stages he spoke against Caesar but was later reconciled with him. He went on to become the governor of the Roman province of Bithynia. (Lucretius' contemporary, the poet Catullus, travelled there too and seems to have taken a violent dislike to him.) He was later found guilty of electoral bribery and went into exile at Athens. Memmius' up-and-down political career, his administrative experience and his fickle political allegiance are typical of politics in first-century Rome: his stressful experiences are just the sort that Lucretius will later (**2.1–19**) recommend be avoided. It is a bold move on Lucretius' part to choose Memmius as the addressee of his poem and his target for conversion to Epicureanism, for he would be unlikely to sympathize with a philosophy that advocated the rejection of political ambition. What is more, Cicero records that Memmius had the opportunity to preserve the remains of Epicurus' house in Athens by organizing the handover of the site to the head of the Epicurean School, but planned instead to put up a building of his own there (*Letters to Friends* 13.1). Venus was featured as 'protectress' on coins minted by Memmius' family, when the minting of Rome's coinage was in the hands of private families who could choose what was stamped on them.

brute business of war Lucretius has already experienced the bloody civil war between the generals Sulla and Marius in the 80s BC and Rome is now on the brink of an equally terrible civil war between the politically ambitious generals Caesar and Pompey – if it has not already started, for the exact years of the poem's composition are unknown.

Mars disarmed by Venus, *1824, by Jacques-Louis David.*

Mars is directing the brute business of battle. At those moments when his incurable **love-wound** overpowers him, he flings himself into your lap: arching his smooth neck as he looks up, staring as he feasts his eyes on you, greedy with love, he lies back with his breath hanging on your lips. Lean down, goddess, and embrace him with your sacred body as he lies there; pour sweet words from your lips and request an untroubled peace for the Romans, sublime goddess. In these harrowing days for my country I cannot go about my work with an untroubled

35

40

Mars the Roman god of war and the supposed father of Rome's founder Romulus. Here he may represent strife, destruction and war, just as Venus did love, creation and peace. The military-minded Romans took pride in their descent from Mars, but here he is pictured at his most unwarlike and in thrall to Venus, who was also a divine ancestor of the Roman race through her son Aeneas.

love-wound Roman religion was polytheistic and its gods were anthropomorphic. Gods and goddesses enjoyed the pleasure of many relationships, both with each other and with mortals, and these relationships feature frequently in Greek and Roman literature. Mars and Venus were traditionally lovers: the story of their affair is told in *Odyssey* 8.255–366. Lucretius' description, reminiscent of the erotic Roman love elegy of the poets Catullus or Ovid, illustrates the difference between ancient and modern Western ideas of what is acceptable in the portrayal of divinity.

mind nor during such times can the illustrious offspring of the Memmii shirk his duty to the common good.

> 1 What clues does Lucretius give in this opening passage to the subject-matter of his poem?
>
> 2 Why do you think Lucretius chooses Venus to represent spring? How does he convey the excitement felt by the natural world at her arrival? You may wish to look at the opening lines of Chaucer's General Prologue to the *Canterbury Tales* to see how a great English poet handles this kind of theme.
>
> 3 What might modern writers cite as their inspiration instead of the Muses?
>
> 4 What do you think tales about a love affair between one god and another say about a religion's view of its gods?
>
> 5 Which has more impact: this passage's upbeat start or its despondent end?
>
> 6 What impression do you get of the style of the poem from its opening lines? How successful is the invocation to Venus in making you want to read on?
>
> 7 Is it clear why Lucretius invokes Venus rather than the conventional Muse?

Praise of Epicurus; the poem's philosophical subject-matter

1.50–158   To continue, then, clear your ears and rid your keen mind of all its cares and give your attention to the true philosophy. Do not scorn the gift which I have prepared for you with unswerving devotion, discarding it before it is understood. I will begin by describing to you the sublime system of the heavens and gods, and I will reveal the primary elements of matter out of which nature creates, grows 55 and sustains all things, and back into which that same nature breaks all things down when they are dead. In giving my account I shall be calling them 'matter' or 'generative particles' or refer to 'seeds' or give them the term 'primary elements' 60 because from these first beginnings come all things that are.

---

the Memmii   that is, both Gaius Memmius' immediate family and their ancestors. Roman aristocrats took great pride in their family name and achievements: busts of militarily or politically successful ancestors adorned the entrance halls of their houses, and masks of their ancestors were carried in the funeral procession for all to see when a family member died. Livy (*Histories* 1.8) tells us that Romulus, the first king of Rome, chose 100 men to be the first senators; they were later known as *patres* or fathers (hence our word 'patrician'). Some families in Rome claimed to trace their line all the way back to these first senators.

the common good   that is, the safety of the Roman state, now threatened by looming civil war and the self-interest of powerful figures. A Roman aristocrat was expected to partake in political life: hence Memmius will not 'shirk his duty'. Unless Venus distracts Mars and civil war is thus avoided, he will not be able to give proper attention to Lucretius' poem.

matter   Lucretius chooses to use this and the other terms he lists rather than the word 'atom' (Greek *atomos*), the nature and behaviour of which form the subject-matter of the first pair of books of his poem. In choosing to avoid the word atom he distances his poem from the theories of the Atomists (see Glossary, p. 152), for he wants his readers to acknowledge Epicureanism alone as the true philosophy; he also makes his poem more Roman by avoiding Greek terms and inventing Latin ones to replace them.

When human life lay ignominiously on the ground for all to see, **crushed by the weight of religion** which reared its head in the broad sky, its ugly face looming down over mankind, **a man from Greece first** dared to raise mortal eyes in 65 defiance and be the first to make a stand. Neither tales of gods nor lightning bolts nor sky's intimidating thunder silenced him; rather, they provoked his keen, brave mind all the more so that he desired to be the first to **break open the tight locks** 70 **on nature's gates.** So it was that the vibrant vigour of his mind gained a victory and he marched out far beyond the world's **flaming ramparts**, and in mind and thought he ranged across the endless universe. On his return as **conqueror** he 75 reports back to us what can come into being and what cannot: that is, the system

---

crushed by the weight of religion   in accordance with the Epicurean doctrine but in more dramatic language than we find in extant Epicurean texts, Lucretius pictures religion as a kind of monster oppressing mankind. By explaining the workings of the universe and our world, and especially by giving an account of natural phenomena, Epicurus hoped to demonstrate that the world exists and functions quite independently of any gods, for he observed how many people lived in fear of what they believed the gods might do to them at any moment; in addition, when they could not explain the workings of nature, they attributed inexplicable phenomena to divine power.

a man from Greece first   Epicurus. Though he is only mentioned by name once (**3.1042**) in the poem, Lucretius opens each of the six books with a eulogy to Epicurus himself or to his teachings, offering prime position to the philosopher whose writings form the basis for the entire poem. Though Epicurus' scientific thinking owed much to his philosophical predecessors (especially the Atomists), Lucretius can justifiably claim that Epicurus was the first to use theories about the world and universe to try to help his fellow men by removing their fears and anxieties.

break open the tight locks on nature's gates   Lucretius borrows the phrasing and imagery of a line from the *Annales* by the Roman writer Ennius (239–169 BC), a poem of which only fragments remain, which recounted Roman history from Aeneas' flight from Troy through to Ennius' own time. Virgil also used the same image at *Aeneid* 7.620–2. Roman poets frequently allude to their literary predecessors: to do so shows the learning of the poet himself, establishes his place in Rome's literary tradition and allows him to use such references as a starting-point from which to take a new direction if he so wishes. Here Lucretius imagines nature as a locked city which Epicurus is besieging in order to discover her secrets.

flaming ramparts   Epicurus held that our world comprises a hollow sphere with the earth in the centre, surrounded by the air, in which the planets move, which is in turn surrounded by the ether in the outermost part of the sphere, the edges of which are permanently aflame and form a kind of wall.

conqueror   Lucretius portrays Epicurus as a victorious general returning in triumph to Rome to give a report about a defeated nation. Over several hundred years Rome had gradually increased her dominion: first she defeated the cities of Italy, then she began to acquire new lands abroad, beginning with the island of Sicily and its independent Greek city-states.

by which there is a limit to what each thing can do, a **boundary-stone** which cannot be moved. So it is the turn of religion to lie crushed underfoot while his victory lifts us up to the heavens.

1	What indications are there in the passage that Memmius may not be a ready listener?
2	How does Lucretius convey his views on religion, his pity for humankind and his admiration for Epicurus in this passage?
3	Why does Lucretius mention that Epicurus was 'the first to make a stand': is there something inherently worthwhile in being the first to do something?
4	Can you find any similarities between Lucretius' praise of Venus at 1.1–43 and this passage?

One thing am I afraid of in these matters: that you might think you are taking 80 up the principles of some **unholy system** and setting down a path of wickedness. Quite the opposite – too often this religion has given birth to deeds both criminal and unholy. Just so at Aulis did the chosen commanders of the Danaans, the pick of the heroes, foully stain the altar of the **virgin goddess of the crossroads** with 85 **the blood of Iphianassa**.

---

boundary-stone (Latin *terminus*) the ancients marked property lines, such as those between the fields of one farmer and those of another, with stone markers, monoliths or cairns. Many statues of gods served the function of guarding property lines; the Roman god Terminus personified and protected these boundary markers. Lucretius employs touches like this, the address to Memmius and allusion to Ennius, to help Romanize the poem and thereby set the reader at ease, as he prepares to expound the unfamiliar ideas of Epicurean philosophy.

unholy system   philosophy had clashed with religion in the past: Socrates (469–399 BC) was accused of impiety and put to death, while misconceptions about the Pythagoreans too led to their being marginalized in the fifth century. In defending the record of Epicureanism, Lucretius goes on the attack against religion, challenging its core claim of holiness with what seems almost an oxymoron: the claim that religion can be unholy.

virgin goddess of the crossroads   Diana (Greek Artemis), goddess of chastity, the woods and the moon. More commonly the crossroads are identified with Hecate, an underworld goddess associated with magic and closely connected to Diana.

the blood of Iphianassa   the Greeks (Danaans) assembled at Aulis to sail for Troy in their quest to retrieve Helen (who had eloped with the Trojan prince Paris), but in the absence of a favourable wind remained stuck in the harbour. The soothsayer Calchas explained that Artemis was angry at the Greeks and required the sacrifice of king Agamemnon's daughter Iphianassa (more commonly called Iphigeneia) before she would grant a favourable wind to allow the departure of the fleet. Agamemnon sent for her on the pretext that she would marry the hero Achilles, but when she reached the altar she was sacrificed instead. This pitiful tale forms the subject-matter of the Chorus' first song in Aeschylus' tragedy *Agamemnon* and the whole of Euripides' tragedy *Iphigeneia at Aulis*.

As soon as the **woollen band** encircling her virgin hair streamed down each cheek in equal lengths, as soon as she noticed her father was standing sorrowfully at the altar, that near him attendants were hiding knives and that her countrymen were weeping profusely at the sight of her, silent from shock she sank to her knees and slumped to the ground. At such a time it was no use to the **hapless girl** that she had been the first to give the name 'father' to the king. Snatched up in men's hands she was conveyed trembling to the altar, not to be accompanied by a loud cheer of 'Hymen' as the solemn and sacred ritual was completed, but to slump down at the very moment of being wed, pure in the midst of impurity, a sorrowful victim slain by her father, so that a **successful and auspicious** outcome might be granted to the fleet. Such terrible acts could religion lead men to commit.

> - 'Such terrible acts could religion lead men to commit' became a famous line and a rallying-cry for atheists down the ages. Would you agree that religion has led men to commit terrible acts?

You yourself may at some point be won over again by the dire-sounding warnings of the holy men and will then look to desert me. Indeed, what numerous fancies they are conjuring up for you at this very moment, which could undermine your life's principles and confound all your fortunes with fears – and with good reason.

woollen band   brides did wear a band (the *vitta*) around their heads, but the word Lucretius uses here (*infula*) describes the band put round the head of a sacrificial animal. However, Iphianassa's sacrifice is forced on her against her will and is at odds with Roman religious practice, since the Romans entertained the conceit that the sacrificial animal should nod its assent before being slaughtered. Throughout lines 84–101 Lucretius interweaves the language of sacrifice and wedding. For example, at a Roman wedding it was the custom for the bride to be symbolically pulled away from her mother's embrace ('snatched up in men's hands'), for the newly-weds to be 'conveyed' by wagon to the groom's house and accompanied by the marriage-song of Hymen, the Greek god of marriage (this song features in poem 61 by Lucretius' contemporary Catullus); there was also a sacrifice at the marriage ceremony itself, so that Iphianassa might have expected to see one attendant holding a knife, but not all of them doing so and trying to hide them.

hapless girl   the sacrifice is now related from the standpoint of Iphianassa; other accounts emphasized the terrible tragic choice which her father faced (this comes to the fore in Aeschylus' *Agamemnon* and in Electra's defence of her father's actions in Sophocles' *Electra*). However, in this case it is important for Lucretius' argument that there be no redeeming aspect to this act, and in his moving description of the tableau, filled as it is with pathos, he succeeds in demonstrating that all those involved suffer (not only Iphianassa herself, but also her father and his accomplices).

successful and auspicious   a formula from Roman divination, which Lucretius uses in pointed contrast to the tragic event it describes, perhaps in order to undermine the credibility of religion.

A vase-painting of the Trojan princess Polyxena being sacrificed in a manner similar to Iphianassa; black-figure Tyrrhenian amphora, 570 BC.

Yet, if people could see that there was a definite endpoint to their troubles, they would have some rational basis to take a firm stand against the terrors of religion and the warnings of the holy men. But, as it is, they have no strategy for resisting nor 110 the means to do so, since they must fear **eternal punishment after death**. For they do not know what the nature of the spirit is: whether it undergoes birth or whether instead it slips in as we are being born; likewise, whether it is broken down at death and perishes with us or whether it visits Orcus' darkness and desolate swamps or 115 whether it can slip into another animal by the gods' doing, as **our Ennius** sang.

---

eternal punishment after death   fear of this and the fear of the gods mentioned earlier are the two supreme fears which impair our experience of life, and the aim of Epicureanism and consequently of Lucretius' poem is to dispel them both. If Lucretius can demonstrate that both the spirit and the mind come into being and cease to exist when we do, then we will fear neither punishment after death nor, he hopes, death itself. Most Greeks and Romans held that after death, though the body decomposed, the spirit descended to the underworld. There were several names for the underworld: some began as the name of a god of the dead (Hades, Tartarus and Orcus – the last being a specifically Roman name) but came to signify the place too; others were features of the underworld (the rivers Styx and Acheron) or its entrance (Lake Avernus).

our Ennius   after borrowing from Ennius at 70–1 Lucretius now mentions the great author by name. Ennius was from southern Italy and knew both Latin and Greek. He wrote a wide variety of works in Latin, including comedies and tragedies, as well as the aforementioned epic poem, *Annales*. He was considered by the Romans to be the father of Latin epic poetry because he was the first to write in Latin, though he kept the metre of all Greek epic, the dactylic hexameter. Ennius believed in the transmigration of the spirit at death: in *Annales* he claimed that Homer had revealed to him that his (Ennius') spirit had previously resided in the body of a peacock, in the body of Homer himself and in that of Pythagoras, who also believed in transmigration.

He was the first to carry an eternal wreath down from lovely **Helicon** and so to win bright fame among the peoples of Italy. Yet even he, while pronouncing his immortal verses, asserts that Acheron does exist, though neither our spirits nor our bodies abide there, but rather a kind of likeness, amazingly pale. He relates how the image of **Homer**, forever in his prime, ascended from there and began to shed salt tears and to reveal the nature of things through his words. This forces me to give **a proper explanation** of what happens in the skies, by what system the sun and moon follow their paths, and the power by which everything on earth occurs. Then, most importantly, we must use astute reasoning to discover the origins of the spirit and the nature of the mind, what it is that appears to us when we are awake but our minds are sick, or again when we are buried in sleep, so that in front of us we seem to see and hear **those who have met death** and whose bones are embraced by the earth.

The difficulties of elucidating the opaque discoveries of the Greeks in a poem in Latin do not escape my notice, especially as many require **a new vocabulary** when dealing with them because of the poverty of our language and the originality of the

120

125

130

135

Helicon   a mountain in mainland Greece where the Muses were said to live and where Ennius claimed his vision of Homer appeared to him. To make a metaphorical wreath out of flowers picked on Mount Helicon is to succeed in writing great poetry: Lucretius himself expresses his hopes of doing the same at 4.3–4.

Homer   to the Greeks Homer, poet of the *Iliad* and *Odyssey*, was not just the greatest poet but also a source of much knowledge, hence he might reveal 'the nature of things'; to the Romans the former judgement still held true, but by Lucretius' time science and philosophy had advanced to such a degree that the latter might not have done. To Ennius Homer remains in his prime because his reputation and his spirit are both immortal.

a proper explanation   these lines give a preview of some of the content of the rest of the poem: Lucretius will explain 'what happens in the skies' in Book 6, 'the nature of the mind' in Book 3 and 'what it is that appears to us' in Book 4.

those who have met death   Epicurus realized that people see images of the dead in their dreams or, if they are sick, even while awake, and that such visions are one cause of the belief in an afterlife. He aimed to provide a rational explanation for how these visions come about and thereby to rid us of that belief.

a new vocabulary   'Lucretius like his contemporary Cicero was preoccupied with the task of presenting Greek philosophy in Latin' remarks Tatum (p. 136). Lucretius, however, does import technical Greek terms when it suits him to do so, such as *homoiomeria* (a condition whereby the parts of a thing are like each other and like the whole) at 1.830. He may wish to show off his virtuosity as a poet by devising new terms, but he may also wish to distance his poem from the theories associated with the philosophers who devised the original ones. Three times in his poem Lucretius complains about the poverty of the Latin language (here, 1.832, 3.260); however, Kenney (*CCL* p. 97) feels that this is 'not an apology but an implicit boast' of his own powers of invention. *Physics*, *atoms* and *theory* are all Greek scientific terms still used by us today and we too import technical philosophical vocabulary along with its subject-matter: there are no English words for *karma* or *nirvana*, for example.

subject-matter. Nevertheless, your upright character and the pleasure of the sweet 140
friendship that I hope to have with you convince me to carry out my task and lead
me to remain awake through the quiet nights, looking for the words and above all
the poetry which will enable me to hold up a shining light before your mind, to
enable you to see right through into matters which are hidden. 145

Well, what we need to scatter the terrifying darkness of the mind are not the sun's
rays or the day's bright light but an understanding of nature's outward form and
inner workings. As a fundamental principle of this I will take as my starting-point
the following: **no thing is ever created out of nothing** by the gods. For indeed I see 150
how firmly fear takes hold of all mortals when they see many things happening in
the sky and on land for which they cannot give any rational explanation and which
they think are caused by divine powers. Therefore, when we have seen that there
is no possibility that a thing be created out of nothing, we will then have a clearer 155
insight into the object of our search: the possible origins of each individual thing
and the way each thing comes into being quite independently of the gods.

---

1 Do religious figures utter 'warnings' nowadays? If they do, what are they
warning their followers about?

2 Do you think people would be less afraid of death if they were certain that
there is no afterlife? How might that knowledge affect their conduct in life?
Is eternal punishment the only fear people might have about the afterlife?

3 Lucretius has mentioned Homer and Ennius and so established the literary
(but not philosophical) tradition of which he wishes to be a part. Does
it lessen the value of a work of literature if it echoes earlier ones? Is it
necessary or important for an author to be aware of previous literature?

4 How many words associated with vision, light and darkness can you find in
136–58? Why do you think Lucretius uses so many?

5 'Looking for the words and above all the poetry' – what is it about science
or philosophy that means they have rarely been the subject-matter of a
poem? Can you find any examples of a poem with scientific subject-matter
that was not written in antiquity?

6 Scientists in modern times have coined words such as 'proton' and 'quark'
for new discoveries. How are such terms decided upon nowadays?

---

friendship   this was held by Epicurus to be one of life's pleasures, and to contemplate the
world in the company of friends was one of the greatest pleasures available to the mind,
though he did also put forward a practical benefit of friendship, that it affords protection
in times of trouble. He wrote: 'Of the things which wisdom provides for the blessedness of
one's whole life, by far the greatest is the possession of friendship' (*Principal Doctrines* 27).
Lucretius hopes to be a friend to Memmius, though we do not know whether his hopes
were ever realized.

no thing is ever created out of nothing   if Lucretius can establish this Epicurean principle,
then he will have shown that the universe is controlled by laws of physics rather than
divine whim and that the gods are therefore not to be feared. It forms a parallel with the
principle that 'no thing can ever be reduced to nothing' (1.215–16).

Lucretius argues that if a thing could be born from nothing, no thing would need a specific seed but anything could be born from anything. This would lead to some ludicrous hybrids, whereas in fact we see that things are only born from fixed seeds according to fixed laws. What is more, nature breaks things down into their constituent atoms rather than destroying them completely; if she did not, there would not be sufficient atoms to make new things and all things would disappear over time. Such is the cycle of being: nature supplies matter for the creation and growth of new things from matter released upon the decay and destruction of old ones.

The existence of invisible matter and of void

1.265–369   Well then, since I have shown that no thing can be created out of nothing and likewise that no thing once created can be reduced to nothing, so that **you do not begin to doubt** what I have said, on the grounds that primary elements are not visible to the eye, consider other matter which you **yourself will have to admit** does exist in the world and yet cannot be seen. First of all: a powerful wind, once   270 roused to full force, will scourge the sea, overwhelm mighty ships and scatter the clouds. At times it will tear along in a ravenous tornado, strewing mighty trees across the plains and tormenting the mountain-tops with tree-cracking blasts: 275 such is the wind's fury, bellowing loudly, and such is its savagery, growling with menace. So wind does undoubtedly consist of invisible bodies which sweep over the sea, the land and, of course, the clouds in the sky, tormenting and snatching them up in a sudden tornado.

you do not begin to doubt   Lucretius has explained that all things are fundamentally made up of the same primary elements: these are the bodies which Democritus and Leucippus called atoms (Greek *atomos* means uncuttable). Yet, like any good teacher, he anticipates potential objections to an unfamiliar idea: here, that things which are too small to be seen cannot be corporeal, i.e. cannot have physical form. To convince his reader, he chooses a simple and helpful analogy from the natural world – wind. No one can see wind itself, but we can see its devastating physical power, as described here by Lucretius in vivid and dramatic language.

you yourself will have to admit   a phrase of the sort used in a Roman lawcourt. The prosecution would speak first and then the defence; the former would therefore often try to anticipate and deal with arguments likely to be put forward by the latter, just as Lucretius does here. Roman boys from wealthy families finished their education under the tuition of a *rhetor*, a teacher (often Greek) who trained them in the art of public speaking, crucial to success in the courts and the Senate.

These bodies flow out to create destruction **in the same way** that water, placid by 280
nature, suddenly swells after heavy rains into a rushing torrent and pours down
from the heights of the mountains in full spate. It smashes whole trees and forest
debris into each other and sturdy bridges cannot endure the sudden force of its 285
coursing waters. With powerful force the surge of seething storm-water rushes at
the bridge's supports; with a great roar it carries out its destruction as it rolls great
boulders under its surface and overwhelms whatever stands in the way of its flood.
Blasts of wind must be borne along in the same way and when they charge in a 290
particular direction like a powerful torrent, they propel objects forward and then
overwhelm them with repeated onslaught; sometimes they snatch objects up in
their spinning tornado and swiftly carry them off, whirling and twisting. So it needs
repeating that wind is composed of invisible bodies, given that its behaviour and 295
effects evidently rival those of a mighty river, whose body is manifest.

Next after that, we sense the different smells of things yet we never see them as
they come towards our nose; we cannot see sweltering heat; we cannot latch onto 300
the cold with our eyes; it is not our practice to see sounds. Nevertheless, it must
be the nature of all of them to have physical form, since they are able to **strike the
senses**. For unless it is corporeal, nothing can touch or be touched. Again, clothes
are hung up on the wave-beaten shore and grow wet: those same clothes, spread 305
out in the sun, grow dry. Yet we do not see how the moisture of the water sinks
in or again how it escapes in the heat, so the moisture must be dispersed into tiny
particles which the eyes have no way to see. There is yet more: over many years of 310
the journeying sun, the underneath of the **ring** on one's finger thins out from being

---

in the same way we can see the body of a river and observe its behaviour and its
destructive power; we observe the similar behaviour and destructive power of the wind
and should conclude that it too has body, though that is invisible. While Epicurus will
state a scientific point, such as the existence of atoms, in quite matter-of-fact terms, it is
typical of Lucretius that he tries to help his readers by illustrating it with a powerful and
evocative simile; he is both inspired teacher and great poet in the tradition of Homer,
who made frequent use of similes drawn from the familiar and natural world to illustrate
events in his narrative.

strike the senses Epicurus is a materialist: if we smell cheese, for example, it is because
minuscule bodies of cheese have left to travel through the air to strike the sense organs
in our nose. We do not see the invisible bodies but the fact that we perceive them in
other ways is proof of their existence, for 'nothing can touch or be touched' unless it has
physical form. Lucretius devotes Book 4 to an explanation of the process of sensation,
treating smell at **4.673–705**.

ring as well as being worn as an ornament by a woman, a ring might also be worn by the
head of a Roman family, who would wear a ring in which was set a gemstone engraved
with the family emblem. He would seal letters by applying a blob of wax and then making
an impression of his ring into it, or sign a document in the same way. When he died, the
ring passed to his heir and this pattern was repeated down the generations.

The existence of atoms and void **19**

worn; falling drips of water hollow out stone, the iron of a curved ploughshare shrinks in the fields; we notice that the paved stones in the road are worn away by 315 the feet of the crowd, while bronze statues near the city-gates display right hands that are being worn down by the touch of people repeatedly greeting them as they pass by. So we see these objects become smaller because they have been worn away. However, the grudging nature of our sight blocks out the spectacle of the atoms 320 leaving at any one time.

Finally, however much we strain our eyes, we cannot perceive whatever matter time and nature have gradually added to things, coaxing them to grow up to their limits. Nor, indeed, can you see what is being lost at a particular moment either by 325 the rocks which overhang the sea and are eaten away by the corrosive salt, or by anything which grows old with time and decay. So, nature acts through invisible matter.

However, it is not the case that objects are hemmed in on all sides and packed close together: **void exists** in the world too. Knowing this will help you in many contexts; 330 it will also prevent erroneous doubt, ceaseless questioning about the universe, and misgivings about what I say. So, intangible space exists, empty and void. **If it did not**, nothing would have the means to be able to move. For it is the nature of each 335 solid object to stand in the way and form an obstacle – this principle applies to all objects all the time – and in that case it would be impossible for anything to move forwards, since nothing could allow an object to begin doing so by moving aside. Yet across land and sea and lofty sky we see with our own eyes many things moving 340 in different ways for a variety of reasons: but if there were no void, these would not so much be robbed and bereft of their harried motions but rather would not have had the means ever to have been born at all, since on all sides matter would be 345 packed close together and immobile.

Indeed, however solid some things may be believed to be, you will nevertheless understand from the following that they contain void. In caves, beads of dripping water seep through the rock and everything weeps with drops aplenty. Food distributes itself down the entire length of the bodies of living creatures. Trees grow 350 and in season bring forth fruit because nourishment is passed right down into their every part, from the lowest roots through to their trunks and along every branch. Noises pass through walls and fly through the closed rooms of a house. Freezing

---

void exists   the only component of the Epicurean universe other than the atom is void. Lucretius uses the term void in two ways: sometimes he means the void we call 'space', i.e. what lies beyond our atmosphere; otherwise he means the void or space between the atoms inside an object.

If it did not   Epicurus argued that void must exist if objects are to move; others were not so sure. Parmenides, for example, argued in his theory of 'unity' that our world is composed of just one substance, which he called *what is,* and so he denied the existence of void, arguing that space is *what is not* and that *what is not* cannot exist. At 1.370–97 Lucretius rejects any theory which explains motion without reference to the existence of void.

cold reaches right to one's bones. However, if there were no void through which 355
the primary elements in each case could pass, you would not observe any of this
happening to the least degree.

Again, why do we observe that one thing weighs more than another, when its
size is no bigger at all? For if there is as much matter in a ball of wool as a ball 360
of lead, **their weight will be the same**, since it is the **function of matter** to press
everything downwards, whereas the nature of void is to be permanently without
weight. Therefore, because it is of equal size but we observe it to be lighter, the ball
of wool declares that it contains more void, whereas the heavier one on the other 365
hand testifies that it comprises more matter and that it contains much less void.
So undoubtedly there does exist mixed into things what we are searching for with
astute reasoning – that which we call void.

---

1   Wind and water both cause erosion and may both be harnessed as an energy
    source. Can you think of any other properties that they share?
2   In this passage Lucretius provides analogies from the visible world to help the
    reader understand the existence of invisible bodies. What are the advantages
    of this approach? Do modern textbooks make much use of such analogies?
3   How does Lucretius make his analogies engaging?
4   Can you think of statues or stones today which have become worn from
    being touched by travellers or pilgrims?

---

their weight will be the same   Romans would have seen this principle at work in their
markets. Customers who wished to check whether they were being cheated by an
unscrupulous merchant could take along the purported weight of grain, fruit etc. to a
public official nearby, who held the standard measure of various weights, known as the
mensa ponderaria.

function of matter   Epicurus observed that all objects naturally and automatically fall
downwards unless they are prevented from doing so; he concluded that all atoms by their
nature tend to fall downwards (**1.984–91**), so the more matter an object contains, the
greater the downward force it will exert and so the more it will weigh.

So undoubtedly   the preceding 40 lines offer a good example of Lucretius' didactic
technique. He begins by stating his proposition and tries to head off any counter-
argument or refute previously suggested theories. He then provides some familiar and
incontestable examples from the everyday world and makes a reasoned deduction from
them in language which allows the reader little opportunity to disagree. Finally, he rounds
the passage off by reiterating his original proposition. He wishes to explain Epicureanism
rather than simply state it, for he knows that if he is to succeed in his aim of converting his
readers, he will need to convince them by argument. Lucretius' poem fits into a tradition
of didactic poetry which began in the eighth century BC with Hesiod's *Works and Days*,
a poem giving instructions on how to run a farm, and continued for about two hundred
years. The tradition underwent a revival in the third century BC, when poets vied to show
off their poetic skill by rendering the most technical instruction into verse; for example,
Nikander (second century) wrote a poem about poisonous wild animals and another about
mineral and botanical poisons and their antidotes.

1.370–482

Lucretius dismisses those who claim void does not exist with an appeal to reason: how could anything move if there is no space for it to move into? He suggests that those of astute mind will have grasped his point by now and warns Memmius that it is time to press on, for there is yet much material to explain and they do not want to grow old before he has finished his poem. He reiterates that there exist only atoms and void: the universe has no third component. Whatever exists is either corporeal and therefore to some degree able to touch and be touched, or is void and so not able to do either.

The permanence of the atom

1.483–502 Furthermore, some things are made up of atoms, others of a compound of atoms. However, no force can destroy the atoms themselves: their **absolute solidity** 485 means they are **invincible** to the end. And yet it seems hard to believe that there exists in our world something which is absolutely solid. Thunder from heaven will pass through the walls of our houses, as will shouts and other sounds; iron 490 will glow white in fire; rocks will shatter under a fierce, scorching heat; not only will a gold bar soften and melt when it is heated, flames will overpower even the frozen stiffness of **bronze** and turn it to liquid. Heat will permeate silver and so

---

absolute solidity   i.e. they contain no void. Lucretius provides a list of familiar examples to remind his readers that even objects which look solid to the eye are obviously not, as experience shows. It is a fundamental tenet of Atomism that the atoms themselves contain no void and can never be destroyed, but undergo a permanent cycle of bonding together to form an object and then dispersing when those bonds come apart as the object perishes.

invincible   Epicurus explained that objects which look solid in fact contain void and therefore are not 'absolutely solid'; only an atom contains no void. If it contains no void, it is both impermeable (for there is no space for anything, no matter how small, to pass through it) and it cannot be divided and is therefore indivisible. If it is indivisible, it cannot be broken down in any way and is therefore indestructible. If it is indestructible, it is permanent. If it is permanent, it cannot change and is therefore immutable. However, there were other ancient physical theories which held that matter was infinitely divisible. For a long time modern science advocated the indestructibility of matter, but more recent scientists accept that matter can be converted into energy.

bronze   the only example from Lucretius' list that might be less familiar today. A mixture of copper and tin, it was the standard metal during the Bronze Age (c. 3000–1100 BC) but was superseded by iron owing to the latter's superior strength, though bronze continued to be used in coins, statues, ceremonial vessels and other items where the appearance of the metal was more important than its tensile strength or the cost of production.

A silver cup unearthed at Boscoreale near Vesuvius.

will piercing cold – as we feel when we hold a **ceremonial** cup in our hands and 495
cool water is poured down into it. With such surety do we observe that nothing in
our world is absolutely solid. However, since a true understanding of the nature of
things demands it, attend closely for a few lines as I explain that things which are 500
both permanent and absolutely solid do exist and they are, as I am in the process
of showing, the seeds and **primary elements** from which the whole universe was
formed and is now composed.

> **1** 'When we hold a ceremonial cup in our hands' – although Lucretius is
> critical of many of the beliefs associated with religion, he readily draws from
> religious practices for his illustrations. Why do you think he does this?
>
> **2** Do you think it a good use of resources to continue the search to discover the
> smallest particle of matter? Why do scientists think it so important to do so?

ceremonial a reference to a libation to the gods, when a person would pour onto the
ground a small offering of water of sufficient purity to be used in a religious ceremony,
or more specifically to the libation made at a Roman banquet, where a guest, reclining
on a couch, held out his drinking-cup to be filled by the slave standing over him.

primary elements the CERN (*Conseil Européen pour la Recherche Nucléaire*) project,
started in 1954 near Geneva, continues to research the 'building-blocks of the universe', as
its website explains: 'At CERN, the world's largest and most complex scientific instruments
are used to study the basic constituents of matter – the fundamental particles. By studying
what happens when these particles collide, physicists learn about the laws of Nature.'

1.503–920

Lucretius repeats that atoms contain no void and void contains no atoms: the two are exclusive, though everything else comprises both. Since atoms contain no void, they are indestructible and therefore immortal. Otherwise, no thing would exist as all matter would by now have decayed over the infinite passing of time. He moves on to the theories proposed by Heraclitus, Empedocles and Anaxagoras; he accepts some of their propositions, but criticizes them for denying the existence of void and suggesting that matter is infinitely divisible.

The poetry of Lucretius' writing; the infinity of the universe

1.921–1007   Well then, discover my remaining subject-matter and hear it expressed more clearly. The obscurity of my material has not escaped my notice; but a fervent hope of winning fame has rapped loudly at my heart with its **staff**, and in doing so has struck my breast with sweet love for the Muses. This is what now inspires   925 me as **my keen mind explores** the remote paths of Pieria that **no foot** has trodden before. It thrills me to approach virgin springs and drink, it thrills me to pick

staff   the *thyrsus* was a staff wrapped with ivy and vine-shoots, which the female followers of the Greek god Dionysus would carry and beat rhythmically on the ground and in unison, often to work themselves into a trance or frenzy. By using the Greek word *thyrsus* for staff Lucretius here evokes the passion of the Dionysiac cult alongside the inspiration of the Muses.

my keen mind explores   in an extended metaphor Lucretius wanders the land of Pieria in northern Greece, said to be home to the Muses, drawing inspiration for his poem by drinking from its springs and picking its flowers. This image closely echoes those of the proem to the third-century Greek poet Callimachus' *Aetia* (a poem about the 'origins' of cults, festivals and cities) which also features an untrodden path, an untouched spring and a garland of fresh flowers, all of which also appear in a similar passage in Ennius' *Annales*. The metaphors which Lucretius uses are connected to poetic artistry: the font of inspiration, the image of choice flowers and the wreath which crowned victors in ancient poetical and musical competitions (still today we metaphorically crown a 'poet laureate' i.e. with a laurel wreath).

no foot   Lucretius cannot claim to be the first to expound philosophy and science in verse (both Parmenides and Empedocles wrote in verse), but he can rightfully claim to be the first both to write a philosophical poem in Latin and to choose Epicurus' teachings as his subject-matter. He also differs from his Epicurean contemporaries: 'in using poetry to expound Epicureanism, Lucretius made a conscious and significant innovation', as Tatum comments (p. 145).

unknown flowers and seek for my brows a **distinguished wreath** with which the 930
Muses have never before crowned anyone: **first**, because I teach of important
matters and go on to **set the mind free from the tight bonds of religion**; then,
because I produce such lucid poetry from such obscure material and infuse it
all with the charm of the Muses – and I have good reason for doing so. When 935
doctors try to administer a foul-tasting herb to children, they first smear the
rim around the cup with some **sweet golden honey**, so the children in their

distinguished wreath   in the ancient world victors of competitions were crowned with
a wreath: Lucretius imagines he will win a wreath from the Muses in recognition of the
quality and innovation of his poem. We heard at **1.118** that the Muses gave Ennius a
wreath, but the one they will award Lucretius is different because his poetic material is
different; the term 'distinguished' qualifies the fame he will win as well as the wreath
itself.

first   there has been some debate whether Lucretius is primarily a poet who has chosen
to write about Epicureanism or an Epicurean who chose to write in verse, though here he
states that his Epicureanism is more important: it is the reason he is writing at all and the
inspiration behind his poem. However, an author is not always best placed to judge his or
her work and we might feel that had Lucretius merely translated Epicurus' works without
'sweetening' them with the 'honey' of his poetry, the Muses would not have awarded
him his wreath. When Milton or Dante wrote their epics, they too may have felt that their
subject-matter was more important than their poetry, yet we may judge that it is the
poetry that makes their works masterpieces.

set the mind free from the tight bonds of religion   Lucretius plays on the Latin words
religio meaning religion and its supposed etymological root *religare* meaning to tie up.

doctors   the Greek Hippocrates (c. 460–377 BC) is credited with founding the study of
medicine: until recently doctors in modern times still had to swear the Hippocratic oath,
promising to treat patients to the best of their ability and to respect their confidentiality.
Pliny comments that 'the Romans got along without doctors for six hundred years' (*Natural
History* 29.5), and records that the first Greek doctor in Rome was one Archagathus in
219 BC. When doctors began to arrive in increasing numbers at the start of the first
century BC (during Lucretius' youth), the Romans were at first reluctant to trust these
Greek immigrants, the most famous of whom was Asclepiades, who arrived in 91 BC. He
rejected the traditional folk-medicine and emphasized diet, exercise and fresh air; he also
practised surgery. However, by 46 BC Greek doctors had established themselves to such an
extent that Julius Caesar gave all practising doctors Roman citizenship.

sweet golden honey   this analogy works on several levels: first, the honey of poetry
makes the 'grim' philosophy more palatable. Second, just as a doctor understands science
and children do not, so Epicurus understands the world and his readers do not. Then,
children are reluctant to take their medicine – the herb is wormwood – in the same way
that 'the common man shies away' from Epicureanism. Finally, children are returned to
health after taking the medicine in the same way that readers will be cured of their fears
after swallowing Epicureanism. Lucretius is not the first to use this image: it appeared in
Plato's *Laws* 2.659e. 'The honey on the cup has a different function from the medicine
inside, but both work together to ensure that the child gets better' (Gale, *CCL* p. 74).

unsuspecting youth are fooled into sipping and then drinking up the herb's bitter 940
juice. They are tricked but not harmed: rather, by this means they are restored to
health and recover. Likewise, since often this philosophy seems too grim to those
who are not familiar with it and the common man shies away from it, I wanted 945
to explain my **philosophy** to you in the **eloquent verse** of the Muses, to smear it
with their sweet honey, as it were, to see if perhaps by such means I could keep
your mind on my poem, as all the while you gain a clear view of the universe and
the configuration in which it stands arranged. 950

Now, since **I have explained** that atoms are absolutely solid and indestructible
and are permanently flying about for all eternity – well then, let us **unravel**
whether there is some limit to their number or not. Likewise, let us see clearly
whether the void now discovered, the place or the space in which things happen, 955
is wholly finite in sum or whether its width spreads without limit and its depths
are immeasurable. The universe is infinite in every direction it travels; otherwise
it would have to have an end point. Now it is clear that nothing can have an
end point unless there is something beyond to mark where it ends; in addition, 960
we would have to be able to identify a point where we perceived the object to
stop. Now since we must admit there is nothing outside the universe, it must

---

philosophy   modern readers might consider the treatment of atoms and void to be part
of science rather than philosophy, but in the ancient world less distinction was made
between the two fields. People wanted to know what the world was made of, how it
worked, what their place in it was and consequently how they should behave. For many,
including Epicurus, to answer the first two questions was prerequisite to answering the
last two. He argued that the purpose of natural science was to rid us of our fear of the
gods and of death, a purpose we might today assign to philosophy.

eloquent verse   in his desire to make his material as palatable as possible by writing in
poetry, Lucretius differs from Epicurus himself, who seems to have disliked that art form,
insisting that clarity of expression was more important than an attractive style; Epicurus'
matter-of-fact style becomes apparent if one reads his *Letter to Herodotus*, for example,
in which he gives a summary of the entire system of his physical doctrine. However,
Lucretius sets himself two goals: to write lucidly and yet with charm.

I have explained   Lucretius has indeed already treated the solidity and permanence of
atoms, but he will only discuss their eternal motion later at 2.80–141. Such inconsistencies
have led many editors to argue that for some reason Lucretius never revised his poem.

unravel   in the ancient world literary works were often written on sheets of papyrus
which were bound together to form one continuous roll, each end of which was attached
to a rod. The reader would scroll across the roll while reading, rolling the section already
read round the left rod and unrolling the right one to reveal the next lines. Lucretius
makes reference in his poem to the act of reading his poem in the same way that a novelist
might suggest to the reader that he or she turn the page to find out what happens next.
The literary self-consciousness here fits with Lucretius' poetic self-awareness earlier in this
passage (935–50).

be infinite, lacking any limit or restriction. Nor does it matter in which part you stand: wherever one takes up position, in all directions its extent is equally and absolutely infinite. 965

Besides, **suppose for a moment** that the universe had a boundary. If a person right at that very boundary took a run up and **threw a spear**, do you think it more 970 likely that the spear, spinning under the force of his throw, would travel in the direction it had been sent and fly some distance, or do you think that something would be able to impede it, blocking its way? For you have to admit and choose one of the two options. Neither of them gives you a way out and each forces you 975 to concede that the universe is infinite. For either there is something to block the spear and prevent its reaching its destination and finding its target, or the spear will keep going, proof it did not start out from the edge of the universe. In this manner I shall stalk you and wherever you mark the universe's edge, I will 980 ask what happens to the spear after that. What will happen is that nowhere can a boundary be established and the space for it to fly on into always prolongs the spear's flight.

Moreover, if the universe and all space lay within fixed boundaries and was not infinite in all directions, the entire sum of matter, being solid and heavy, would 985 have streamed to the bottom and there could be no activity under the broad sky – nor would sky or sunlight exist in any form, since all matter would by now have 990 sunk and be lying in a heap for all eternity. But atoms are undoubtedly given no rest, since there is absolutely no lowest point where they might, as it were, gather and bed down. All things are forever carried on in constant motion: on 995 all sides and from below atoms are stirred up and supplied from infinite space. Finally, we see for ourselves how one thing will mark the end of another. The sky rings the hills, the mountains ring the sky, land defines sea and sea land. Yet 1000

---

suppose for a moment   the issue is the infinity of the universe. Lucretius imagines that a person stands on the edge of the universe: if that person then throws a javelin, either it flies on or something blocks it. It cannot have started at the edge of the universe, if there is space beyond for it to fly into, yet there can be nothing outside the universe to block it, for that thing would necessarily be part of the universe, according to the definition of universe as the sum of all things. The content of these lines is not in the section (41) of Epicurus' *Letter to Herodotus* which discusses the infinity of the universe and so provides a good example of how Lucretius tries harder than Epicurus to make Epicureanism more palatable to the ordinary reader, though it may be that in his *Letter* Epicurus is writing to someone who was already a convert and therefore wanted a brief account of his philosophical system rather than an explanation sweetened with 'honey'.

threw a spear   an image probably drawn from traditional Roman ritual and consequently familiar to the Roman reader. For war to be declared, a Roman priest would go to the boundary of enemy territory, utter a ritual formula and then hurl a spear across into it (Livy, *Histories* 1.32). To the Romans, this ritual ensured that it was a just war, since proper notice had been given.

the truth is that there is nothing outside the universe to bound it. The nature of space and the enormity of its depths are such that a dazzling flash of lightning, shooting across the endless sweep of time, could neither traverse them nor even, 1005 despite its progress, lessen the remaining distance one bit, so far and wide does the enormous amount of room for matter stretch everywhere in all directions without limit.

---

1   Why might Lucretius be so proud of being the first to treat Epicureanism in Latin verse?

2   Does he spoil the trick of the effect of the poetry by explaining it? Do you think Memmius might feel more patronized or flattered?

3   After your reading of the poem so far, do you think he is correct in referring to the 'obscurity' of his subject-matter and describing it as 'too grim'?

4   In your estimation, does Lucretius succeed in making his subject-matter palatable?

5   After reading this passage, do you think Lucretius is more passionate about Epicureanism or proud of his poetical achievement in delivering it? Or are the two inseparable?

6   When do philosophy and science overlap in modern life?

7   Is it ever the role of philosophy to try to rein in scientific development? For example, should society look to philosophers for guidance on whether to control scientific experimentation such as genetic engineering and stem-cell research?

8   As an attempt to demonstrate the infinity of the universe, do you find Lucretius' example of the spear-thrower helpful in its clarity or naive in its simplicity?

9   Would any of lines 951–1007 be out of place in a modern textbook? If so, which lines and why?

1.1008–1117

Having demonstrated that the universe is infinite, Lucretius argues that the number of atoms too must be infinite and that there must be a ready supply of them to hand at all times in order for things to be constantly renewed. If there were a finite number of atoms, every thing would by now have broken down over time and the entire number of atoms would be spread across the universe. He ends Book 1 with a rejection of the proposition that our world has a centre towards which all things are moving of their own accord and that our world is at the centre of the universe, for an infinite universe cannot have a centre.

2 Atomic motion, shape and properties

The power of Epicurean philosophy

2.1–54   **Sweet it is**, when the winds are churning the waves in heavy seas, to watch another's hard struggle from dry land – not because there is any joyful pleasure in someone being in trouble, but because to observe problems that you yourself are free from is sweet. Sweet it is too to watch a great battle being fought out across 5 the plains when you have no part in the danger. But nothing is **a source of greater joy** than to live protected in **serene realms** constructed from the teachings of the wise, from where **you can look down** and see others wandering aimlessly in their 10

Sweet it is   just as Lucretius began Book 1 with a prelude – the invocation to Venus and address to Memmius – before turning to his main subject-matter, so he opens Book 2 with a eulogy to Epicurean philosophy: lines 1–54 are a prominent excursus interrupting the discussion of atoms which precedes and follows them. Similarly, the opening lines of each of the remaining four books also have a broader literary or philosophical focus.

a source of greater joy   Lucretius first speaks of immediate, physical danger. The relief of the onlooker not to have any part in this is obvious to us. He then makes a significant comparison: if the aforementioned relief is sweet, how much sweeter is the relief of the onlooker who is free from activities which cause anxiety or misery. Such activities may not be physically dangerous like a shipwreck or battle, but for Epicurus they were in fact the greater threat, because they were part of daily life and undermined one's happiness and serenity.

serene realms   for Epicurus serenity is the goal of life and is attained when life's disturbances do not trouble the one who experiences them. The Greek word for this state is *ataraxia*. He intended that his teachings should help his followers achieve this state and Lucretius' poem therefore has the same purpose. However, when Lucretius advises his readers to avoid certain activities if they wish to attain *ataraxia*, he has in mind ones which Romans inherently respected and which many of his readers would consider to be their duty: a career in politics or the army, owning and overseeing property and land, regular participation in religious ritual. Lucretius' poem is more controversial and radical in its message to its readers than Epicurus' teachings were in their time.

you can look down   while the sight of a person in difficulty at sea or of a battle is real, this third view is metaphorical. De Lacy suggests Lucretius means that men may distance themselves from physical danger, but they fail to distance themselves from the anxieties of life. He argues (*ORCSL* p. 149) that Lucretius means for us to 'take the distant view, the perspective gained by philosophical vision'.

---

search for direction to a drifting life, competing intellectually, vying politically, striving day and night with extraordinary effort to attain the pinnacle of wealth and become master of their world. O wretched minds of men! What blind hearts! How dark, how dangerous is the life in which we live out our time, however long 15 it may be! Do you not see that human nature **barks** for nothing for itself other than that the body be quite free from **pain** and the mind enjoy the sensation of **pleasure**, having banished worry and fear?

For we see that our bodies by nature have **few needs**: merely whatever will remove 20 suffering and can supply a few delights for us to experience. Human nature itself does not require any **greater pleasure** at such times, even if there are no **golden**

---

barks   this surprising and innovative verb conveys the notion of an incessant, insistent and forceful call.

pain   defined by Epicurus as a disturbance to the atoms of the body, spirit or mind, for example the sensation we feel when we long for something, such as food. He called the absence of bodily pain *aponia*.

pleasure   defined by Epicurus as the sensation either of a process – while a longing is being satisfied; or of a state – when all pain is absent: for example, when that longing has been satisfied and is therefore gone. The latter affords the greater pleasure because it comprises a state (the absence of pain – Greek *ataraxia*), whereas the former is a process and therefore still involves atomic disturbance. Greek philosophers often had a primary organizing principle that defined their philosophy: for example, Socrates argued that the purpose of life was to find virtue or excellence (Greek *aretē*). Epicurus claimed that the aim of human life is the pleasure (Greek *hēdonē*, whence comes our English word hedonist) which arises when one has attained *ataraxia*. He was much criticized for this and his name has been unfairly linked ever since to indulgence and extravagance, even though his definition of true pleasure was simply the absence of pain. The philosopher John Stuart Mill (AD 1806–73) underpinned his utilitarian philosophy of the 'greatest good' with a similar pleasure principle.

few needs   Epicurus suggested that our longing falls into three categories. First, we long for things that are physically necessary for us to have, such as food, clothing and shelter. Second, we long for things that are not physically necessary for us to have but which our bodies naturally crave, such as sex: the wise person will master these longings through prudent indulgence. Third, we long for things which are neither physically necessary nor which we naturally crave, such as expensive luxuries, political power or intellectual supremacy. Such longings are never properly satisfied and a person in their grip is in constant pain: they are therefore to be shunned.

greater pleasure   pleasure is the absence of pain, so greater pleasure must be the greater absence of pain, a notion that makes no sense, of course, for one cannot have a greater absence (i.e. less) of nothing. Epicurus therefore proposed that pleasure cannot be increased, only varied, and that all attempts to increase pleasure must consequently be futile and more likely to increase pain instead.

---

statues of young men about the halls, clutching blazing torches in their right 25
hands to provide light at the night's feast, even if the house does not shine with
silver or glisten with gold and there are no gilded ceilings to echo to the lyre – so
long as people can gather and spread themselves out in the soft grass under the
boughs of a lofty tree near a flowing stream and refresh themselves pleasantly **at** 30
no great cost, all the better if the weather smiles down on them and it is the time
of year when the luxuriant grass is dotted with flowers. A burning fever will not
quit your body any more quickly if you toss and turn on embroidered fabric or 35
blushing crimson than if you have to lie on common cloth.

Consequently, since neither wealth nor noble birth nor the glory of being a king
are of any benefit to the body, we must realize that **they are of no benefit to
the mind** either – unless, when your legions overrun the plain of the **Campus** 40
engaging in practice battles or when you draw them up fully armed and equally
motivated, and reinforced by numerous auxiliaries and a force of cavalry – unless

---

golden statues Lucretius describes a lavish dinner held in a grand house and contrasts
it with a simple picnic held in an idyllic country spot: there may be large disparity in
the cost and the setting, but the amount of pleasure each affords is the same. In the
second and first centuries BC, as tribute from newly conquered provinces began to flow
in and Romans became more wealthy, many rejected the austere lifestyle and values
inherited from more frugal generations and looked for ways to spend that wealth. Lavish
banquets became fashionable, causing the poet Horace (65–8 BC), for example, to attack
such extravagance in *Satires* 2.2.

at no great cost Epicurus argued that it is easy and cheap for us to satisfy our longing
for those things which are physically necessary. For example, it is easy to satisfy our
hunger by eating and we do not need to be wealthy to do so, for we satisfy it no more
quickly or easily with expensive food than we do with cheap food. The type of idyllic
rural gathering which Lucretius describes here has philosophical and literary overtones,
for there was a long tradition of an 'idyllic location' (Latin *locus amoenus*) as the place
for serious reflection, which goes back to Socrates' iconic decision (related in Plato's
Phaedrus) to leave the confines of the city of Athens for more peaceful and productive
surroundings. There was also a moral dimension to the opposition to conspicuous and
profligate spending in the Roman literary tradition, which often held up examples of
frugality and simple living as being quintessentially Roman.

they are of no benefit to the mind neither military power nor political success nor
wealth can remove the two fears which prevent us from attaining *ataraxia*: fear of the
gods and fear of death. Lucretius explains that all such power belongs to philosophy
alone. Epicurus suggested that a principal reason why men seek power or wealth is
to gain some protection against the threat of others, so that it is fear of death which
motivates their ambition.

Campus the Campus Martius, a plain outside Rome, where generals often exercised
their troops while waiting to go on campaign. In 58 BC Caesar kept an army for three
months on the Campus Martius and was criticized by Memmius for this threatening
reminder of the forces he controlled.

---

at that point the terrors of religion are panic-stricken at the sight and run away   45
from your mind in fear, while at the same time fear of death takes its leave of your
heart, now empty and freed from anxiety. But if we do see that such a notion is
frivolous and laughable, and that in truth men's fears and the cares that pursue
them fear neither the sound of battle nor its grim weaponry, but go boldly amongst   50
kings and potentates, respecting neither the shine of their gold nor their purple
mantle's bright splendour, do you have any doubt that all such power belongs to
reason alone? – especially when one's whole life is a struggle in the dark.

---

1   Do you think it is cruel to observe others' misfortunes and feel relief that you
    are not in danger? Does not some television comedy want its audience to
    laugh at a character's misfortunes? Is such laughter born of cruelty or is there
    another explanation for it?

2   For Lucretius, Epicureanism gives life direction (**2.11**). Where do people turn
    nowadays to seek direction for their lives?

3   Lucretius claims that Epicureanism offers its followers protection, serenity,
    wisdom. Is there any indication in the passage that he considers Epicureans
    superior to non-Epicureans? Is a feeling of superiority over non-believers an
    inherent part of any religion or philosophy, whether ancient or modern?

4   Are there ideological or religious groups today who advocate a life of
    disengagement from politics?

5   Lucretius observes that participation in business or politics can cause anxiety
    and therefore prevents one from attaining *ataraxia*. Might a modern
    politician or person of business understand his concerns? Is it possible to
    follow either path and yet avoid disturbance to one's serenity?

6   'How dark, how dangerous is the life in which we live out our time' – are
    our lives today dark and dangerous? If they are, what factors make them so?
    Can these be addressed by religion and philosophy? If not, do religion and
    philosophy lose their purpose?

7   Do you agree with Epicurus that pleasure is merely the absence of pain? Even
    if you do not, do you agree with his logic that any absence is absolute and
    therefore cannot be increased?

8   What do you think are our basic needs today? Are they as readily and cheaply
    satisfied as Epicurus believed? Do you think they will have changed much
    since his time?

9   On the evidence of this passage, do you think Epicurus' reputation for
    advocating indulgence and extravagance is deserved?

2.55–111

Lucretius now starts his treatment of the motion of atoms. He begins by
explaining that all atoms are in constant motion. Their own weight bears them
downwards through the infinite void, but they often collide with one another.
Then they will either latch onto each other and bond (though they continue
to be in motion, but their movement is in harmony with the whole object), or
they will bounce off in a different direction and so continue to wander through
the infinite void, clashing with other atoms and rebounding off them.

Atomic movement

2.112–41   As I say, a similar example of this very process is constantly to hand, taking place before our very eyes. **Take time to watch closely** when rays of sunlight are let into a dark house and stream in: within these shafts of light you will see countless particles 115 of dust rushing around through the emptiness in all directions, entering into **skirmishes and clashes**, as if in some never-ending battle, fighting in squadrons without pause, engaging and disengaging in frequent succession. You may surmise 120 from this the manner in which atoms are constantly hurled about in an expanse of void; to some degree the small can replicate the big and serve to illustrate a concept.

There is **a further reason** why it is even more fitting that you study these specks as 125 they charge about in the sunbeams before your eyes: because their rushing around also indicates to us that similar movements are also occurring, hidden and invisible, within matter. For there you will see the particles constantly changing direction as 130 they are struck by invisible blows and, **as they rebound**, heading off hither and thither in all directions all over the place. This random motion undoubtedly comes to them all from the atoms. For atoms move of their own accord first. Then those bodies which are formed from the bonding of a few atoms and are, so to speak, most susceptible to their atomic energy, are jolted by invisible knocks and set in 135 motion; they in turn knock into other bodies slightly bigger than themselves. Thus

---

Take time to watch closely   Lucretius frequently uses phrases such as this one or 'do you not see?' to grab his readers' attention and to point out that, since the existence of atoms and how they behave is difficult to grasp, there are phenomena in the visible world (as at **1.265–328**, for example), which we should observe to gain a better understanding of the nature of the atom.

skirmishes and clashes   Lucretius frequently uses military metaphor, partly to enliven his explanations – 'to infuse it all with the charm of the Muses' (**1.934**) – and partly to put his reader at ease with an unfamiliar and abstract idea by describing it in familiar and concrete language, for a Roman noble would be likely to have had some military experience as part of his political career. De Lacy (pp. 150–3) shows that in previous philosophical writings the cosmic order had often been compared to the careful order of an army and that Lucretius here (and elsewhere) inverts that tradition by portraying an army as a disorderly and chaotic entity.

a further reason   not only does Lucretius' illustration show how the atoms move if we could only see them, it also provides an example which we can see of that very movement itself, although at a few levels above the atomic.

as they rebound   when investigating the principle of Brownian motion, many students at school nowadays will have used a microscope to observe tiny particles of smoke move in a way which is similar to that of the motes in the sunbeam described by Lucretius.

motion passes **up from the atomic level** and gradually emerges into our sight, with the result that particles which we are able to see in the sunlight are also set in motion, though the blows which move them are still hidden. 140

> • Do you find the example which Lucretius has chosen to illustrate atomic motion easy to follow? What might be considered poetic in his description of the particles in the sunlight? Do you find any of it distracting? He hoped that such poetry would help readers master his material: has he been successful here?

2.142–215

Lucretius points out how quickly the sun's warmth and light travel through the air once the sun has risen, and argues that the atoms travelling through void must be able to move much more quickly still. He attempts to prove that nothing moves upwards of its own accord: even flames contain a force driving them upwards or they would naturally fall: the natural movement of all atoms is downwards, a movement caused by their own weight.

The atomic swerve

2.216–62   On the same subject, I want you also to realize this: when atoms are borne straight down through the void by their own weight, at a wholly unknown time and unknown point they **swerve** a little from their course, just enough that you could say they had 220 changed their direction. Because if they did not, they would fall like drops of rain through the yawning void and no collision of atoms would ever have occurred, no blows been caused: in which case nature would never have created anything. But

---

up from the atomic level   in the first place, the atoms are constantly moving; they form molecules, which themselves move because they contain the energy of those atoms; the molecules form particles, which move under the force of the molecules and so on until the movement reaches a level that we can perceive. The atoms, their movements and their collisions are all invisible, but the particles, their movements and collisions are all visible. Modern science has since shown that at one level below that of the atomic, electrons too are in constant motion.

swerve   if all atoms fall straight downwards under their own weight, they will never collide, never bond and so never create things; therefore Epicurus suggested that atoms randomly swerve as they fall. This suggestion was the object of much criticism in the ancient world – Cicero called it childish (*On the Definitions of Good and Evil* 1.6.109) – for it contradicts one of Epicurus' main principles, that nothing in the universe happens without a cause; however, Epicurus did allow chance itself to be a cause.

if anyone believes that heavier atoms travel more quickly straight down through a vacuum and so can drop down onto lighter ones, in that way causing the collisions which initiate the movements necessary for creation, he is off track and moving far away from true reasoning. For whatever the object that is falling through water or thin air, the speed of its fall depends on its weight, for the reason that the density of water and the rarefied nature of air cannot slow every object equally, but both are forced to give way to heavier objects more quickly. However, an empty vacuum cannot offer any resistance to anything in any direction at any time. No, its nature permits it to offer no hindrance, which means that all things must proceed through the stillness of the vacuum at the same speed, even though propelled by different weights. Therefore heavier objects will never be able to drop down from above onto lighter ones nor of their own accord to cause the collisions which generate the various motions for nature to carry things on.

So it needs repeating: atoms must swerve a little – not more than the tiniest amount, or I will seem to be inventing movements sideways and will be proved wrong by what happens in reality. For we clearly observe the following, plain to see: heavy objects cannot drift sideways of their own accord, when they fall headlong from above – so far as you can perceive. But who has **the ability to perceive** that they do not swerve from their path even the least amount? Then, if every movement is linked to the next, each new one following the previous one in a fixed order, and if atoms do not swerve to cause motions which break the bonds of fate, so that cause and effect are not determined for infinite time, how can free will exist in living creatures throughout the world? How, I ask, does **free will** come about, wrested

---

the ability to perceive Epicurus held that perception by the senses was the criterion for truth, but all the scientific theory which Lucretius has explained so far concerns the imperceptible. In such cases, Epicurus argued, it is legitimate to suggest a theory, provided that nothing we can perceive contradicts that theory. However, we observe that objects fall straight downwards, so he suggested the convenient explanation that in fact they may swerve imperceptibly as they fall: Lucretius is conscious that he may seem 'to be inventing movements sideways'.

free will an essential part of Epicurus' moral system (all his theories about natural science are directed towards supporting his moral philosophy). In his physical system he therefore allowed for a random swerve from the downward atomic motion, an element of chance within the laws of nature – 'wrested from the Fates', as Lucretius dramatically puts it. This random swerve means that our actions are not predetermined, for if all atomic motion followed an established pattern, all activity would be fixed according to that pattern and we would have no free will. Epicurus claimed (*Letter to Menoecus* 134) that he would prefer to live at the mercy of divine whim than under the shadow of the oppressive notion that all is fixed by fate. The Atomists (see Glossary, p. 152), however, believed that the atoms fall straight down and that all motion and action is therefore predetermined.

from the Fates, free will by which we go wherever our pleasure takes us and we too make a swerve, not at a determined moment or a determined place, but wherever 260 we have a mind to? For it is a person's free will, without doubt, which is the origin of such movements, and which then **channels movement** down the limbs.

---

1   Do you feel that Epicurus' invention of the atomic swerve is an acceptable means of allowing for creation and the existence of free will, or does it in fact undermine the credibility of his philosophical system?

2   Do you agree with Epicurus that there is no point arguing for a moral system if we are not free to follow it?

3   Which do you think would be more frightening to live in: a world where everything was predetermined or one governed by capricious gods such as the Romans worshipped?

4   Which scientists have made the greatest contributions to the understanding of gravity and motion? Which of their discoveries does Lucretius anticipate here?

2.263–307

In his treatment of will and movement Lucretius observes that at the races horses wish to leap out of the starting-gates with greater urgency than their bodies can manage; and that when we are given a push, first the desire to resist it arises and only after that do our bodies react: these examples demonstrate that motion is initiated by a wish to move, which then sends signals down our limbs. He reiterates that it is the atomic swerve which allows the mind to have free will. He then moves to a new point in his treatment of atomic behaviour: the universe has always been the same size, because there is no space for it, being infinite, to expand into, and so atoms have always behaved in the same way, because there cannot be anything outside the universe to inflict change on its fixed laws. He finishes his treatment of the motion of atoms as follows.

Atomic movement and shape

2.308–66   On the same subject, one thing is not to be wondered at: why, when all the individual atoms of a body are in motion, nevertheless the body as a whole 310

---

channels movement   after this passage Lucretius goes on to explain how it is our will which sets in motion the process by which we move: since the mind is composed of atoms (he explains this at **3.161–76**), our will has the power to stimulate atomic movement, which travels down the limbs and initiates the movement of our body.

seems to be standing **absolutely still** – unless the body is itself moving. For the substance of an atom lies far below our senses; therefore, since you cannot see the atoms themselves, their movements too must elude you, especially since even 315 when we can see a thing, often we cannot detect at a distance that it is moving. For often **while grazing** the lush pastures on the hillside, woolly sheep will roam wherever the grass, sparkling with fresh dew, beckons them invitingly, while the lambs sport and gambol coyly after feeding: yet all of them seem to us from a 320 distance to blur into one and to be standing still like a patch of white on the green hill. Or again, when mighty legions fill the space of a plain with their charge, as they go through a battle drill, while the glare reaches right to the heavens and the 325 countryside all around glimmers with the shine of bronze, a din arises from the pounding of men's feet and the mountains are struck by their shouting and echo their cries to the stars; cavalry dart about, then suddenly cut across the middle, thundering over the flat of the ground at a vigorous gallop. Even so there is a 330 spot high in the mountains from where the whole glittering mass seems to stand stationary on the plain.

Well then, learn next about the qualities of the primary elements of all things and the wide variety of their forms and the diversity of their multifarious shapes; 335 the shapes of many may be similar, but they are not all exactly the same as each other – nor is this surprising. For when atoms exist in such profusion that they have neither maximum number nor limit, as I have shown, surely

---

absolutely still   Lucretius explained at **2.125–8** that all atoms are constantly in motion, even atoms that have bonded to form a solid object. Ever conscious of the obscurity of his subject-matter, he is aware that his readers might find such a proposition hard to accept – given that a rock, for example, appears to be the embodiment of inertness – so once again he offers an analogy to demonstrate that a similar phenomenon occurs in the visible world: something may appear to be inert though it contains many moving parts. Such analogies are common in didactic poetry, just as similes are in epic. Both are part of the poet's repertoire: in narrative epic they help readers – or listeners, for any poetry was likely to be read aloud in the ancient world – to picture the scene, while in didactic epic they help them to understand a point.

while grazing   in another display of poetic virtuosity Lucretius chooses two contrasting analogies to illustrate his point (sheep being quite different from soldiers). The first analogy comprises a peaceful, idyllic country scene, the second (almost twice as long and reminiscent of **2.118–20**) is warlike and full of the vigour of the din, the glare, the shouting and the thundering of hooves. The bleating of the sheep contrasts with the men's shouting, the wool they bear with the men's armour, their gambolling with the men's charging and the cavalry's thundering, the white patch with the dazzling glare, and the hill with the plain.

it cannot be the case that they are all absolutely alike, identical in structure and 340
furnished with the same shape. Moreover, the human race and the dumb shoals of
scaly fish, the fat cattle and the wild beasts, the various birds which fill the refreshing
wetlands along river-banks, springs and ponds, and which love to flit around 345
secluded groves: whichever of these you care to pick, you will still find that they
differ from one another in appearance. Otherwise offspring could not recognize
their mother nor a mother her offspring; but we see that they can and that they are 350
no less recognizable to each other than humans are. For often in front of ornate
shrines to the gods, next to **incense-burning** altars, **a calf is struck down** and emits
a warm torrent of blood from its breast as it falls. But its bereaved mother wanders 355
the green glades, searching the ground for the imprints of its cleft hoofs; her gaze
scrutinizes every spot in hope of catching sight of her lost offspring anywhere; she
halts and fills the leafy grove with her lament and often goes back to the stable

it cannot be the case at **2.112–41** and at the start of this passage, Lucretius employed
deductive reasoning: he stated Epicurean theory about an aspect of the imperceptible
world and inferred that a particular phenomenon in the visible world was one instance of
that theory in practice. Now he reverses his methodology and employs inductive reasoning:
he cites a particular phenomenon in the visible world and infers a general law from it, that
atoms have a large variety of shapes. However, although there are an infinite number of
atoms of any given shape, there must be a finite variety of shapes, since otherwise atoms
would exist that were large enough to be visible, as he explains at **2.478–99**.

incense-burning Lucretius has probably coined this word (Latin *turicremas*). Virgil, Ovid,
Statius and Lucan all went on to use it, giving us a small but useful way of gauging how this
poem influenced later writers; in addition, lines 352–66 as a whole inspired similar pieces
by Virgil (*Eclogues* 8.85–90) and by Ovid (*Fasti* 4.459–81). The smell of incense was believed
to rise to the heavens and alert the gods to the sacrifice, as well as afford them pleasure in
its own right; down on the ground it would also provide the practical benefit of masking
the smell of the slaughtered calf.

a calf is struck down another extended illustration like those at the start of the passage.
A calf is sacrificed at the altar; its mother misses her offspring terribly and no other calf
can take its place, even though we might think that all calves look the same. This extended
illustration is another example of how Lucretius can take the most prosaic subject-matter
– the proposition that atoms have different shapes – and work it into a moving and
memorable vignette, making readers sympathetic to the mother and perhaps at the same
time hostile to the religious act which caused her loss. It is illustrations such as these (and
there are many in the poem) which make Lucretius the brilliant poet and teacher that he is.
It is also a good instance of a 'purple passage' (an ornate or elaborate passage of writing),
one in which some critics suggest that Lucretius departs from his argument to flex his
creative muscle: Bailey comments (p. 861): 'it shows how the picture in his mind gets the
better of him, since much of the detail is irrelevant to the argument'; in response to such
passages some critics have suggested that Lucretius is primarily a poet and only secondarily
an Epicurean. We have heard from Lucretius himself, however, that although he will write
with lucidity and charm (**1.933–4**), the Muses will give him a crown primarily (**1.931**) for the
poem's content, i.e. because he imparts Epicurean philosophy.

pierced with longing for her young. The succulent willows, the grass bathed in dew, 360
the familiar rivers gliding past in full flow – none can cheer her spirits or prevent
her sudden anxiety, nor can the presence of other calves all across the rich pastures
divert her attention and alleviate her distress, so intensely does she seek something 365
that is familiar and her own.

---

1   Note how far Lucretius develops each analogy. Why do you think he uses two
    analogies instead of one and what is gained by their being so detailed?

2   Do you agree that in these extended analogies Lucretius gets carried away
    and is side-tracked from his argument?

3   In what ways do the content and style of this passage belong to a poem more
    than a scientific textbook?

4   Do you agree with Epicurus' argument that, if there is variety among
    different atomic combinations, there is necessarily variety among the atoms
    themselves too?

5   Why do you think Lucretius chooses a calf for his illustration? Do you think all
    animals within a species look the same? How do we learn to tell them apart?

6   Which details of his description of the grieving mother are necessary for
    Lucretius to explain his point? Which details contribute to the scene's
    poignancy? What human qualities does he ascribe to the mother?

7   Do you think the scene stands out or is it typical of the way Lucretius 'honeys
    the cup' of his subject-matter through the poem?

8   Why do you think these lines influenced later poets?

2.367–599

Lucretius continues to treat the shapes of atoms: just as in the visible world
many sea-shells look the same, but on closer inspection are seen to be different,
so the atoms must all be different, if only slightly. Wine and olive oil are both
liquids yet clearly have different properties, while a difference in atomic shape
causes some foods to taste pleasant, but others awful, because atoms of the
latter foodstuffs are rough and jagged. However, though there may be many
types of atom, there are not infinite types, for otherwise there would have to be
included in those infinite types visible atoms. There are, however, an infinite
number of atoms of any particular type, for if there were not, atoms of each
type would be spread across the infinite vastness of the universe and would not
be present in sufficient numbers to renew each particular thing. For all things
are born, grow and then perish in a fixed cycle. Lucretius moves on to a new
point: anything that comprises only one type of atom has the smallest range of
atomic combination and movement and so has the least potency: the wider the
variety of atoms in a thing, the greater its force and power. So the earth, which
is the most powerful of all beings, contains the seeds of fire, water, crops, trees
and animals and is called the 'Great Mother'.

Worship of the Great Mother

2.600–60   Of Cybele the learned Greek poets of old sang that, from a throne in her chariot, she drove a pair of yoked lions, thereby **showing that** the great earth hangs in mid-air and that earth cannot rest on earth. **They** harnessed animals which were wild to show that young, however wild, ought so to be tamed and made gentle by 605 the attentions of their parents. They encircled the top of her head with a crown of battlements, because in her fortified guise she preserves towns on prominent hill-tops. Still endowed with this symbol **today**, the image of the divine mother **is carried** around great lands to the awe of all. On her as Mother of Ida the various 610 nations call in the sacred ancient manner and they give her bands of Phrygians

Of Cybele   ancient worship of the goddess Cybele or Great Mother originated in Phrygia in eastern Turkey. In this passage Cybele is equated with the goddesses Gaia (the Greek 'Mother Earth') and Rhea (mother of Jupiter and Juno), both of whom were also earth goddess figures. During processions held in Cybele's honour her statue was transported in a chariot drawn by lions and her priests, many of whom had castrated themselves as a sign of their devotion, danced wildly and noisily. Catullus conveys the frenzy of such self-mutilation in his remarkable poem 63.

showing that   though Lucretius will not allow that the earth is a goddess, he is ready to accept her worship as an allegory for the ideas, which he enunciates here; he was willing to invoke Venus for similar reasons at the start of the poem (**1.1–43**).

They   it is not quite clear who 'they' are. Lucretius may mean the 'learned Greek poets of old' that he has already mentioned: the tragedians Sophocles (*Philoctetes* 391–402) and Euripides (*Bacchae* 65) refer to Cybele and her rituals. Alternatively, Lucretius may mean other poets, unknown to us, who gave an allegorical interpretation of the ritual along the lines of the one Lucretius offers here.

today   the sacred Sibylline Books, acquired by the last king of Rome, Tarquinius Superbus (reigning 534–510 BC), were thought to contain information about the future (in much the same way that the prophecies of Nostradamus (AD 1503–66) have received attention in modern times). In them was a prophecy that the cult of the Great Mother should be imported to Rome, so in 202 BC her cult officially became part of Roman state religion and the sacred black stone, kept at her cult centre of Pessinus in central Asia Minor (modern Turkey), was brought to the city. It was decreed that there would be an annual procession in March in her honour, though conducted by Phrygian priests (Latin *Galli*) because Romans themselves were banned from being part of it, lest their morals or self-discipline be corrupted by the wildness and frenzy of the procession. Similar processions but on a smaller scale were held throughout Italy.

is carried   processions were a common part of worship in ancient Greece and Rome. The focal point of the procession was the statue of the god or goddess, recognizable by his or her traditional symbols, which was carried by attendants; also in the procession might be other devotees and priests, musicians, select members of the public, and animals to be sacrificed. In contrast to more stately processions (like the one portrayed on the frieze which surrounded the Parthenon), the one in honour of Cybele must have made a strong impression on its spectators.

A Roman statue of Cybele in her chariot drawn by lions; second century BC.

as companions, because they declare that from those lands first corn began to be grown throughout the world. **Eunuchs** they appoint for her, because they want to show that those who offend the majesty of the Mother and prove ungrateful to 615 their parents must be considered unworthy to bring children into daylight's realm. Taut tympana thunder in their hands and curved cymbals clash all around, horns blare out a raucous warning and hollow pipes goad their minds to a Phrygian 620 rhythm. They hold out knives in front of them, reminders of the violence of their frenzy, so that through the goddess's majesty they can frighten the ungrateful minds and impious hearts of the crowd and fill them with fear.

So, as she is carried through mighty cities and silently bestows her mute blessing 625 on mortals, people strew the entire route of her journey with bronze and silver, lavishly enriching her with coins, and they make a blizzard of rose-petals which

---

Eunuchs Lucretius' explanation of the eunuchs' castration is tendentious and does not explain its actual rationale (there is no explanation of how the eunuchs have offended the majesty of the Mother), but instead reflects Roman prejudice against eunuchs and a fear of unfamiliar ritual practices. Lucretius chooses the most bizarre, un-Roman and questionable cult as his example, which he then deconstructs.

---

creates shade for the Mother and her band of companions. Then, whenever **an armed troop**, called Curetes by the Greeks, go cavorting amidst the bands of the Phrygians and jump to the rhythm in delight at the blood, nodding and shaking the terrifying crests on their heads, they bring to mind the Dictaean Curetes, who are said once to have drowned out Jupiter and his cries on **Crete**. Surrounding the infant boy, boys in armour clashed brass on brass to the rhythm of their nimble dance, so Saturn would not get hold of him and swallow him up, thereby causing a permanent injury deep in the Mother's heart. For that reason they accompany the Great Mother in their armour – or because they show that the goddess proclaims they should be willing to defend their native land with arms and with courage, and that they should prepare to be a protection and source of pride for their parents. However worthily and excellently chronicled and retold such a notion is, nevertheless it is **far removed from a true understanding**.

For by its very nature **divinity** must enjoy life everlasting in utmost tranquillity, far removed and detached from our own world. Free from all suffering, free from

---

an armed troop   though the cult of the Great Mother originated in Phrygia, eastern Turkey, a Mother-figure goddess with similar characteristics was worshipped on Crete, and the two traditions were often conflated, helped by the coincidence of there being a Mount Ida both in Phrygia and on Crete.

Crete   when Saturn – or in Greek mythology Kronos, father of Zeus – was king of the gods, he received a prophecy that he would have a son who would overthrow him. To prevent this he would eat each of his sons at birth, but Jupiter's mother Rhea managed to replace the new-born infant Jupiter with a stone, which Saturn swallowed in his place. Meanwhile, she gave Jupiter to Gaia, who hid him in a cave on Crete, but his cries would have still been loud enough to attract Saturn's attention, had some boys not danced around the infant boy and clashed their cymbals to drown them out. Stories such as this one of musical din during Jupiter's infancy are aetiologies explaining cult practice through myth (i.e. why cymbals are used in the worship of Cybele). Brown (*ORCSL* pp. 343–5) demonstrates that these lines echo Callimachus' *Hymn to Zeus* (1.52–4) and shows that, when taken with certain other passages dotted about the poem, Lucretius was familiar with the third-century Greek poetry later known as Alexandrian (so called because the most famous poets lived in Alexandria, which was then the capital of the Greek-speaking world).

far removed from a true understanding   Lucretius describes the procession in all its exotic glory but then 'abruptly brings the reader up short' (Farrell, p. 89). By following such a virtuoso display of his powers of description with this anticlimax, Lucretius emphasizes the point that the procession is misguided in portraying such a picture of a Mother goddess: as Kenney puts it, 'Lucretius debunks even as he delights' (*CCL* p. 106).

divinity   for the first time in the poem Lucretius relates Epicurus' view of the gods. Epicurus proposed that they exist in a permanent state of *aponia* (freedom from bodily pain) and *ataraxia* (freedom from mental pain) and that they can have nothing at all to do with our world; nor do they feel anger or pleasure. Thus there is no need either to fear them or to appease them, and so one of the two biggest causes of human anxiety is removed.

danger, powerful in its own resources, **it has no need of us** and it is unmoved by good   650
deeds and unsusceptible to anger. For in truth, the earth never has been possessed
of **consciousness** at any time, but only because it contains atoms of many types can
it send them up into the light of day in great numbers in many ways. Given this,
if anyone decides to **call the sea Neptune** or grain Ceres, or prefers to abuse the   655
name of Bacchus rather than mention the actual word wine, we should let him go
on referring to the earth as Mother of the gods, provided, that is, that deep down
he refrains from tainting his mind with the corruption of religion.   660

---

1. How does Lucretius convey the drama, spectacle and energy of Cybele's procession?

2. What processions might one encounter nowadays? Are they all religious?

3. Lucretius gives a detailed description of a procession in the goddess's honour, but his description does not detail or advance any aspect of Epicureanism. Why do you think he includes it?

4. Why did early civilizations worship a 'Mother Earth' deity? Where might one find such a figure worshipped today? Why in those societies particularly?

5. Is our own 'green' movement in some way a return to such a belief? In what ways is it different?

6. Epicurus' gods are 'unmoved by good deeds and unsusceptible to anger'. Which of today's religions views its gods in the same way?

7. Is the concept of 'good' bound to religious beliefs? How would people with no religious belief define 'good'? What does motivate people to do 'good deeds' if not religious belief?

8. Is the ancient purpose of prayer – to ask assistance from (a) god in return for an offering – still valid in any of today's religions? In religions where it is not, what does motivate prayer?

9. Does polytheism inevitably lead to gods having characteristics not found in monotheism? If so, what are they?

---

it has no need of us   this statement constitutes a challenge to the basis on which Greek and Roman worship was founded, namely a contract between a god and the worshipper. The latter would offer or promise the god a tangible gift, such as a sacrifice, a libation or an offering, in return for divine assistance – the so-called principle of *do ut des*, meaning 'I give so that you may give'. If the gods have no need of or interest in humans, worship is pointless and without it religion of an official and organized kind is rendered redundant. Epicurus did, however, value individual spiritual contemplation.

consciousness   Lucretius is at pains to point out that worship of the earth as a sentient being is mistaken: the earth is simply an enormous store of a vast number of atoms, and releases them according to fixed laws and not with any goal of being useful to mankind. Lucretius thus undermines both popular belief and Stoic doctrine, which held that a divine spirit permeates all things in this world including the earth itself.

call the sea Neptune   both Greeks and Romans allocated spheres of influence and responsibilities to each individual god within their polytheistic systems. Neptune was the god of the sea, Ceres the goddess of grain and Bacchus the god of wine; the Romans might refer to grain or bread as Ceres, for example, in a figure of speech known as metonymy.

2.661–99

> Having broken off to describe and comment on worship of the Great Mother, Lucretius now returns to his treatment of the shapes and arrangements of atoms. He reiterates that things are different from one another because they are composed of different atoms or of atoms combined in different ways.

Atomic combinations

2.700–29   However, no one should think that all atoms can be combined **in all ways**. Then you would quite commonly see freaks being born; a species of half-animal, half-human creatures would exist, living bodies would sometimes grow tall branches and many animal legs would sprout fins, and throughout the lands which are parents to all creatures, nature would rear **Chimaeras** too, breathing fire from   705
their hideous mouths. Obviously, not one of these exists. We see that all things are born from specific seeds and specific parents and grow up able to preserve their species. Undoubtedly their growth must occur according to a fixed method: 710
the atoms which are compatible with the limbs separate out from whatever is eaten and pass into them and latch on to produce the **appropriate movements**. On the other hand, matter which is incompatible we see nature throw back to the ground; in addition, many atoms, **driven out by blows**, flee the body unseen,   715
unable to bond onto any part or, once inside, to join in sensing the vital motions and copy them.

---

in all ways   it is important to Epicurean philosophy that there are natural laws which are knowable and which cannot be broken, so that fear of divine whim and its capacity to harm is removed. Lucretius explained that all things are born from specific seeds at 1.159–214.

Chimaeras   in mythology the Chimaera was a fire-breathing monster (one-third lion, one-third goat and one-third snake) which was killed by the hero Bellerophon. In popular accounts of creation such as Hesiod's *Theogony*, many of the early divinities were such hybrid creatures. Again in passing Lucretius debunks popularly held beliefs (see note on p. 42).

appropriate movements   atoms are in constant motion. When they combine with other atoms they continue to move, but their movements combine with those of the atoms they have joined to produce a harmony which becomes the movement of the whole. When we replenish our stock of atoms, only some of those from what we eat will move in the same way as those already in place and therefore be absorbed; the others which move in a different way are rejected, often by excretion onto the ground (as here).

driven out by blows   according to Epicurus the atoms around us are in constant motion and therefore our bodies are subject to constant blows, which dislodge those atoms which could not properly combine with the body.

The Chimaera: one-third lion, one-third goat, one-third snake. An Etruscan bronze votive statue, c. 380–360 BC, discovered at Arezzo, Tuscany, in 1553.

Lest you happen to think that only living creatures are bound by these laws: the same system limits everything. For just as each thing which is born is different 720 in its nature as a whole from all others, so it must be that the shape of their atoms is different too: in no way do all atoms have the same shape, though there is an abundant supply of atoms of each shape. Furthermore, since the atoms 725 are different, different also must be the spacing between them, their course, combinations, weight, blows, collisions and movements. These factors not only differentiate living things but mean that land is quite distinct from sea, and sky quite separate from land.

2.730–990

After finishing his discussion of the shapes and effects of atoms, Lucretius explains that atoms have no secondary properties of their own such as colour or sensation, but they only gain these when combined with other atoms and lose them again when those combinations are broken up. His first proposition is that atoms themselves have no colour. He observes that some things change colour when viewed in different light: this would not be possible if atoms had their own colour, for what is permanent cannot change. Just as atoms have no colour, so they possess no warmth, cold, sound or taste of their own. Nor can the atoms themselves experience sensation, unless they are part of a whole living being: then it is possible for the insentient to combine to form a sentient being. Otherwise, if atoms were independently sentient, they might be happy or sad just like the being they were part of, which is a ridiculous notion.

The cycle of the atoms

2.991–1022 Finally, we must all spring from seed from the sky. Every thing has **the same father**, whose moist drops of rain are received by nurturing mother earth. In her fertility she gives birth to rich crops and vigorous trees, to the human race and all breeds of creatures. She provides food too so they may nourish their bodies and lead a happy life and bring forth their offspring; for this reason she has rightly received the name of mother. Likewise, the same matter that originally came from the earth returns to it, and what was sent down from the regions of the sky is **sent back up** and received in its broad realm. 995 1000

For **death does not destroy things** in such a way that it eradicates atoms; rather it only undoes the bonds between them. Then it re-combines those atoms with

the same father   like other Indo-European cultures, the Romans also had a sky-god: first Uranus and then Jupiter, who deposed his father Saturn to become king of the gods. In mythology it is the union of sky and earth which produces living beings: the sky-god sends down the rain, which constitutes the life-giving seed that fertilizes the earth by providing moisture. In the creation account in Hesiod's *Theogony* (176–90) the drops of blood which fell on earth at the castration of Uranus also generated life-forms. Epicureanism does not admit such an explanation, of course, but we have seen from Lucretius' description of the Great Mother at **2.600–60** and his invocation to Venus at **1.1–43** that he is willing to acknowledge traditional religious beliefs in order to indulge in allegorical cosmologies. This description of the union of sky-god and mother earth echoes lines from *Chrysippus* (fragment 839) by the tragic playwright Euripides, who himself may have been drawing from the writings of Anaxagoras.

sent back up   Epicurus held that, when we die, not only do our bodies' atoms return to the earth once we have been buried – a notion we can readily accept today – but also the atoms of the spirit (which Lucretius discusses in more detail at 3.231–57) return to their source, those which are heat and air returning to the sky.

death does not destroy things   Lucretius refers to such recycling of atoms at three other points in the poem (1.250–64, **3.964–71**, 5.235–305) and it is a point that is fundamental to his argument that being dead is nothing to be feared, for if we can understand that the atoms which constitute 'us' will disperse and be reused elsewhere after our death, we will not be at all afraid of being dead, for there will be no 'us' to experience it. Compare this idea to the one expressed by Hamlet:

> Alexander died, Alexander was buried, Alexander returneth into dust; the dust is earth; of earth we make loam; and why of that loam, whereto he was converted, might they not stop a beer-barrel?
> Imperious Caesar, dead and turn'd to clay,
> Might stop a hole to keep the wind away:
> O, that that earth, which kept the world in awe,
> Should patch a wall to expel the winter's flaw!

Hamlet, Act 5, scene 1

others and in this way causes all atoms to reappear in a new arrangement and in   1005
new colours, and once again to experience sensation – and later of a sudden to
relinquish all such qualities.

So you should understand that what makes the difference is which of the others those
atoms combine with and in what arrangement, and what movements they pass on
to and receive from one another, and you should not think that the characteristics   1010
we see **floating on the surface** of things, now being born and now suddenly
perishing, remain the fixed properties of the atoms. No – what makes the difference
in my poem too is which letters others combine with and in what arrangement, for
the same letters contribute to the words sky, sea, land, rivers, sun, or they can spell   1015
out crops, trees, animals. If not all, then the majority of those used are the same
but it is their arrangement that gives them different meaning. So likewise with the
things themselves: when there is a change in the combination, movement, order,   1020
position or shape of their atoms, the things too must be changed.

- Do you think Lucretius' description of the recycling of atoms could be
  classed as a kind of reincarnation?

---

floating on the surface   Lucretius ends this part of Book 2 with a reminder that, while
atoms have permanent properties of size, shape and weight, other properties, such as
colour and the ability to experience sensation, are gained for a time when atoms combine,
and are then lost again upon the death and disintegration of the body they form. It is a
central tenet of Epicureanism that whole beings are sentient but individual atoms are
insentient.

the same letters   atoms have few properties in and of themselves: it is their arrangement
which creates a being and gives it visible characteristics. Just as words often share some or
all of the same letters, but have different meanings according to the order in which those
letters are placed, so too things may share some or all of the same atoms, but their different
arrangement makes those things different. Modern chemistry confirms this: for example,
diamond and graphite both contain only carbon atoms, but are so different because of the
different arrangement of those atoms. Lucretius uses this analogy of the letters four other
times in the poem: at 1.197, 1.823–6, 912–14 and 2.688 (it may be of interest to note that
the letters in the name Lucretius can be rearranged to form 'is culture'!). Consequently,
arguing that there is also nothing in this passage that Lucretius has not treated before,
Bailey remarks (p. 958) that 'then follows the familiar illustration from the letters in words,
repeated here in phrases already used and less aptly fitted than elsewhere to the context.
Editors are probably right in thinking that this was a patchwork passage hastily composed
by Lucretius as he was seized with the thought of using his illustration once again.' Gale
thinks differently (*ORCSL* p. 7): 'what had once been regarded as an indication of the
poem's unfinished state came to be seen as a tool … for impressing important scenes or
passages of ideological significance on the reader.'

2.1023–47

Lucretius now begins the last part of Book 2, in which he advocates the existence of an infinite number of worlds, and explains how worlds came to form and later perish. Before he does so, though, he issues a reminder that we should not be amazed at or afraid of Epicureanism just because Epicurus' teachings are new to us, in the way that primitive people were awestruck when they first saw the sky or stars or sun. Just as we are quite accustomed to those latter phenomena, so people will grow used to the marvels of Epicureanism. If after careful consideration readers are convinced by his philosophy, they should accept it; if not, they are free to reject it. He then moves to the next and final subject-matter of Book 2.

Other worlds exist

2.1048–89

First of all: there is no end to the universe in any direction anywhere, this way or that, above or below. I have shown this, the truth of it speaks loudly and the 1050 nature of the depths shines forth. Now, since space lies empty and infinite in all directions and since atoms in countless numbers fly every which way through its furthest reaches driven on in perpetual motion, it is **utterly unrealistic** to 1055 think that ours are the only world and sky to have been born and that so many atoms outside our world are doing nothing. All the more so, since this world was made by nature and since the atoms which form it collided by **chance**

---

utterly unrealistic   a rare example from ancient literature of an author looking beyond our world. Because so much of the earth had yet to be explored in ancient times, from the *Odyssey* onwards poets tended to set fantastical stories beyond the edges of the known world but still on earth. The author Lucian (second century AD) wrote a fantastical description of space travel, but he was primarily parodying earlier fantasies about travel in unknown lands on earth. Now that our planet has been fully explored, in the last 60 years writers have turned in ever greater numbers to space as the final frontier.

chance   in admitting the element of chance to his philosophical system, Epicurus differed from the Atomists, who held that 'necessity' alone was the guiding force which would lead to the creation of a world: if certain conditions were met, a world would of necessity form. Lucretius introduced readers to the Epicurean concept of chance at **2.216–62** when he explained the atomic swerve.

of their own accord, and were driven to bond in various ways, accidentally, 1060
without pattern or design; at length there combined those atoms of the sort which,
when suddenly driven together, will always form the beginnings of planets, of
land and sea and sky and living creatures. So it needs repeating: you must admit
that elsewhere there are **other accumulations of matter** like our one which is 1065
held by the ether in tight embrace.

Besides, wherever there are abundant atoms to hand, where space is available and
where no matter or cause prevents it, undoubtedly **there will be activity** and things
will be formed. Now, since the number of atoms is so great that all generations of 1070
living creatures would not be able to count them all up, and since the same natural
forces exist elsewhere which could drive atoms together in a similar way to what
has happened here, you then have to admit that there are other worlds in other 1075
parts of the universe, different races of humans and species of animals.

---

of their own accord Lucretius reminds us of the randomness of cosmic phenomena.
On this point too Epicurus differed from the Atomists, whose explanations were all
deterministic: they believed there was a mechanism and order to the universe. In the
twenty-first century the Big Bang theory is currently the dominant scientific explanation
of the origins of the universe. Among those who espouse it, there are some who believe in
Intelligent Design, i.e. that a divine intelligence provided the first cause for the Big Bang,
while others believe, like Lucretius, that it was a natural occurrence which took place
'without pattern or design'. It could be argued that the Epicurean swerve is equivalent
to a 'Big Bang' theory, for if just one atom were to swerve just once, and collide with
another so that the second atom was driven off course, and so on ad infinitum, it would
be enough for a world to be created. Epicurus, however, claimed that these swerves take
place often.

other accumulations of matter that is, other planets. Until Copernicus and Galileo in
the fifteenth and sixteenth centuries, the generally held understanding of the universe
was firmly geocentric: our world was held to be unique and the centrepiece of creation.
Although some had argued against this view – not least the early Greek philosophers
– it was only with the invention of the telescope that this belief was finally disproved.
As Lucretius predicted at 2.1024–9, this radical reconception of the universe met stiff
resistance, not least because it was new, though the Catholic Church rejected it primarily
because it seemed to lessen mankind's importance in the scheme of creation.

there will be activity having established the element of chance, Lucretius now introduces
the Atomists' principle of 'necessity': if the conditions are right (i.e. there is sufficient matter,
space enough and the necessary force) then there will be atomic collision and bonding,
and things will be formed. After that has happened and a world has been created, it will
be subject to natural laws – or necessity – but chance events will still occur, brought about
by the atomic swerve.

On top of this, **nothing in the universe is unique**, nothing is born unique or grows up unique, the only one of its kind. No, everything belongs to a type and there are many things in each class. Think first of living creatures: you find this 1080 to be true of the **class of animals** that roam the mountains, true of the human race, true too of the mute shoals of scaly fish and of all types of birds. You must therefore admit by the same token that out of sky, land, sun, moon and sea, and 1085 everything else, none is unique but rather there are a countless number of each, that indeed a firmly fixed boundary-stone of life awaits them too, and that their bodies came into being just as much as those of all the races whose members proliferate in kind here on earth.

---

1 Epicurus was adamant that there is no guiding hand to the formation of a world. Do you think it is worse to live in a world without purpose and governed by chance than one ruled by benign gods?

2 Does Lucretius seem troubled by his certainty that other planets and life forms might exist elsewhere?

3 Do you think it is possible or probable that other life forms exist on other planets? Does it intrigue or trouble you?

4 Would the existence of other worlds affect our view of our own in any way?

---

nothing in the universe is unique in his first two arguments Lucretius employs a deductive argument, explaining how, if the conditions are right, a world will and must come into being. Now he changes his approach (see note on p. 38) by employing an inductive argument based on observation of our existing world: no creature in our world is unique, so it follows that nothing else of our world is unique either, so there must be other suns and skies elsewhere, for anything that can come into being in our world can equally come into being in another world, given the same conditions; in an infinite universe with an infinite number of other worlds, those same conditions certainly occur elsewhere. The invention of the telescope has proved Epicurus right: there are countless planets, stars and even galaxies, though we have yet to find another one which supports life.

class of animals systematic taxonomies were created by the Greek philosopher Aristotle (384–322 BC) and these continued as the basis for zoology and botany until the mid-eighteenth century, when the Swedish scholar Linnaeus provided the modern system for classifying plants and animals by genus and species.

2.1090–1143

Lucretius suggests that if we understand that our world is not unique but one of a type, then we will accept that nature governs everything according to a system and without the gods' participation. Moreover, like the creatures on it, our world came into being and grows through the addition of matter. Then, once it has reached maturity, it will become so large that it will begin to cast off more matter than it takes on, just as each being which grows does. For the nourishment it absorbs will not spread easily across its increasing bulk and so it will begin to weaken. Then it will perish, sapped by that loss of nourishment and the continual blows from atoms in the surrounding air.

The deterioration of the earth

2.1144–74

So the walls of the mighty world will be breached **in the same way** and collapse in crumbling ruins around us. For everything needs food to replenish and renew it, food to sustain and support it. Yet to no avail, for the veins cannot endure it in sufficient quantity and nature does not provide the required amount. The earth's life is now so broken and she herself so worn out that she can scarcely produce tiny creatures, where once she produced all species and gave birth to beasts of prodigious size. For it is not my belief that mortal creatures were lowered down from the sky onto the fields by **a golden rope** or that they were born from the sea or the waves that pound the rocks: no, this same earth bore what she now sustains from her own self.

What is more, in the beginning she herself freely produced bounteous crops and rich vines for mortals, she herself made a gift of the sweet fruits and rich pastures. Now these scarcely grow to a good size even when we labour to increase them, and we tire out our oxen and the farmers' energy is sapped; we wear down the plough in fields which barely provide for us, so much do they begrudge their fruit

1145

1150

1155

1160

---

in the same way Lucretius explains that the earth is like a living creature and follows the same cycle: it is born, takes on nourishment and grows, then it begins to fail, as it cannot take on enough nourishment to feed its growing self, and it becomes weak; finally it collapses from lack of nourishment, because its veins have been unable to distribute that nourishment properly. According to Epicurus, just as nourishment is distributed down the veins of living creatures, so in similar fashion nourishment for life on earth (particles which replenish matter) travels down the fissures and channels inside the earth.

a golden rope this rather strange notion may have its origin in a passage from *Iliad* 8.19, where the gods suggest pulling Zeus down from the heavens to earth with a golden rope; this has been interpreted as an allegory that life had its origins in the sky, an idea which can be explained much more easily when one considers that water is the source of life (**2.991–8**) and it most obviously reaches the fields and forests as rain.

A Roman marble relief of a weary farmer and his cow, first century BC; in the background is a shrine in a state of decay. The artist may wish to show a link between the decline of the traditional Roman citizen farmer (threatened by large-scale production) and the decline of traditional Roman religion (threatened by the arrival of foreign culture into Rome, particularly Greek).

and thereby increase our hard work. These days the aged ploughman shakes his head and sighs ever more often that his hard work has proven fruitless; when he compares the present age with those of the past, he regularly applauds his parents' good fortune. So too, the man who plants the old and wrinkled vines sadly denounces **the downward trend** of his times, and upbraids the heavens and

1165

---

the downward trend   the preceding lines are in all likelihood a reference to the Roman belief in a Golden Age in the history of mankind, when the earth supposedly of her own accord produced enough food to satisfy human needs and the back-breaking work of cultivating the land was not required. Linked to the notion of a Golden Age was the belief that the earth was as generous as her inhabitants were honest and unpretentious. This representation of an early Golden Age that regressed to morally corrupt lesser ages stands in contrast with other accounts of human progress. Here Lucretius may hint particularly at a phenomenon of his own lifetime, namely the land confiscations of the first century. Generals promised rewards to their legionaries while on campaign abroad and needed to make good those promises upon return to Italy. They often did so by allocating land to those soldiers; if that land was already occupied, the owner or tenant was forced to move out. Two of Virgil's *Eclogues* (1 and 9) have as their theme the land confiscations carried out by Octavian and Antony after the battle of Philippi in 42 BC.

mutters how **earlier respectful generations** managed to subsist quite easily on
small lots, when each man used to own **much less land**. He does not realize that
everything is gradually wasting away and heading for the grave, worn out by the
passage of old age.

1	Do you think the planet is closer to extinction than it was in Lucretius' time?
2	Is Epicurus right that everything which grows must necessarily also decay?
3	In what tone does Lucretius express his prophecy: matter-of-fact or sensational?
4	According to Epicurus the world will die out at some point: does his argument mean that the efforts currently being made to save our planet are futile? Does modern science agree with Epicureanism that our planet had a beginning and is set to come to an end?
5	Does the earth currently provide enough food for its inhabitants? Would you agree that it becomes ever harder to extract natural resources from the earth, with agriculture in particular proving increasingly difficult? Do you think technology of food production will be able to keep pace with population growth?

earlier respectful generations for centuries the fields of Italy had been tilled by
smallholders; it was these sturdy farmers who used to down tools and pick up weapons
and who formed the backbone of Rome's legions before she established a standing army.
A famous example of the 'gentleman farmer' was Lucius Quinctius Cincinnatus (fifth
century BC), a Roman senator who retired from politics and set to working his own fields.
In 458 when Rome was at war with her neighbours, the Aequi, and was in desperate
straits, the Senate sent a delegation to his farm to ask him to take on the emergency
position of *dictator*. He agreed, put down his farming implements to put on his toga, led
the army to victory against the Aequi and 16 days after his appointment returned to his
farm and became an ordinary citizen once more (Livy, *Histories* 3.26–7).

much less land the second century BC saw the rise of the large farming estates or
latifundia. As Rome gradually conquered more lands both in and outside of Italy, much
of the newly acquired land was bought up by members of the senatorial class. In addition,
by virtue of their being officers in the Roman army they acquired large quantities of gold
and slaves as booty, enabling them to purchase yet more land and then to farm it at very
little cost. The consequence was that the traditional smallholders up and down Italy, but
particularly in the south, could not compete with such large and cheaply run farms, so
more and more of them sold their farms to the owners of the *latifundia* and moved to
Rome, or enlisted in the army.

3 The nature of the spirit and mind

Fear of death; the physical nature of mind and spirit

3.1–176   **O you** who amid such utter darkness raised on high a light so bright and who were the first one able to reveal the good things in life, it is you I follow! **You, the pride of the Greeks**, laid the footprints in which I now firmly plant my own feet – not from a desire to compete with you but because in my devotion 5 I long **to imitate** you. For why would a swallow challenge a swan? How could the feeble legs of a kid ever match the power of a mighty horse in a race? You are the father, the author of truth; you give me a father's instruction, glorious

---

O you   Lucretius began Book 1 with an invocation to Venus and Book 2 with a eulogy to Epicurean philosophy; he now begins Book 3 with a eulogy to Epicurus himself; though mortal, he is here addressed in the language of a prayer. 'O' was a common way to begin a prayer in ancient times: it was hoped that the power of its monosyllabic urgency would attract the god's attention.

You, the pride of the Greeks   it is interesting to compare this passage to the invocation to Venus at **1.1–28**. Not only does Lucretius implicitly award Epicurus divine status by invoking him in language suited to prayer, but there are other similarities between them: he uses imagery drawn from nature and light (the clarity that fills Lucretius' mind after encountering Epicurus' philosophy is reminiscent of the luminosity that accompanies a divine epiphany when a god makes himself manifest to mortals); he calls Venus mother and Epicurus father; he asks Venus to be his mentor and sees Epicurus as his instructor; and both passages are full of excitement and awe at the power of their respective addressees.

to imitate   Roman writers frequently took a Greek work as their model: the *Aeneid* is based on the *Iliad* and *Odyssey*, Horace's poems on the Greek lyric poets, some of Cicero's speeches on those of Demosthenes and so on. However, authors made a distinction between *imitatio* (imitation – with its desire to pay respects to the model) and *aemulatio* (emulation – with its goal of surpassing the model). Lucretius' philosophical model is Epicurus' body of writings (or summaries contained in various letters); his literary model is ostensibly Empedocles' poem *On Nature* but he ranges far beyond it to include the epics of Homer and Ennius, the didactic poetry of Hesiod and the later Hellenistic poets, and Greek lyric poetry and tragedy: he will borrow from all of these and adapt them to suit his purposes (see Introduction, pp. 3–4).

lord, and from your **pages**, as **bees sip** at every flower in the meadow, so too 10
will I feed on every one of your golden sayings – golden, most worthy to live on
always and for ever. For no sooner does your philosophy, born of your godlike 15
intellect, start to proclaim the nature of things, than the fears in my mind are
dispelled, the barriers of the universe come down and I see what is transpiring
throughout space. The gods in their majesty appear, as do **their peaceful homes**
which no winds ever buffet, no clouds drench with rain, which are never spoilt by

---

pages   Lucretius would have read Epicurus' works on scrolls of papyrus; it was around
the time Lucretius was writing that the first Roman collectors were beginning to assemble
their own private libraries of Greek works. The remains of one such library have been
discovered in the Villa of the Papyri in Herculaneum, buried by the eruption of Mount
Vesuvius (AD 79); it contains a large number of carbonized scrolls of papyrus, which have
been and continue to be painstakingly deciphered and some of which have been found
to be works by Philodemus, an Epicurean contemporary of Lucretius.

bees sip   a poet finding inspiration in the Muses was commonly compared in ancient
literature to a bee sipping at flowers (e.g. Plato, *Ion* 534a) and the comparison is
appropriate here because Lucretius draws on a variety of different earlier works in writing
his poem. An anthology of poems is so called from the Greek word for flower, *anthos*: it is
a collection of poetic flowers. By likening bees sipping at flowers to his finding inspiration
in Epicurus' writings (in place of the Muses), Lucretius further associates Epicurus with the
divine, as he does too by the phrase 'born of your godlike intellect', where the Latin
wording implicitly recalls the birth of Athena, who was born from Jupiter's head.

their peaceful homes   traditionally, the gods of the upper world were thought to reside
on the top of Mount Olympus (2,917 m, 9,570 ft), a mountain in northern Greece, often
shrouded in cloud, beset by wind and rain, and cloaked in snow in winter. In popular
imagination, the Olympian gods lived a life of ease on Mount Olympus, removed from
the human realm and human concerns but able to look down on human activities with a
bird's-eye perspective and readily able to descend and intervene directly. Lucretius wrote
about the nature of the gods at **2.645–51**; here he describes their abodes. Epicurus located
the homes of the gods between worlds and quite separate from them, and he held that
the gods therefore have no interest in or connection to our world or any other, so that
their worship is redundant. Lucretius describes their homes as 'peaceful', for the gods are
permanently in a state of *ataraxia*. These lines echo Homer's archetypal description of the
homes of the gods at *Odyssey* 6.41–5, leading Farrell to remark (p. 88) that once again we
find 'Epicurean argument framed by non-Epicurean material'.

The English poet Tennyson (1809–92) echoes these lines in his poem *Lucretius*:

> The Gods, who haunt
> The lucid interspace of world and world,
> Where never creeps a cloud, or moves a wind,
> Nor ever falls the least white star of snow
> Nor ever lowest roll of thunder moans,
> Nor sound of human sorrow mounts to mar
> Their sacred everlasting calm!

A view of Mount Olympus, traditionally the home of the gods.

the hard, harsh frost of the white snow's fall – the sky which roofs them over is 20
cloudless at all times and smiles with an all-embracing radiance. Moreover, **nature
provides** them with everything, and nothing eats away at their peace of mind at any
time. Whereas nowhere do the regions of **Acheron** appear, though the ground does 25

---

nature provides   according to Epicurus the gods are self-sufficient. They live outside
our world and therefore need nothing from us, neither food from a sacrifice nor honour
from a prayer or dedication. This view was at odds with the traditional belief that the
anthropomorphic gods do desire both sacrifice and honour from humans, as Aphrodite
explains at the start of Euripides' tragedy *Hippolytus* (1–8), for example.

Acheron   a river in the underworld and then one of the names for the underworld as a
whole; Tartarus was another name for it, though more specifically the deepest region.
Typically Romans believed that at death the spirit went down to the underworld, where
it stayed for eternity, and that some parts of the underworld were better than others. In
Book 6 of his *Aeneid* Virgil portrays the underworld in mostly unpleasant terms, explaining
that only the great heroes enjoy a pleasant afterlife in the Elysian fields. He imagines the
dead as insubstantial (Aeneas is told that it would be pointless for him to rush with his
sword at the shadows of dead monsters) but somehow still able to be unhappy and to
suffer physical punishment. However, some Romans participated in adopted foreign cults
introduced into Rome in the first century BC, such as that of Egyptian Isis – and later those
of Persian Mithraism and Christianity – which offered an alternative view of the afterlife,
whereby those initiated into the cult could look forward to a blessed existence after death.
Epicurus and Lucretius, of course, reject out of hand all belief in an afterlife.

not stop me from seeing through to all that is happening in the void far below my feet. Thereupon a **divine pleasure and a shudder** come over me, because **by your power** nature lies uncovered, clear and open to view on all sides.   30

---

1 How are the homes of the gods imagined in the iconography of other religions, both ancient and modern? In what ways is Epicurus' picture different?

2 Can you imagine any teacher or guru in today's world inspiring such enthusiasm as Lucretius feels? If so, who and why?

Now, **I have demonstrated** the properties of the beginnings of all things and how those vary in their different forms, how they fly around of their own accord, propelled by their unceasing motion, and in what way each thing can be created from them. Following on, I must now shed light in my poem   35 on **the nature of the mind and the spirit** and I must drive out headlong that

---

divine pleasure and a shudder   two sensations which a Roman might experience during worship: pleasure at the ceremony itself and being part of it, and a shudder of awe at the god's power, perhaps as suggested by a magnificent statue or temple. Lucretius uses the imagery of mystic revelation but daringly subverts it: he himself experiences such sensations as he contemplates not the conventional Roman gods – whose existence he denies – but the mortal Epicurus' philosophy.

by your power   Lucretius brings the invocation full circle: he began by praising Epicurus' powers ('the first one able to') and ends by doing the same again – an artistic device known as 'ring composition'.

I have demonstrated   these summaries of what has gone before serve both to remind the reader of ground already covered and to mark the introduction of new material. It was not easy for Roman readers themselves to look back to an earlier part of the text, for they would have to unroll an unwieldy papyrus scroll to find particular lines. The subject-matter of Books 1 and 2 was the atom, its behaviour and properties; in Books 3 and 4 Lucretius will use what he has established about the atom to consider human nature: the mind, the spirit and the process of sensation.

the nature of the mind and the spirit   Epicurus, rejecting the traditional Greek distinction between the mind (*nous*) and the spirit (*psychē*), considered the mind to be the rational part of the otherwise irrational spirit. Lucretius follows Epicurus, suggesting that the mind (Latin *animus*) is in fact part of the spirit (*anima*). It is difficult to reflect in translation the shared etymology of the Latin terms: both derive from the Greek *anemos* meaning wind or breath. Lucretius explains in the course of Book 3 that atoms of spirit are distributed throughout the body and are responsible for sensation, but that in the breast (**3.140**) there is a concentration of atoms of spirit which he calls 'mind' and which is responsible for thought and emotion.

fear of Acheron which undermines human life at its very roots, muddying everything with the blackness of death and allowing no pleasure to be straightforward or untainted. For people often declare that sickness and shame 40 are more to be feared than Tartarus of the dead, and that they know the nature of the spirit is **blood – or even air**, if that happens to be their whim – and that they have absolutely no need of our philosophy. You will realize from the following 45 observations that these are just boasts to earn admiration rather than acceptance of the actual truth.

Those very people, **exiled from their homeland** and banished far away from men's sight, polluted by a shameful crime, tormented by all kinds of anxiety, 50 nonetheless go on living and, whatever point of despair they reach, they still make sacrifices and slaughter **black cattle** and send down offerings to the immortal dead and in bitter times turn their attention all the more eagerly to religion. For

fear of Acheron   in early Roman religion individual shades were not believed to retain their identity in the underworld, and it was thought that the dead continued as a collective group, known as *manes*; later Roman belief that individual spirits existed and were punished in the underworld was Greek in origin. Cicero writes that Epicurus assumed people were afraid of punishment after death, but he states that in fact few people are troubled by it (*On the Gods* 1.31.86); of course, as Bailey points out (p. 994), such fears may well have troubled ordinary people, whose opinions are not recorded in the erudite literature which has survived. Lucretius has already disposed of the fear that we will be conscious when the body is destroyed (2.870–93) and that being dead will be a miserable experience (2.894–930), and later he will describe death as a state of rest (3.211, **910, 977**).

blood – or even air   there were several theories about the composition of the spirit: Empedocles claimed that the spirit is composed of blood, Anaximenes (who lived in the second half of the sixth century BC) that it is composed of air. However, Lucretius may be citing popular ideas about the spirit rather than those ones specifically: hence he writes 'if that happens to be their whim'. Many Greeks believed that a person's spirit survived death to go down to the underworld, there to experience happiness, misery or nothing much; others, such as Pythagoras, claimed that the spirit entered a new being. Epicurus, however, insisted that the spirit was made up of atoms and was broken up at death like any other part of the body.

exiled from their homeland   Lucretius portrays exile as a miserable existence. However, for Roman nobles banished for wrongdoing, exile could be comfortable enough: they were allowed to keep their fortunes and could continue to keep in touch with Roman politics. For example, Cicero went into exile from Rome for a time (58–57 BC) and, though he was unhappy to be away from the city, his letters show that he continued to correspond with the leading statesmen of the day on matters of politics.

black cattle   these were sacrificed to the dead more frequently than other cattle. Romans sacrificed to the dead mainly from a desire to honour them, but also in some cases from a wish to appease them, in the belief that otherwise they might appear on earth to haunt the living.

this reason it is better to observe a man under duress and in danger and to find 55
out what sort of man he is in adversity; for then at last his true feelings will be
coaxed up from the bottom of his heart and his mask will be torn off: what is left is
the truth. Again, greed and a blind desire for honours, which force wretched men 60
to cross the boundaries of what is right, sometimes as accomplices or partners
in crime, straining night and day with extraordinary effort to reach the summit
of power – these sores of life are in no small part kept raw by fear of death. For
the shame of disgrace and the grimness of poverty seem for the most part to 65
keep their distance from a pleasant and settled life and they feel more like a wait
outside the gates of death. So, while men, driven by misguided fear, wish to have
fled far away and to have distanced themselves from such ills, they amass their
wealth through **the deaths of fellow citizens** and greedily multiply their riches, 70
heaping murder on murder; in their cruelty they rejoice at a brother's grim death
and they hate and fear dining with relatives.

In similar vein, because of that same fear often they are consumed with envy 75
because this man is so obviously powerful, that man catches the eye as he strides

---

to cross the boundaries of what is right   Lucretius does not specify how fear of death
could lead a person to commit crimes. However, according to Epicurus, some men believe
that being famous and conspicuous might afford them protection from others, a belief
Lucretius refers to later at 5.1120–35. They therefore commit terrible crimes in their desire
to attain the fame and status which would provide this security: the historian Sallust
(86–35 BC) describes this very phenomenon in his account of the Catilinarian conspiracy
of 63 at *Catiline* 10.3–5 and Barbour notes (p. 150) that generally in Lucretius' poem
'assessments of the motives to political power and ambition are simply and scathingly
negative'. Epicurus taught that the best protection from being harmed by other men was
to have friends and to live the quiet life, i.e. not to become involved in politics: he advised
his followers to 'live unnoticed' – an attitude quite at odds with that of the majority
of well-born Romans. One notable exception was Titus Pomponius Atticus (110–32 BC),
Lucretius' contemporary and Cicero's great friend and correspondent, who abandoned
all thoughts of a political career, sold his assets in Italy and moved to Athens in 85, both
to escape the political troubles that were brewing in Rome and to study Epicureanism.

the deaths of fellow citizens   a phrase echoed by Sallust at *Catiline* 14.1–3 when
describing Sulla's proscriptions (when lists of supposed public enemies were posted in
the Forum so that those proscribed would be captured or killed by people hoping for
a reward). Lucretius lived through some of the most turbulent times of Roman history
(see Introduction, pp. 1–2), when Roman killed Roman in the civil wars between Marius
and Sulla (in the late 80s BC), and then (if he was still alive) between Pompey and Caesar
(49–48 BC): 'freebooting political ambition was bringing the Roman commonwealth
to its knees' (Kenney, commentary p. 81). There were even incidents of brother killing
brother, which Virgil laments at *Georgics* 2.510, and people might well fear dining with
relatives in case they were poisoned – usually so that the perpetrators could claim a
reward (commonly a significant portion of their victim's estate, with the remainder going
into the coffers of one of the aforementioned generals).

'They are consumed with envy because this man is so obviously powerful' (3.75): Cassius (John Gielgud, left) and Brutus (James Mason) resent Julius Caesar's power, and plot to kill him, in MGM's 1953 production of Shakespeare's Julius Caesar.

forth in **the colours of his rank**, while they themselves complain that they live in obscurity and filth. So some of them die for statues and fame, while often in fear of death others become so firmly gripped by a loathing of life and of looking on   80 the light of day that with sorrowing heart they commit suicide, forgetting that it is from this fear that their anxieties spring – it will persuade one man to stain his honour, another to sever the bonds of friendship: in short **to overthrow all respect**. For often before now men have betrayed their country and their parents in an   85

---

the colours of his rank   senators wore a toga with a broad purple stripe (*toga praetexta*); men who were wealthy but not in the Senate (*equites*) sported a thin stripe. A *dictator* (appointed by the Senate, freely or under duress, in times of emergency so that Rome would be ruled by one man, thus avoiding a split between the two consuls) also wore the *toga praetexta*. Sulla was appointed *dictator* for the year 81 BC.

to overthrow all respect   the concept of *pietas* (respect for and duty to one's family, friends, country and gods) was central to the Roman psyche. Virgil made it central to the *Aeneid* and he regularly describes Aeneas as dutiful (*pius*), while Livy's *Histories* are full of examples of virtuous Roman men and women fulfilling their duty to Rome (such as the stories of Brutus at 1.59–2.1 and Cloelia at 2.13).

'the colours of his rank' (**3.78**): senators were distinguished by a purple stripe on their togas (see note on p. 60). A scene from the 2005 television series Rome, produced by the BBC, HBO and RAI.

attempt to avoid the realms of Acheron. **For just as children tremble** and in blind darkness are afraid of everything, so even in the light we too are sometimes afraid of things which are absolutely no more to be feared than those which the children 90 are afraid of in the darkness and imagine will happen. So what we need to scatter the terrifying darkness of the mind are not the sun's rays or the day's bright light but an understanding of nature's outward form and inner workings.

1 'People often declare that sickness and shame are more to be feared' – do you think that nowadays there is anything else that people would prefer to die rather than experience?

2 'Some of them die for statues and fame' – how do people today try to ensure that their name lives on after they die?

3 Do you feel that your duty lies most towards family, friends, country or god? Do you think your own view is the predominant one nowadays?

For just as children tremble   these lines have already occurred in part at **1.146–8** and in full at 2.55–61 and will do so again at **6.35–41**. Such repetitions have led many editors to argue that our text of Lucretius is unfinished and corrupt (see notes on p. 47 and p. 131); more recent scholarship has come to regard repeated passages to be within the tradition of narrative and didactic epic – in the latter such repetition has a didactic purpose, as Kenney makes clear (*CCL* p. 94): 'the repetition of lines and passages which occur throughout the poem is intended to score fundamental principles on the reader's memory.'

My first point is that the mind, which we often call the **intellect**, where our reasoning 95
and our life's guiding principles are located, is absolutely no less a bodily part than
the hand and foot and eyes which constitute parts of a whole living being. Even so,
others have suggested that the mind's power of sensation is located in no particular
place but is a condition of the living body – and the Greeks call this **'harmony'** – 100
which causes us to live and to experience sensation while alive, and that the intellect
does not reside in any one part, just as good health is said to be a condition of the
body and yet it is not any specific part of a healthy man. So they do not locate
the mind's perception in a particular place – in which respect they seem to me 105
to be very wide of the mark. For often the body, which can be clearly observed,
is sick, even though we are happy in a different part which cannot be seen; while
on the other hand it is the case that in turn the reverse often occurs, that a person
downcast in mind feels pleasure all over his body – this is no different from when 110
a sick person has a pain in his foot but in the meantime his head is perhaps in no
pain. Furthermore, when the limbs have been surrendered to gentle sleep and the
weight of the body lies relaxed and insensible, there is nevertheless something else
inside us which during that time is stimulated in all kinds of ways and receives all 115
the motions of happiness and the unfounded cares of the heart.

Now, to enable you to understand that the spirit too is situated in the limbs and
that it is not through 'harmony' that the body experiences sensation: first, even
when the body has lost a number of limbs, it is the case that life often remains in 120
our frame nevertheless – and again, when just a few particles of warmth escape
and a little air is exhaled out **through the mouth**, that same life suddenly deserts
the veins and abandons the bones. From this you will realize that not all particles

---

intellect Lucretius makes a distinction between the mind as a whole (Latin *animus*),
responsible for emotion as well as thought, and the intellect (Latin *mens*), the part of the
mind responsible solely for thought.

'harmony' Aristoxenus (fourth century BC), a pupil of Aristotle with an expertise in music,
had put forward the theory that 'spirit' is an abstract quality which the body possesses
when all elements within it are working together – like 'good health' – in the same way
that music can have harmony. However, the Atomists had earlier suggested that the
spirit was a physical entity composed of atoms, and Epicurus himself wrote that the spirit
is corporeal. It is rare for Lucretius to transliterate an original Greek philosophical term:
he does so here to be quite clear which doctrine he is rejecting and also possibly because
the Greek word *harmonia* occurs only rarely in Latin and therefore serves to reinforce the
supposed peculiarity of the idea it denotes.

through the mouth in the next few lines Lucretius explains that the spirit is composed
of atoms of wind, heat and air (later at 3.241–51 he will add a fourth element). When
someone dies, it is clear for all to observe that breath and warmth leave the body, but
when Lucretius turns to treat the nature of the *anima* in more detail, he explains that the
anima exits through all the pores of the body at death, not just the mouth (3.254–5).

play an equal role, not all prop up our wellbeing to an equal degree, but rather the 125
ones that are the seeds of breath and warmth see to it that life remains in the limbs.
Therefore there is a warmth and a vital breath within the body itself which desert
our frame as we die. For this reason, since the nature of the mind and spirit has 130
been found to be like any other part of the body, give up the term 'harmony' that
was handed down to the musicians from lofty Helicon – or they themselves may
have dragged it up from somewhere else and applied it to that concept, which had
no name of its own at the time. However it happened, **let them keep it**, but, **you**, 135
pay attention to what else I have to say.

Now I maintain that the mind and the spirit are bound tightly together and
combine to make up a single entity, but that our reason – what we mean when
we talk about the mind or intellect – lords it over all of the body and is its head,
so to speak. It is firmly rooted in the middle part of the body, **in the chest**. Here 140
pulsate panic and fear, here is located the joy that delights us: here, therefore, lie
the intellect and the mind. The rest of the spirit, which permeates the whole of
the body, obeys the mind, responding to its will and inclination. Only the mind
can independently experience awareness or feel happy independently, when there 145
is no stimulus affecting the spirit or the body. We may be hurt in the head or the
eye and assailed by pain, but our whole body does not suffer in agony; so too the
mind on its own can suffer or be full of happiness, while the rest of the spirit in the 150
body and limbs undergoes no change. In contrast, when the mind is overcome by
some more potent fear, we see that the entire spirit throughout the body shares in

let them keep it Epicurus asserted the importance of using clear and simple language to
express ideas and Lucretius rounds off this argument with a 'brusque and unceremonious'
(Kenney, commentary p. 94) dismissal of the unhelpful and potentially confusing term
'harmony', borrowed from music, or even medicine or carpentry (hence 'dragged it up
from somewhere else').

you a reference to Memmius or to the general reader. Memmius, however, after being
addressed four times in Book 1 (**26**, **42**, 411, 1052) and twice in Book 2 (143, 182), is not
mentioned again by name until Book 5 (**8**, 93, **164**, 867, 1282) – and not at all in Book 6.
Bailey comments (p. 33) that 'the natural inference is that 1, 2 and 5 are closely connected
and that while Lucretius had Memmius in mind in these three Books, which he wrote first,
in the later Books he was always addressing the general reader'.

in the chest ancient philosophers argued about the location of the mind and emotions.
Some located them in the head, others – including Epicurus – located them in the chest; in
Homer emotions are located in the midriff (next to the diaphragm). This may be because
the Greeks believed both our thoughts and our emotions emanate from the same source,
and it is true that we feel emotions not in the head but in the chest or stomach. Lucretius
draws attention to his point that the *animus* is not located in the head with some typical
word-play, calling it the body's 'head, so to speak'.

the sensation: the whole body **goes pale** and starts sweating, the tongue cracks and 155
the voice fails, the eyes mist over, the ears ring and the limbs give way: indeed, we
often see men faint with terror. From this anyone can easily realize that the spirit is
bound tightly to the mind, for when it is struck by the mind's force, it immediately 160
pushes the body and makes it move.

This same reasoning shows that both mind and spirit are corporeal, for we can
see that the mind makes the body move and rouses it from sleep, it changes the
facial expression and guides and steers the whole person. Yet, since we see that
none of this can take place without being caused by touch, and in turn all touch 165
is physical, surely one has to admit that the mind and the spirit are corporeal in
nature? Moreover, you can see that the mind suffers what the body suffers and

---

goes pale   these lines echo a poem (fragment 31) by the Greek poetess Sappho which was
also imitated by Lucretius' contemporary, the poet Catullus (poem 51). Sappho (seventh
century BC) is describing the sensations of being in love, but Lucretius radically alters
their context by making them symptoms of fear, for he disapproves of love's passion;
Gale remarks (*CCL* p. 70) that 'there is a marked tendency in the *de rerum natura* toward
a highly critical engagement with earlier literature'. The ancient world held emotion to
be more of a physical than mental process: for example, words for 'grief' primarily mean
physical pain rather than mental despair. The following translation of Sappho's poem is
by William Carlos Williams (1958).

> Peer of the gods is that man, who
> face to face, sits listening
> to your sweet speech and lovely
> laughter.
>
> It is this that rouses a tumult
> in my breast. At mere sight of you
> my voice falters, my tongue
> is broken.
>
> Straightway a delicate fire runs in
> my limbs, my eyes
> are blinded and my ears
> thunder.
>
> Sweat pours out: a trembling hunts
> me down. I grow paler
> than dry grass and lack little
> of dying.

This same reasoning   the *anima* causes the body to move: it must therefore have
substance itself, for only atoms can move other atoms (void cannot, and the only things
in the universe are atoms and void). Lucretius then resumes the main argument: bodily
pain affects the *anima*; it too must therefore be corporeal like the body. Epicurus argued
from the opposite starting-point: if the *anima* is not corporeal, it must be void, which is
impossible if the *anima* is to perform any of the functions assigned to it or indeed any
functions at all.

feels what the body feels. When a weapon brutally forces its way in and opens up 170
sinew and bone, it may not threaten one's life, yet faintness ensues and it is a relief
to swoon to the ground; there is confusion of mind once one is on the ground and
sometimes a vague wish to stand up. Therefore it must be that the nature of the 175
mind is corporeal, since a blow from a weapon, also corporeal, will trouble it.

> **1** Do you agree with the tripartite division of a person into body, mind and
> spirit? If so, what do you mean by spirit? Do you agree with Epicurus that
> the mind is part of the spirit?
>
> **2** Nowadays there is agreement that the mind is located in the brain, but
> is there consensus about where the emotions are located? Where, for
> example, would you place nervousness or excitement?
>
> **3** Would you agree that thoughts and emotions have actual substance? If not,
> in what way can they be said to exist?

3.177–322

Lucretius explains the composition of the mind and spirit. The mind is made up
of the tiniest atoms, for the thought process is extraordinarily quick and smaller
atoms are capable of moving more quickly than larger ones. Furthermore, when
we die, the mind and spirit depart the body, yet it loses nothing perceptible of
its size or weight: in the same way, wine will lose its flavour or perfume its scent
and yet neither undergoes a perceptible change. The spirit is composed of four
elements: breath, heat, air and a fourth element, smaller, thinner and more
mobile than the other three. The other three are inextricably intermingled and
they are spread throughout the body. The proportion of each element in us
affects our character and disposition, though it need not affect how we live, for
the parts which philosophy cannot reach are so insignificant that all of us are
capable of attaining the divine state of *ataraxia*.

The shared nature of spirit and body

3.323–69   So the spirit with **its particular traits** is enclosed within the body and is itself the
body's guardian and cause of its life: for they cling to one another with shared 325
roots, and we see that they cannot be forcibly separated without being destroyed.
Just as it is impossible to separate the scent from a lump of **frankincense** without

---

its particular traits   a reference to the subject-matter of the preceding lines, namely that
the proportions of atoms of heat, air and breath in each person's *anima* cause them to be
prone to anger, perhaps, or to fear, or to be very calm.

frankincense   imported from the east and therefore expensive (hence in the Christian
New Testament it was a gift brought to the infant Christ by one of the Magi, and was
considered comparable to another's gift of gold). Frankincense was burned during cultic
ceremonies as a special honour to the deity; in addition, to keep out the smells from the
street it was burned in the town houses of the rich, often in ornate metal braziers, some of
which have been found in the excavations at Pompeii and Herculaneum.

the lump itself being destroyed too, so it is impossible to remove mind and spirit completely from the body without all three disintegrating. Their atoms are so intermingled right from the start that their existence depends upon the partnership they share. Clearly the body and the mind are not endowed with **the ability to experience sensation** without each other's aid, but through shared movements common to them both, sensation is kindled and fanned throughout our flesh. What is more, it is clear that the body is neither born nor grows without the spirit, nor does it survive after death without it. For it is not like water, which remains intact as it loses heat which was given to it, and is itself undamaged by the process. Unlike water, I repeat, the limbs left behind cannot survive the disintegration of the spirit: once deprived of it they completely wither and rot away. From the moment the body and spirit come into being, they learn the motions of life in mutual embrace while still hidden inside a mother's womb, so that disintegration could not occur without all being lost. So you can see that since they share the origin of life, they will also share a common nature.

What is more, if someone denies that our actual body experiences sensation and believes instead that the spirit, which permeates all parts of the body, experiences the movement we call sensation, he is battling against a plain and obvious truth. For who can ever tell us what bodily sensation really is, if it is not what our senses plainly demonstrate and teach us? '**But when its spirit is removed**, the body cannot feel anything at all.' Yes, for the body is losing an ability which was not inherently its own in its lifetime, and it loses **plenty besides** when banished from life. Moreover, it is **hard to argue** that the eyes have no ability to see anything and that it is the mind that looks through them as though a door had been opened, when the sensations in our eyes indicate the opposite. For such sensations

330

335

340

345

350

355

360

---

the ability to experience sensation according to Epicurus, the process of sensation occurs as follows: an object touches the body, the atoms of the body both are knocked and simultaneously knock the atoms of the spirit, which are distributed throughout the body. The spirit cannot experience sensation (or indeed exist) without the body to encase it and the body cannot experience sensation without the atoms of the spirit to interpret it. The processes by which we smell, taste, hear and see form the main subject-matter of Book 4.

But when its spirit is removed an imaginary opponent poses a question – Bailey comments (p. 1053) that 'it is a little abrupt, but all this passage is loosely written'. Lucretius is here rejecting the Stoic view stated by Cicero (*Tusculan Disputations* 1.20.46) that only the spirit has the ability to sense touch.

plenty besides for example, the body loses colour and movement when the spirit disintegrates: for, like sensation, the body itself did not possess these independently, but only for the time the *anima* was present.

hard to argue Lucretius states a logical extension of the argument put by his imagined opponent: to argue that it is the spirit and not the body which experiences touch is like arguing that it is the mind and not the eye which experiences sight, which cannot be true, because our actual eyes feel physical pain when looking at bright lights.

point to the eyes, leading us right to the eyeballs themselves – in particular, we generally cannot look straight into a bright light, since our eyes are hampered by the brightness. This does not happen with doors, for the door through which we might be looking out would not experience any such handicap when opened. Moreover, if the eyes are like doors, clearly the mind should see better **if the eyes were removed**, taken out doorposts and all.

365

---

1 Why can we not look straight at the sun? Is it because our eyes cannot cope with the intense light or because the brain cannot cope with so strong a signal?

2 Is Lucretius' use of *reductio ad absurdum* helpful or does it spoil the tone of the passage?

3 Think of the situation of a person who is in a coma: does the patient's condition support Lucretius' claim that 'the body and the mind are not endowed with the ability to experience sensation without each other's aid'?

3.370–444

Lucretius urges us not to accept Democritus' proposal that the atoms of the body and the spirit are found in the body in alternate arrangement side by side, for in fact the atoms of the spirit are fewer and smaller. We can be sure, though, that the distance between each atom of the spirit is no greater than the size of the smallest bodies which we can sense when they touch us, though there are, of course, many objects whose touch we do not sense: dust, powdered chalk, feathers, tiny insects and so on. Furthermore, the mind must be more vital to life than the spirit, for a person will die if the atoms of the mind disperse, but one can lose many of the spirit's atoms and still be alive. Lucretius then sets out to show that both mind and spirit form at birth and break up at death: he repeats that what he says about one applies just as much to the other too. He has already explained that the atoms of the mind are far smaller than those of liquid or smoke: so, if liquid will escape when a vessel is smashed and smoke will disperse into the air, why should we believe that the atoms of the mind would not equally disperse into the air when the body is wounded and blood flows out?

The mortality of the spirit

3.445–86   Moreover, we can see that our minds and bodies are born at the same time, develop together and grow old at the same time. Infants stumble because their bodies are unsteady and weak and this is matched by their feeble powers of reasoning. Then,

---

if the eyes were removed   Lucretius extends the argument even further to a *reductio ad absurdum*, a device whereby the person criticizing an argument suggests such an extreme extension of it as to make it look ridiculous and so utterly undermine it. Lucretius also uses this device at 1.919–20, 2.976–84 and **3.776–83** (see note on p. 71).

as they reach maturity and become physically strong, their judgement is more   450
sound and their mental powers increase. Later, when the body has been shaken
by the powerful might of time and the limbs grow weak as their strength is worn
down, then the intellect hobbles along, the tongue babbles, the mind stumbles:
everything founders and fails all at once. It would therefore be consistent for the   455
atoms of the spirit too to come apart, like smoke, into the upper reaches of the air,
given that we can see how the spirit and body are born together, develop together
and, as I have shown, at the same time as each other become tired and exhausted
by age.

In addition, we see that just as the body itself will experience serious illness and   460
painful agonies, so the mind experiences bitter anxiety, fear and grief; therefore
it must be that the mind has death in common too. That is not all: when the body
is sick, the mind too often wanders waywardly; it becomes irrational and speaks
nonsense, and in a heavy torpor is sometimes carried off into **an endless deep**   465
sleep, eyes and head drooping, to a place where it hears no voices nor is able to
recognize the features of those who stand round calling it back to life, their faces
and cheeks wet with tears. Therefore you must admit that the mind too does break   470
up, when the contagion of disease strikes at its core. For pain and disease are the
artisans of death, as the deaths of many before now have taught us. Furthermore,
when **the fierce power of wine** makes its way into a man, diffusing its warmth   475
as it travels **down the veins**, why does a heaviness come over his limbs, why do

---

painful agonies   Epicurus explained that pain is either intense but short-lived or long-lasting but less intense: in each case it is therefore bearable (*Principal Doctrines* 4).

an endless deep sleep   Lucretius conflates two situations. First, he seems to be describing people who are standing by someone in a coma or 'torpor' and trying to call him or her back to consciousness. Second, his description also recalls the Roman custom whereby mourners surrounded a corpse and as part of the mourning rite attempted to call the dead person back to life.

the fierce power of wine   the Romans were great drinkers of wine, from the rough of the street tavern to the smooth of a vintage from Falernum in southern Italy. However, like the Greeks, the Romans always diluted their wine with water and the drinking of undiluted wine was the sign of a barbarian; in summer the super-rich might also cool their wines with ice carefully kept frozen since winter. At a dinner party, slaves would therefore bring in a large bowl of mixed wine and water, which they would ladle out to guests. As well as drinking wine for pleasure, Romans would often drink it as part of religious ceremonies, in particular to honour the god of wine, Dionysus, to whom they gave the title 'liberator' (Latin *Liber*).

down the veins   Lucretius explained at 2.1125 that the nourishment taken from food travels along the veins: here he asserts that the power of wine does the same.

his legs trip over each other as he staggers along? His tongue turns sluggish, his mental faculties drown, his eyes swim; increasingly he shouts, sobs, argues – and all the usual sorts of thing which happen next. Why is this so, if not because the violent assault of the wine confounds the spirit inside the body? No – when a thing can be confused and confounded, it shows that it can be robbed of further life and will **perish**, if a rather more harmful agent works its way in.

480

485

---

1 Do you agree that the mind always deteriorates with age?

2 'When the body is sick, the mind too often wanders waywardly' – what links has modern science made between diseases of the mind and body? Can you think of any diseases of the mind that have physical manifestations?

3 Wine often played a central part in the religious rites of ancient Greeks and Romans. Is this true of any religions today? Why do you think that in some religions nowadays the consumption of alcohol is discouraged or even banned?

3.487–740

Lucretius observes that when epileptics have seizures, their minds are affected too, which shows that the mind is physical. The mind and the spirit need the body if they are to exist and function, for they can do nothing apart from the body: thus, when the body dies, so do they. At death the bonds of the atoms of the spirit are dissolved and the atoms disperse, all of which is true of the mind too. He adds that the spirit must permeate the body, for when a limb is hacked off, often it continues to twitch independently: therefore either a person has two spirits or just one which can be divided into parts and so must be mortal. If the spirit is immortal and enters the body at birth, why can we not remember our past? Likewise, if that were so, the spirit would not develop in parallel with the body but would be distinct. Yet we find the spirit located throughout the body: a tooth hurts when it comes into contact with cold water, for example. If it is spread throughout the body, it will dissolve all the more easily at death. If it departs intact at death, why would it then seek another body, which would only expose it to more pain, disease and other discomforts?

---

perish we know (see note on p. 22) that if a thing can change, it can be broken up and therefore can perish. Since we observe that the spirit can be changed by wine, the same must be true of the spirit and it must be mortal, proof of which claim is the primary aim of Book 3.

To believe in the transmigration of the spirit is illogical

3.741–83   Furthermore, why is the fierce lion family always of aggressive and brutal disposition and the fox cunning? Why do deer **inherit from their fathers** an inclination to run away, why does a paternal timidity course through their legs? Indeed, why do all other traits of this kind develop in both the body and the character as a life begins, 745 unless it is because, in each seed and in each species, the character of the mind is fixed and grows together with the body? But if a spirit were immortal and in the habit of **changing its host body**, creatures' behaviour would be swapped about. A hound of **Hyrcanian** stock would often turn and run at the attack of an antlered 750 stag; a hawk would quake in the breeze at the arrival of a dove and fly off; men would lack reason, the wild breed of wild beasts would be rational.

For it is a proposition based on false logic when people say that **an immortal** 755 **spirit is altered** by being in a different body; for what is altered is broken and

---

inherit from their fathers Lucretius argues here that the mind (*animus*), which determines what we would call character, is passed down from father to offspring in the father's seed and that therefore it must be a physical entity. At **4.1218–32** Lucretius explains in more detail that the characteristics of a parent – or even a grandparent – are passed on to a child and he discusses whether the seed of the mother or the father plays the greater role in this.

changing its host body Lucretius moves to his second argument and now attacks those who believe in the transmigration of the spirit. He argues that if the spirit (*anima*) has a character of its own, its character must surely remain the same even if it moves to a new body, leading to some ridiculous situations of the sort he lists. The most prominent proponent of the transmigration of the spirit was the Greek polymath Pythagoras (sixth century BC), whose interests were wide-ranging and included philosophy, science, mathematics and religion, though nowadays he is best known for his geometric theorem. Pythagoras held that the spirit is immortal and upon the death of its host body moves to a new host (see note on Ennius, p. 15). As a result Pythagoras (and his followers) strictly avoided eating meat (Diodorus Siculus, *Library* 10.6.1).

Hyrcanian Hyrcania was an area south of the Caspian sea, in modern-day Turkey. In the ancient world Hyrcanian dogs were notorious for their ferocity, much like a Dobermann or Rottweiler today: it was even thought that they were part tiger. Lucretius chooses pairs of animals whose character traits are polar opposites, to emphasize the absurdity of Pythagoras' theory. At *Aeneid* 4.367 when Queen Dido discovers that Aeneas is going to leave, thereby dashing her hopes of marriage, she exclaims that it must have been Hyrcanian tigresses that suckled him, so cruel is he.

an immortal spirit is altered Lucretius anticipates the counter-argument that a spirit will change its disposition to fit its new body. His response is that anything which changes has by definition been broken in some way and therefore cannot be immortal. Similarly, if a spirit enters a new body of the same sort as its previous one – transferring from cat to cat, for example – it still loses its 'former life and awareness' and has therefore changed, and so must be mortal.

therefore no longer exists itself. For the spirit's components are rearranged and move away from their station, and it must then be possible for them to disperse along the limbs, so that ultimately they will all die when the body does. But if those people argue that human spirits always enter human bodies, I will still ask how a spirit is able to become foolish again after being wise – why is no child wise, why is the foal of a mare not as schooled as a strong and powerful horse? Of course, they will take refuge in the argument that the mind returns to infancy to suit its young host. But if that is what happens, they must admit that the spirit is mortal, since it is so extensively altered throughout the limbs, giving up its former life and awareness. How will each mind be able to grow strong in parallel with each body and attain the flowering of youth it desires, if the two are not partners right from the very start? Why do the spirits of the old want to leave the confines of their body? Is the spirit afraid to stay locked up inside a decrepit shell, lest its housing, tired by the passage of old age, crash down on it? Yet nothing can endanger what is immortal. Furthermore, it seems **ridiculous** that spirits should be standing by during the union rites of Venus or at the births of wild beasts, or that an unnumbered number of immortal spirits should be waiting for mortal bodies and then rush hotfoot to compete amongst themselves for which of them all should get inside first – unless by chance the spirits have come to some formal agreement that the first to fly along will be the first to get in, to avoid any hint of a competition of strength with one another.

760

765

770

775

780

---

1   Do you think that the tone of the last few lines is derisive? If so, does that undermine the scientific credibility of Lucretius' other arguments?

2   With the discovery of DNA we know that certain physical characteristics are inherited, but are we certain how our character traits are formed?

3   Do people still believe in the transmigration of the soul today? If so, how might they counter Lucretius' arguments?

3.784–829

Lucretius argues that it is nonsense for people to join what they know is mortal (the body) to what they believe is immortal (the spirit). Only individual atoms and void are immortal; since the spirit comprises a collection of atoms, it can therefore be broken back down into those individual atoms. In addition, it is affected by disease, fear and care and what can be so affected cannot be immortal.

---

ridiculous   Lucretius again (**3.359–69**) uses *reductio ad absurdum* (see note on p. 67), taking the argument which he is seeking to puncture and teasing out its implications in a way that makes it seem absurd. Here he gives us a vivid visual vignette of souls standing by as they wait for a human or animal to conceive, and he suggests that they either stampede to be the first to possess the newly conceived offspring or abide by some pre-arranged contract that the first spirit to arrive will have that right.

There is no 'us' after death

3.830–69   Therefore **death is nothing to us** and **does not concern us at all**, seeing that the nature of the mind is mortal. We felt no dismay in times gone by when from all directions the **Carthaginians** came to fight, when the whole world was shaken in 835 a quivering ferment of war, shivering and trembling under the sky's lofty realm: no one knew whether power over all human affairs on land and sea would fall to this side or that. In just the same way, when we are no longer alive, when body and spirit, which together make up **our single self**, are separated, absolutely nothing

---

death is nothing to us   this resonant statement is the culmination of the arguments put forward in the first half of Book 3 (which demonstrated that the spirit and mind are material and therefore break up after death) to address the fear of punishment and suffering after death; now Lucretius turns to the fear of death itself. Epicurus writes (*Letter to Menoecus* 125): 'So death, the most terrifying of ills, is nothing to us, since, when we exist, death is not yet present, and when death is present, then we do not exist.' Such thoughts about death were often, as here, voiced in the form of a *consolatio*, a standard literary and philosophical device by which an author tries to provide reassurance or consolation to a reader on some grave subject, perhaps death or exile. Often a *consolatio* was addressed to someone with recent personal experience of the subject-matter, for example the Roman philosopher Seneca's (AD c.1–65) Letter 63 on the death of Flaccus or Letter 107 on the pain of life.

does not concern us at all   Epicurus' attitude to death would have been quite alien to that of many of Lucretius' contemporaries. Romans paid a great deal of attention to their dead: they venerated their ancestors by adorning their halls with busts of members of earlier generations, they carried those busts in funeral processions of later family members, and they spent large sums of money building lavish tombs. Poorer Romans might be members of funeral clubs, whereby for small but regular payment members were guaranteed cremation and a place for their ashes to rest, normally a niche in a communal memorial, known as a *columbarium* for its resemblance to a dovecote (Latin *columbus*, dove).

Carthaginians   a race descended from the famous sea-faring traders the Phoenicians (Latin *Punici*), they fought against Rome in the three Punic wars. In the first Punic war (264–241 BC) the Carthaginians and Romans competed for control of Sicily and South Italy: the Romans quickly mastered the art of naval warfare and defeated the Carthaginians at sea to gain their first province, Sicily. It was during the second Punic war that Rome suffered severe defeats at the hands of Hannibal, the Carthaginian commander, including what was to be the worst in her history, at Cannae (216 BC), when approximately 45,000 men were killed in a single day (Livy, *Histories* 22.49). Hence the Romans saw the Carthaginians as the most terrible enemy they had ever faced.

our single self   Lucretius suggests that our identity is formed by a union of spirit and body. Before that union has occurred 'we' do not exist; nor do 'we' exist after it has been dissolved. Thus after death we cannot sense anything, just as we sense nothing before birth. This notion formed the second of Epicurus' *Principal Doctrines*: 'Death is nothing to us. For what has been dissolved has no sense-experience, and what has no sense-experience is nothing to us.' Lucretius goes on to explain that, even if he were to accept hypothetically that the spirit could experience sensation after death, because it would have left our body, it would not be 'we' who were experiencing it.

will be able to happen to us either, since we will not be alive at that point, or to 840
stimulate our senses – not even if land is merged with sea and sea with sky. Even
supposing for a moment that the nature of the mind and power of the spirit can
experience sensation when they have been torn from the body, that is still nothing 845
to us, whose existence as a single self depends on the combination and marriage
of body and spirit. Next, if time gathered together our atoms after our death and
returned them to their current combination and we were thus given the spark of
life anew: even if this were done, it would be of absolutely no concern to us, when 850
once the memory of who we were had been broken into pieces. The people we were
before are of no interest to us now; we suffer no anguish because of them.

For when you look back at the whole expanse of infinite time that has passed and
at the diverse movements which atoms make, you could readily believe that the 855
same atoms from which we are now formed have often been arranged in the same
combination before as they are now. Even so, our minds are unable to remember
it, for a break has been interposed in our existence and all the movements of the 860
atoms in all directions have taken them far from the path of sensation. Even if there
is misery and wretchedness ahead, a person must be alive at the time to be able to
experience those troubles. But since death precludes this and prevents the existence
of the man to whom misfortune might attach itself, we can be sure that there is 865
nothing to be feared in death, that someone who is not alive cannot be miserable
and that it is not at all different from what it would have been if a man had never
been born, once immortal death has taken away his mortal life.

1	Do you think that people are afraid of being dead? If so, what is it they fear: the unknown in general or more specifically the possibility of punishment?
2	Would anyone find Lucretius' arguments reassuring nowadays or are we very different from his Roman audience?
3	Epicurus argued that after death there is nothing. What is lost by such a belief?
4	If Epicurus is correct and there is nothing after death, would that necessarily stop people fearing it?
5	Do you think it likely that at some time in the past or the future atoms have combined or will do so to produce another 'you'? In what ways might that 'you' be the same as and in what ways different from the current 'you'?
6	Lucretius says nothing about those who seek death rather than fear it. Why might a person want to die? Would Lucretius' arguments affect that wish?

---

returned them to their current combination Lucretius introduces another hypothetical situation: the atoms might chance to recombine in just the same way to re-create another 'us', but even then our current self and our future self will have no consciousness of one another, just as we have no recollection now of ever being anyone before. The Stoics proposed the unusual doctrine that at some time in the future atoms could combine in such a way that our spirit is reassembled: this suggestion formed a part of their belief in a general recurrence of events in regular cycles. Epicurus accepted the possibility and even likelihood of such a reassembling of the spirit but ascribed it to chance instead and he denied that this second manifestation of our spirit had any connection to 'us'.

3.870–93

Lucretius observes that it is illogical to feel anxiety that after death one's body might be devoured by wild beasts and yet to have no such anxiety about being cremated or buried: in all such cases one will equally feel nothing.

Death is nothing; hell is up here with us; we are never content

3.894–1094 'No more, no more will your happy home welcome you, nor will the best of wives; sweet children will not **rush up to snatch the first kiss** and so touch your 895 heart with silent joy. You will no longer be able to protect your thriving interests or your family. You are pitiable – how pitiably,' they say, 'one malevolent day has taken from you all the numerous rewards of life.' One thing in all this they do not 900 add: 'Nor does any longing for those things possess you any more.' But if they saw this clearly in their minds and **matched this with their words**, they would release themselves from great anguish and fear. 'Just as you have fallen asleep in death, so you will be rid of all pain and sadness for the rest of time. But as for us, while 905 you were **reduced to ash** on a terrifying pyre nearby, we wept on insatiably – and

rush up to snatch the first kiss Lucretius continues to put forward arguments why death is nothing to us and so not to be feared. Here he puts conventional words of mourning into the speaker's mouth and then curtly dismisses them. However, these lines may be imbued with genuine pathos and have often been quoted out of their satirical context: Virgil imitated them at *Georgics* 2.523–4, as did Thomas Gray in the eighteenth century in his *Elegy Written in a Country Churchyard* (21–4):

> For them no more the blazing hearth shall burn
> Or busy housewife ply her evening care:
> No children run to lisp their sire's return,
> Or climb his knees the envied kiss to share.

matched this with their words it was a tradition for Roman funerary inscriptions to include an imagined conversation between the deceased and the person reading the inscription. Roman funerary inscriptions might well include set phrases such as 'best of wives' (Latin *uxor optima*) which Lucretius uses here.

reduced to ash a single word in Latin (*cinefactum*) and one coined by Lucretius; he may intend that its unfamiliarity should bring the reader up short, and so lessen the speech's potential pathos. This second imagined speech again follows conventional sentiments of mourning, but is phrased in such a way as to undermine their pathos: Kenney remarks (comm. p. 206) that 'the speaker is made to express the feelings of the bereaved in unmistakably satirical terms'. The word 'insatiably' is only used one other time by Lucretius, of pigs enjoying a good wallow in some mud (6.978), while the whole line (907) consists of only three words and its last three syllables are all long: two features which Kenney claims (p. 207) would have had a 'grotesque' effect on the Roman ear. In addition, we find the conventional and exaggerated claim that the mourners will never overcome their grief.

*'they recline at the table, cup in hand' (**3.912**): a silver drinking cup (first century AD) decorated with partying skeletons to warn revellers to enjoy life while they can; from Boscoreale, near Vesuvius.*

no day will ever take this everlasting sorrow from our hearts.' Well, we should ask this of these mourners: what is so bitter, if all things return to sleep and peace, that anyone should waste away **in endless grief**? 910

This too they often do, when they **recline at the table**, cup in hand and brows shaded with garlands: they speak from the heart: 'Brief are such pleasures for paltry mankind; soon they are gone, never to be called back thereafter.' As if in death this 915

---

in endless grief   Diogenes Laertius (*Life of Epicurus* 10.119) reports that Epicurus accepted the need to grieve and decried those who tried to suppress their grief on rational grounds. Lucretius here attacks extreme expression of grief rather than grief itself.

recline at the table   Romans used to lie down on couches to eat; diners might wear a wreath or garland on their heads as part of the festivities. Lucretius has moved from mourners grieving at a funeral to diners indulging in philosophical observation over the dinner-table, and the issue is no longer sorrow for the death of a loved one but regret that the dead are no longer able to enjoy life's pleasures. Petronius (first century AD) describes a similar scene in his novel *Satyricon*, where the wealthy freedman Trimalchio invites rich friends to dinner-parties and pontificates on the meaning of life, drawing on a mish-mash of philosophical ideas: for example (chapter 34), 'Alas for us wretches, how the whole of puny mankind is nothing! So will we all be, after Death takes us away. So let us live, while we can live well.'

---

were the greatest hardship, that thirst would burn the wretches and its dryness parch them, or that a longing for anything else would possess them! In fact no one misses himself and his life when mind and body sleep equally at rest. As far as we could care then, our sleep could go on for ever and we would still not be affected by any longing for ourselves. Yet when we sleep the atoms along our limbs **hardly depart at all** from the motions which bring sensation, and thus a man can start up from sleep and get himself together. Therefore we must think that death is much less to us – if there can be less than what we see to be nothing – for at death there follows a more thorough dispersal of the crowd of our atoms and no one awakens and stands up, once life's chill end has caught up with them. 920 925 930

---

1 Do you think there is any pathos in what the mourners say here or does Lucretius make them utterly overblown protestations of grief? If you think the former is the case, do you think that the emotion you find in the passage undermines Lucretius' argument?

2 When people mourn nowadays, are they mourning out of pity for the dead person or from their own sense of loss? If they pity the dead, on what grounds do they do so?

Furthermore, suppose that **Nature herself** should suddenly speak up and complain to one of us as follows: 'Why does death matter so much to you, mortal, that you indulge in such inordinate and bitter grief? Why do you moan and weep at your mortality? If the life you have lived up till now has been enjoyable and the good things in life have not all leaked away, poured into **a vase full of holes**, so to speak, and have not passed away without being enjoyed, why do you not leave, like a guest who has had his fill of life, and calmly accept a peace free of 935

---

hardly depart at all Lucretius treats the mechanics of sleep at 4.907–61. There he explains that sleep ensues when the atoms of the spirit depart from the body or recede deep within it, though he does not explain the process of waking up. His argument here is that if we already feel no longing for existence while asleep, when the atoms of the spirit have gone only a little way from their usual station and it is easy to wake up, then it is impossible that we can feel any such longing once dead, when the atoms of the spirit have dispersed far and wide and we will never wake up.

Nature herself Lucretius here uses an established rhetorical device whereby a concept is personified and then addresses the audience or reader, which provides dramatic variety from the main narrative; however, Nature, for Lucretius, is no concept but a manifest force. In Cicero's *Catiline* 1.8.19 Rome herself rebukes the errant Catiline and in Plato's *Crito* 50a Socrates imagines that the personified Laws come to rebuke him. As well as providing some variety within his narrative, Lucretius has Nature speak in a critical tone which would possibly seem too strident if he himself were to address his reader so.

a vase full of holes a reference to the daughters of Danaus, whose punishment in the underworld for killing their husbands was to try to fill with water jars which were full of holes.

care, you fool? But if what you have reaped has leaked away and disappeared, and 940
life is hateful, why do you seek to extend it, so that once again everything may
pass away without being enjoyed and miserably disappear? Would you not rather
put an end to life and its troubles? There is nothing more that I can discover or
devise which might give you pleasure: it is always the same old things. The years 945
may have not yet shrivelled your body and your limbs may not be exhausted and
weak: nevertheless, the same old things remain, even if you go on to surpass all
generations by outliving them – or still more, even if you never died.' How do we
reply to this, except to say that Nature is making a fair claim and putting forward 950
in her argument a legitimate case?

Now if at this point some older, more senior person were to complain and
bemoan his impending death with more self-pity than he should, would Nature
not justifiably raise her voice and rebuke him in a harsh tone? 'Away with you and 955
your tears, you imbecile! Curb your whining! After enjoying all of life's rewards,
now you are shrivelling up. But because you always yearn for what is not to hand
and despise what is in front of you, your life has slipped by you unfulfilled and
unenjoyed and now, to your surprise, death has taken up position at your side
before you are ready to leave satisfied and full. Even so, now give up everything 960
unsuited to your age. Come on, make way for the next generation with a calm
mind. You have no choice.' She would have a just case, I think, and just would
be her complaint and reproach. For the old is always pushed aside by the new
and makes way for it. Everything must be built out of something else, no one 965
is surrendered to the abyss of black Tartarus – the atoms are needed for future
generations to arise, all of whom will still go the same way as you, once they
have done with life. Generations have passed away before and will pass away in
future – you are no different. So everything will always continue to spring up out 970
of something else: no one can own life outright, everyone must rent. Just look
back at how the ancient past of the infinite time before we were born has been as
nothing to us. This is **a mirror image** which Nature is showing us of our future 975
after we finally die. Does anything there appear frightening, anything seem grim?
Is it not more free from care than any sleep?

1	What does Nature say in each of her two speeches that Lucretius might hesitate to say directly to his reader?
2	Would you describe the content of Nature's speeches as more reassuring or depressing?
3	Which of the ideas about death might you be just as likely to find expressed today and which are more specific to their Roman context?

---

a mirror image   we can have no experience or sensation of all time which has passed
before our birth: with converse logic, the same will be true of all time which comes after
our death. Thus the answer to the subsequent rhetorical question is 'no', for there is
nothing at all in the mirror image to see.

The punishment of Tityus, *1548–9, by Titian.*

No – all the things which are traditionally said to exist in deepest Acheron are undoubtedly with us here in life. There is no wretched **Tantalus** afraid of a big stone dangling mid-air above him, as the stories have it, and paralysed by an empty fear, but rather it is the case that in real life a futile fear of the gods looms over mortals and they are each afraid of the misfortune which chance may bring

980

Tantalus   said to have stolen nectar and ambrosia from the gods, their drink and food respectively. As a punishment in the underworld, a rock was suspended above his head and he was too afraid of its falling to be able to eat or drink. More familiar to us is an alternative version which is told at *Odyssey* 11.582–92, where Tantalus is constantly hungry or thirsty but food and drink remain just out of his reach, from which image comes our word 'tantalize'.

each of them. No birds make their way inside **Tityus** as he lies in Acheron – and
even if they were to do so and for all eternity, they would never be able to find 985
a single thing to pick over inside his massive chest. However huge an area his
outstretched body covered – even if his sprawling limbs encompassed not just
nine **acres** but the whole of the globe – he would still not be able to endure eternal 990
suffering or to supply food from his own body for ever. Rather, Tityus is here
with us, he is the man who is torn at by birds because he lies prostrate with love
or who is devoured by the anguish of anxiety or cut deep by some other anxious
desire. We see **Sisyphus** too with us here in life; he is the man who thirstily seeks 995
from the people **the rods and cruel axes** but who will always return defeated and

---

Tityus   one of the Giants (children of Earth and Jupiter), who attempted to rape Leto
(the eventual mother by Jupiter of the twin gods Apollo and Diana) and who was
consequently chained down to suffer the agony of vultures gnawing at his liver (held by
the Greeks to be the seat of the passions) every day, at the end of which a new one grew
back each time, ready for the next day's agony; his story is told at *Odyssey* 11.576–81. For
Lucretius, Tityus in the real world is the man in love who is in metaphorical chains, is in
emotional agony and is perpetually gnawed by jealousy; Lucretius sets out his pessimistic
view of love at 4.1058–1287.

acres   Lucretius uses the term *iugera*: a Roman *iugerum* was the amount of land a pair
of oxen could plough in a day, that is, approximately 2,500 square metres (27,000 sq ft).
An acre is a modern measurement of land comprising approximately 4,000 square metres
(43,000 sq ft).

Sisyphus   said to have told Juno when Jupiter was having an affair, to have cheated
death and generally to have offended the gods with continual arrogance and trickery.
His punishment in the underworld was to roll a large rock up a hill: if he managed to do
this successfully, he would be free, but the rock always rolled back down the hill just as
it was on the point of reaching the summit and so his efforts proved permanently futile.
His story is told at *Odyssey* 11.593–600. For Lucretius, Sisyphus in the real world is the
man of political ambition, which he holds to be futile. Epicurus advised against political
ambition (see note on p. 59) – he said one should 'live unnoticed' – on the grounds that
it disturbed one's serenity or *ataraxia*; Lucretius follows him closely and is equally critical
(note on p. 31). However, first-century Rome was quite different from fourth-century
Athens and well-born Romans were expected to pursue a career in politics: Lucretius'
comments here are much more out of tune with his times than Epicurus' would have
been, and Cicero vehemently attacks this attitude (*On the Republic* 1.1–12). Just as he did
in the case of worship (see note on p. 43), Lucretius puts forward an idea quite alien to
the general Roman reader; he is equally dismissive of political ambition again at 5.1120–
35. Hardie observes: 'Lucretius preaches an Epicurean gospel at odds with the core values
and traditions of Rome' (p. 112).

the rods and cruel axes   sticks bundled together with an axe at their centre (Latin *fasces*).
They were carried by the bodyguards of Roman officials as a symbol of their power, the
sticks representing corporal punishment and the axe capital punishment. By Lucretius'
time such punishments were no longer as common, but the bodyguards continued to
carry the *fasces* out of tradition. The twentieth-century Italian leader Mussolini named
his 'Fascists' after them.

downhearted. For to seek power, which is essentially **futile** and temporary, and to that end to expend strenuous and unceasing effort – this is to strain to push a rock uphill, only for it to roll back down again from the summit out of a pressing desire to be back on **the flat of the plain**. 1000

Likewise, to be ever feeding the ungrateful nature of the mind, to fill it with delights and still never satisfy it – just as the seasons in their cycle do for us when 1005 they produce their fruits and other treats, only for us never to feel full of life's delights – this, in my opinion, is the tale they tell of **the girls in the flower of youth** who pour water into a vessel full of holes, even though there is no possibility of 1010 its being filled. As for **Cerberus, the Furies**, Tartarus of the darkness belching forth **a hot terror from its jaws** – nowhere do they exist, nor in fact could they. However, what does exist is the fear of retribution for evil deeds in life, which

---

futile   Epicurus argued that if a man desires power as a means of protection from other men (see note on p. 31), he will find that holding office is not a secure way of protecting himself; in addition, power in Rome was always temporary because Romans legitimately held office for one year only. The system of political appointments was known as the *cursus honorum* (course of honours). Romans of noble birth, men without daily jobs in the modern sense, attempted to climb this political ladder: there were several rungs but at each one the field narrowed: at the bottom rung stood 20 men starting together as quaestors, but at the top there was space for only two consuls. Each post was held for a year only and candidates for the next post would seek it through election rather than appointment by their superiors: thus each year candidates would vie with one another to woo voters.

the flat of the plain   West points out (p. 102) that Lucretius may be playing on words: not only is the plain the destination of Sisyphus' rock, it may also refer to the plain outside Rome known as the Campus Martius, where Roman elections were held. Like Sisyphus' rock, candidates would have to 'roll' down there on election day from houses in pleasant and expensive locations up in the hills of Rome.

the girls in the flower of youth   the daughters of Danaus (see p. 76). This example differs from those of Tantalus and Tityus because the girls are not named by Lucretius nor do they appear in Homer's underworld in *Odyssey* 11.

Cerberus, the Furies   Cerberus was the three-headed dog which guarded the entrance to the underworld. The Furies were avenging goddesses who pursued wrongdoers until they paid for their crimes: they famously form the Chorus of the Greek tragedian Aeschylus' *Eumenides* and pursue Orestes because he killed his mother.

a hot terror from its jaws   there were several places thought to be 'jaws' of the underworld, i.e. its entrance. One was Lake Avernus in southern Italy: the name Avernus may derive from the Greek word for 'birdless' (*aornos*), for supposedly noxious fumes rose up from the lake and deterred birds from flying over it. Nearby are the sites of the Phlegraean Fields and modern Solfatara, the crater of an extinct volcano which continues to emit hot sulphur fumes today, perhaps the 'hot terror' Lucretius describes here.

fear is as potent as those deeds, and the punishments for a crime: **the dungeon**, 1015
the horror of being thrown down from **the rock**, lashes, executioners, stocks,
pitch, the metal plate, torches. Even though none of them is to hand, the mind,
conscious of those deeds, applies a goad to itself in its terror and sears itself with
a whip, nor does it see all the while the boundary-stone limiting its troubles or 1020
indeed any end to its punishment; in fact, it fears that these same things may grow
worse after death. In short, it is life up here that makes a hell for the ignorant.

You can also say this to yourself sometimes: 'Even the eyes of good King Ancus 1025
took their leave of the light, **a man much better than you** in countless ways, you
impudent man. Many other kings and potentates have subsequently perished –

the dungeon   the Roman state prison, situated at the north-east end of the Forum in
the centre of Rome; it was there that captives from abroad might be held until paraded
through the streets (in a procession known as a 'triumph') and then executed. Criminals
were not sentenced to time in prison itself as they are today, though they might be
sentenced to slavery, to work in the mines or to row in the galley of a warship.

the rock   the Tarpeian rock on the Capitoline hill in central Rome, off which murderers
and traitors were thrown to their deaths. Livy (*Histories* 1.11) tells the story of the infamous
Tarpeia, after whom the rock was named. When the Sabines, a neighbouring people,
were besieging Rome in one of her many wars with her neighbours, they persuaded the
commander's daughter Tarpeia to admit them into the citadel, possibly by bribing her
with what they wore on their left arms; she took this to mean their gold bracelets, but
when they entered Rome they threw their shields onto her and so crushed her to death.

pitch, the metal plate, torches   all associated with torture by fire. More normally the end
of a torch was dipped in pitch and set on fire to provide a steady source of light, but no
doubt hot pitch could serve as ready means of torture too. Metal plates were heated in
a fire and applied to the body.

a man much better than you   this echoes the similar sentiment spoken by Achilles to
Lycaon (*Iliad* 21.99–113) to the effect that the far greater hero Patroclus has recently
died and therefore Lycaon should not complain about his own imminent death. Lucretius
here compiles a careful list of great men who have died in the past to make the point
that all mortals, even the most important, must die. Ancus, the fourth of Rome's kings
(642–617 BC), was famed for his goodness. The first few words of the speech are copied
from Ennius' *Annals* 149.

and they commanded great nations. Even **that man** who once laid a road over the mighty sea to provide a route for his armies to cross the deep, who taught them 1030 to travel by foot over salt waters and who scoffed at the roaring sea, trampling it with his horses, he too was robbed of the daylight and breathed out his spirit from his dying body. **Scipio's descendant**, a thunderbolt of war, the terror of Carthage, gave his bones to the earth as though he were the most lowly of slaves. 1035 To these, add inventors in the sciences and the arts, add the friends of the Muses, including **the peerless Homer** who holds a sceptre and yet sleeps as deeply as the rest. Democritus too: warned by his seasoned old age that the motions of his mind 1040 which constitute memory were failing, he voluntarily met death and offered his head. Epicurus himself died when his life's light had run its course, the man who surpassed the human race in intelligence and eclipsed us all, as the risen sun in the sky does the stars. Will you then falter and protest at your death – you, whose life 1045

that man   Xerxes (king of Persia 486–465 BC), whom Lucretius mentions as an example of a man so powerful that he overcame the forces of nature. Xerxes ordered a bridge of ships to be strung across the Hellespont at Abydos in Mysia (modern north-west Turkey) so that his army might march across it into Europe. A storm blew up and destroyed it, so Xerxes had the builders executed and gave orders for his men to walk into the waves and whip them as a punishment, and to throw chains into the sea to symbolize that he would dominate it. He then ordered another bridge to be built. His army was so large that it took seven days and seven nights to cross the 1,200 metres (3/4 mile) separating Europe and Asia. However, his forces nevertheless suffered defeat at the sea-battle of Salamis (480) and the land-battle at Plataea (479), all of which is related by Herodotus in his *Histories* 7–9. Many Greeks thought Xerxes' bridging of the Hellespont was *hubris* (an arrogant act defying the elements and offending the gods) and they interpreted his defeat – and eventual assassination in 465 – as *nemesis* (punishment sent by the gods).

Scipio's descendant   though Scipio had many descendants, Lucretius is probably referring to Publius Cornelius Scipio Africanus (236–183 BC), who defeated Hannibal near Carthage at the battle of Zama in 202, and so Lucretius picks him to represent military success. The expression 'thunderbolt of war' may be a phrase borrowed from Ennius, but there may also be a subtle play on words here: the Latin *scipio* means staff or sceptre, the Greek word for which is *skēptron*, while the Greek word *skēptos* means thunderbolt. At the time Lucretius was writing, it was fashionable for noble Romans to learn Greek and even to travel to Athens to finish their schooling: this kind of pun might appeal to such readers.

the peerless Homer   Lucretius picks Homer to represent the pinnacle of literary merit and Democritus that of science and learning, for he was the father of atomic theory. The order in which Lucretius lists the men reflects the poem's priorities: political and military success mean less than literary achievement, but greatest of all is philosophical teaching. It is no surprise to find Epicurus at the climax of this list of great men, but this is the only time in the poem that he is mentioned by name. Lucretius describes Democritus' decline in the terminology of Democritus himself, who expounded the notion that atoms are in constant motion. He supposedly lived to the age of 109 and starved himself to death, thereby metaphorically 'offering his head' to Death the executioner.

is virtually dead even while you live and breathe? You, who spend the majority of your time asleep, who snore while awake and are continually daydreaming? You, who carry a mind troubled by vain fears and who often cannot discover what 1050 is wrong with you? You, who are drunk with countless anxieties that harry you from all directions, you wretch, who drift along, your mind bobbing aimlessly on a shifting sea?'

1 How does Lucretius make this passage dramatic and interesting? Do you think that it is one of the 'purple passages' which many feel embody Lucretius' skill as a poet but have little to do with Epicureanism?

2 What is the modern attitude to political ambition? Is it as negative as Lucretius'?

3 What connection links the first three great men (Ancus, Xerxes and Scipio) and what the second three (Homer, Democritus and Epicurus)?

4 What is it about this passage that might prompt Lucretius to name Epicurus here and nowhere else in the poem?

5 What is the tone of the words Lucretius suggests you say to yourself (lines 1025–52)? Would you object if someone said these words to you?

6 How effective do you find this *consolatio* (speech of consolation)? Would you agree that, since more prominent people have died before, it is unreasonable to fear one's own death?

If only people, just as they obviously feel a weight on their mind and are worn out from that burden, could also understand what causes it to be there and where that 1055 large block of misery, as it were, in their heart came from, they would not spend their lives in the way we see most of them currently do: nobody knowing what he wants but always looking to change his situation, as if he could thereby offload his burden. The man who is sick of being at home often ventures outdoors from 1060 **his grand residence**; later of a sudden he returns, having felt no better off while away. He runs off to **his country house**, driving his horses at breakneck speed, as

---

his grand residence at the time Lucretius was writing, Rome was rapidly expanding her territories, especially in the eastern Mediterranean. Roman nobles, whose public career often included stints as commanders in the army and provincial administrators, often returned to Italy rich. They might spend that new-found wealth on enlarging their existing properties or constructing new ones.

his country house Rome was (and still is) uncomfortably hot in summer and many Romans would leave the city to avoid consequent health risks, and would spend the summer in a country house in the hills or down on the coast at Baiae (near modern Naples). Such houses were large and expensive; they might encompass a private gymnasium, a swimming-pool and extensive formal gardens. The Roman scholar, businessman and politician Pliny the Younger (AD 61–112) owned one such villa at Laurentum on the coast near Rome and he gives a full description of its layout at *Letters* 2.17. As well as being a luxury retreat, the villa also served as the administrative centre from which the surrounding estate was run (see note on use of land p. 53).

though urgently bringing help for some building on fire; yet as soon as his foot 1065
touches the threshold of his villa, he immediately gives a yawn or falls fast asleep
and seeks oblivion; he may even head hurriedly back to town to be there again. In
such ways does each man try to get away from himself, but since it is absolutely
impossible to escape, he is stuck with himself against his will; moreover **he hates
himself**, since he is ill but cannot explain the cause of his sickness. If he were to 1070
get clear sight of it, each man would drop all his affairs at once and devote himself
first and foremost to learning the nature of things, since it is a question of his state
for eternity and not just one hour – the state in which mortals must await all time 1075
which remains after death.

So what is this terrible desire to be alive which is so powerful as to make us tremble
when under duress and in danger? A fixed limit to life does indeed attend all
mortals: it is impossible to avoid death but we must face it. Moreover, we live in 1080
and amongst the same old things, nor is any new pleasure forged by living longer.
But so long as what we long for is out of our reach, it seems to be more important
than anything else; after we have attained it, we long for something else, and an
undiminished thirst for life possesses us, our mouths always open. What fortune
the days ahead may bring is unknown, as are what chance has in store for us and 1085
how things may turn out. In truth, by prolonging our lives we do not detract
even the tiniest amount from the eternity of death, nor can we skim off the least
amount so that we can be dead for not quite such a long time. So rack up as many 1090
generations as you want: no less will the same eternity of death still await you, nor
will the man whose life ends with today's light be dead for any less length of time
than he who died many months or years ago.

---

1   Lucretius argues that people do not understand the cause of the weight
    on their mind. Yet does knowing the cause of a sickness necessarily lead to
    being able to cure it?

2   Would you agree that wealth and the leisure to enjoy it make people
    restless? Do you think some people travel nowadays to be rid of that
    feeling?

3   Bailey remarks (p. 1173) of lines 1076–94: 'The paragraph consists of a series
    of disconnected points and is unsatisfactory as a conclusion.' Do you agree?
    Which points have already been made in Nature's first speech (lines 933–
    49)? Does that weaken the effect of the paragraph? Do you think it forms a
    satisfactory conclusion to Book 3?

---

he hates himself both Plato (*Republic* 1.352a) and Aristotle (*Nicomachean Ethics*
9.4) claimed that the wicked man would hate himself, but Lucretius widens his net to
include anyone who is metaphorically 'ill' because he has not been cured by Epicurean
philosophy.

4 The processes of sensation and thought

There exist images of things

4.26–109   **Well, since I have explained** what the nature of the mind is, of what matter it is composed, how it grows together with the body, and the way in which it is torn up and returns to its primary elements, I will now explain something to you which is most pertinent to those questions: there exist what I will call **images** of things. Like a skin peeled off from the surface of a body, they fly this way and that through the air. Confronting us while we are awake, these images frighten our minds – and in our sleep too, we often behold fantastic shapes or **images of the lightless dead**, which often wake us in terror when we were lying relaxed in sleep.

30

35

Well, since I have explained   lines 1–25 repeat **1.926–50** (the image of honeying the cup of medicine). Some editors believe Lucretius would have removed them when he came to revise his poem, while others argue that at this half-way stage in the poem he repeats them deliberately, wishing to refocus the reader's attention on the scientific subject-matter, since he addressed matters of moral philosophy so extensively at the end of Book 3.

images   in lines 26–44 'images' refer to mental images (dreams and daydreams); Lucretius then goes on to discuss other types of emission – smell, reflected colour, mirror images, all of which he understands to be similar phenomena. This notion may seem stranger to us than anything we have encountered so far in his poem, but in a material world where all is either atoms or void, the process of perception or sensation must be explained in atomic terms. It is quite easy to comprehend the idea that the atoms of a smell or a sound travel from their source to strike the atoms inside our nose or ear to produce sensation, and even easier to so do in the case of taste and touch, but sight is not so easily explained. The earliest philosophers spoke of 'effluences' given off by objects and subsequently the Atomists explained that these effluences were formed of atoms and travelled across the air to strike the atoms of the eye. They held that all objects are constantly shedding atomic versions of themselves: Lucretius follows Epicurus in calling these 'images' of objects.

images of the lightless dead   in the ancient world dreams were important as omens: for example, pilgrims would stay overnight in the temple of Asclepius (the god of healing) in Epidaurus in Greece, where the god or his agents would appear to them in a dream. The Greek Artemidorus (second century AD) wrote his *Onirocritica*, an encyclopaedia of dream interpretations, after travelling to collect dreams and their outcomes; in Sophocles' tragedy *Electra*, Clytaemnestra has a frightening dream in which her dead husband's spirit comes back to life – Lucretius is here challenging a popular belief when he discounts the religious explanation of dreams, but he is aware that people see images of the dead in their dreams and he must therefore account for this.

This must not lead us to think that spirits escape from Acheron or that ghosts fly around amongst the living, or that something of ourselves can remain after death, when the body and the nature of the mind have together perished and each 40 has been broken down into its atoms. So I say that objects give off **likenesses of themselves**, slender shapes from the surface of their bodies, a concept you will understand, however slow your wits, from the following.

First, in the realms of the visible many things give off bodies, some of which break 55 up and scatter – as wood gives off smoke and fire heat – while others are more strongly and closely bound together: just as cicadas will shed their sleek coats in summer, or when calves are born they shed a membrane from the surface of their body, or just as a slippery snake discards its garb on thorns – we often see these 60 blowing about and adding to the brambles' catch. Since all this happens, it must also be that every thing sends out a slender image from the surface of its body. For why would a dense image come off and move away from things more readily 65 than a slender one? It is impossible to mutter an answer, especially since objects have many tiny particles on their surface which could be dispatched in the same order they were lined up and could maintain the shape of their formation – and all the more quickly, since they are less encumbered, being few and located on 70 the front-line.

For we certainly see many objects cast off particles in profusion, not only from deep inside, as I said before, but in fact often from their surface too, such as their colour. The yellow, red and purple awnings frequently do this, when they flutter 75 and flap, spread out on poles and beams and stretched across large **theatres**. For

---

likenesses of themselves sometimes we perceive the 'images' themselves: when we smell perfume, the atoms emitted by the perfume strike our sense organs and so perception takes place. In such cases, the images originate deep within the object and during their journey to the object's surface they are broken up. However, perception by sight is different: images leave the surface of an object and therefore are not broken up. Lucretius calls such intact visual images 'likenesses'.

theatres drama was a popular form of entertainment in Rome and for two hundred years plays were staged in temporary wooden theatres, specially constructed for a series of performances. In order to shelter the audience from the sun, awnings were stretched across the top of the theatre to form a makeshift roof; this included a complex set of wooden poles and beams, operated by a team in the same way that a crew of sailors might rig large sails. The sockets for such poles can still be seen in the Colosseum in Rome. These temporary theatres might nevertheless be very elaborate: Pliny the Elder (*Natural History* 36.2) tells of one, constructed in AD 58 to stand for just a month, in which the backdrop to the stage was three storeys high, one storey of marble, one of glass and one of gilded planks, and included 360 columns and around 3,000 statues. The audience would be seated according to status: at the back were ordinary citizens, in the reserved seating in front of them sat the wealthy non-senatorial class known as *equites*, and in the front rows near the stage sat the senators.

*A fresco from Pompeii of an amphitheatre, first century AD. Note the awning at the top of the picture (**4.75–6**).*

there they add colour to those in the seated areas below, to those with a close view of the stage and to some of the stage itself, forcing the whole theatre to 80 shimmer in their colours – and the more tightly enclosed by its walls a theatre is, the more cheerful is everything inside, robbed of sunlight and bathed in charm. Therefore, just as an awning emits a tint from its surface, it follows that all things 85 emit likenesses which are slender, since in each case the emissions emanate from the surface. So there are precise traces of shapes, made of a delicate weave, which fly about everywhere but which cannot be seen one at a time.

On the other hand, all smells, smoke, heat and other such emissions from objects 90 disperse far and wide. Because they originate from deep within a thing and rise to its surface, they are split up on their winding journey, for there are no direct exits on their route from which they might swiftly sally forth, once they have mobilized. However, when a thin film of surface colour is emitted, there is nothing that 95 can pull it apart, since it sits at the ready, located right at the surface. Finally, whenever we see something in a mirror, in water or in any shining surface, it must be the case that what we are seeing is made up of these images that have been sent 100 out, since there is a perfect likeness. So there exist **slender images** of the form of each thing and most like it. No one can see these one at a time, but returning in 105 continuous and quick succession, they make up the reflection we see on the surface of a mirror. By no other process could the images be so well preserved that such a true likeness of their original shape was sent back.

---

1   Have you ever dreamed of someone who was dead? Did having that dream suggest to you that the dead person's spirit still exists in some sort of conscious form?

2   Is it logical of Lucretius to suggest that all objects give off images just because a few do?

4.110–291

Lucretius reminds us that things exist which we cannot see: we need only consider creatures which are so small that if they were divided into thirds, they would be invisible to the eye – how much smaller must their heart be, for example. He then begins to give an account of the aforementioned visual likenesses. They flow unceasingly from the surface of things and will pass through some objects, such as glass, break against others, such as rock, or bounce back from yet others, such as mirrors. These likenesses are so slender that they can fly through the air at unimaginable speed: for example, if one puts a bowl of water under a starry sky, the reflection of the stars appears instantly; likewise, we taste salt as soon as we walk near the sea. The likenesses are so thin and slender that we cannot see each individual one but only their sequence in rapid succession – just as we become cold when buffeted by the wind but do not sense the individual particles of the wind. He then treats the subject of mirrors and how they reflect the likenesses, explaining first why an object seen in a mirror seems to stand as far beyond the mirror as it actually stands in front of it.

---

slender images   Lucretius first cites the shedding of its skin by a cicada as analogous to the emission of an 'image' by an object. He then blends analogy and a real instance of such emission, for the colour coming from the theatre awning is the actual colour image emitted from it, but it is not an intact visual likeness because it has lost its shape or form. Finally, he cites a reflection in a mirror, which is an intact visual 'likeness' of its original object because it is composed of the actual atomic images coming off the original object's surface. Each individual atomic likeness remains imperceptible to us, but their bombardment of the mirror in constant and quick succession means they are visible – rather like individual frames in a reel of film: the eye does not perceive each particular one, but the continuous bombardment of the individual pictures together makes up a visible, moving image.

Reflections in a mirror

4.292–323   Now, the right side of our body appears in a mirror as though it were the left for the following reason: when the image arrives at the mirror's surface and strikes it,

it does not come back true but rather is dashed 295
directly back – just as would happen if one were
to slam a **plaster mask** against a pillar or beam
before it was dry; though preserving its proper
shape, the mask would instantly recast itself
so its front was pushed back out towards us.
This would mean that what before was its right 300
eye is now its left and its left eye is swapped to
the right. It is also possible for an image to be
bounced from **mirror to mirror**, so that even
five or six likenesses could easily be made. For
objects may lie hidden inside a house at the
back, but even so, however far back inside they 305
are and around however many corners, all of
them can be properly revealed using a series of
mirrors along a zigzagging route and can be seen
as being in the house. So consistently does the
image beam across from mirror to mirror, and
when one holds out a left hand, it subsequently
becomes one's right hand, but then reverts back 310
again and returns to its original side.

*A Roman nobleman holding the death masks of his
ancestors, c. 30 BC; such masks often adorned the entrance
hall of a wealthy household and were brought out for a
funeral, to accompany the body to the family tomb.*

---

plaster mask   Romans made plaster masks of their relatives, modelled on the face at death, which were then displayed in the home to impress family and visitors; they might also be worn at family funerals. Masks were also made for use in the theatre, where actors, like their Greek counterparts before them, wore masks to represent characters.

mirror to mirror   modern optical fibres work on the same principle. Light rays enter the fibre at one end and bounce off or are 'totally reflected' by the internal glass walls of the fibre all the way along to its other end.

Furthermore, any concave mirror, **curved outwards** like our hips, will send back the **right-handed image** to us: **either because** the image is bounced from one side of the mirror to the other, and only flies out towards us when it has been dashed against it twice; or possibly because the image is reversed before reaching our eye, 315 the curved shape of the mirror having led it to be turned around to face us. In addition, you should realize that the likenesses move forwards and take steps in time with us and **copy our movements**, because whichever section of the mirror 320 you move away from, immediately the likenesses can no longer be reflected from that part – for nature requires that every thing is thrown back **at the same angle**, when reflected and bouncing back from surfaces.

---

1 How do you think Lucretius reached his conclusions on scientific matters? Do you imagine him conducting a series of optical experiments in a makeshift laboratory, or do you think that he observed these phenomena as he went about his daily life?

2 Are there modern-day intellectuals with interests as broad as Lucretius', combining scientific enquiry with philosophical thought?

---

curved outwards   the outside of a concave mirror curves outwards 'like our hips' and is convex; it is the inside which is concave. Ancient mirrors were typically made from a single piece of polished metal; it would be easy enough to push the metal out to form a concave surface inside. Depending on the distance between the object and mirror, concave mirrors will produce an image that is the correct way up but enlarged and are therefore commonly used today as make-up mirrors. The Greek scientist Archimedes is said to have fashioned a concave bronze mirror to trap sunlight and direct it at the enemy Roman ships during their siege of Syracuse and to have succeeded in setting them on fire from a distance.

right-handed image   by which Lucretius means a correctly oriented image, with the right side of the object properly appearing as the right side of the reflected image. Romans observed that few of them were left-handed and therefore thought it odd to be so: *sinister*, the Latin word for left or left-handed, could mean unlucky or even immoral.

either because   at times Lucretius will offer more than one explanation for a phenomenon: the one he puts first has usually turned out to be the correct one (as here) and it may be that he deliberately puts his preferred explanation first. In a concave mirror an object is reflected twice: you will see the correct image if you stand to one side of the mirror and look at the object in the other. In his alternative explanation, Lucretius imagines one side of the image hitting the mirror before the other and bouncing back first, with the result that the image twists round.

copy our movements   from the Marx Brothers' *Duck Soup* through to Bugs Bunny in *Hare Tonic* writers have included a scene in which a character stands in front of a 'mirror' which in fact holds no glass, and makes various movements which another character, hiding behind the glassless mirror, must instantly copy in order to avoid detection.

at the same angle   in modern physics the Law of Reflection states that the angle between the ray that strikes the mirror and the 'normal' – that is, an imaginary line drawn perpendicular to the mirror – is always equal to the angle between the normal and the reflected ray.

4.324–413

Lucretius continues to explain the process of sight: why it hurts our eyes to look at the sun or other bright lights; why we can look out from darkness and see objects which are in the light but not vice versa and why we have a shadow. In all cases, he is at pains to emphasize that the eyes only receive images and can never be mistaken in receiving them, but the mind will sometimes misinterpret that information. For example, when sailing it seems to us that the coast is moving while the ship we are on is standing still; likewise, when children spin round and then stop, it seems to them that the room is spinning. In these cases it is the mind which is deceived and never the eyes, which simply receive likenesses.

Optical illusions; the senses as sole determiners of truth

4.414–521   **A puddle of water** lying between the flagstones on a paved road, though not more than a finger deep, affords a view below the ground that stretches as far down as the   415
yawning expanse of heaven does above. Thus you seem to gaze down on the clouds and sky, and to see bodies miraculously hidden in a sky below the ground. Again, when our spirited horse gets stuck mid-river and we look down at the fast current of   420
the stream, its force seems to drive the body of our stationary horse the other way, **pushing it urgently upstream**, and wherever we cast our glance, everything else

---

A puddle of water Epicurus explained that all sensation involves the atoms of each 'image' striking the sense receptors, a process which cannot be mistaken, and the sense receptors then pass a message to the mind. In this example, we look into the puddle and our eyes see the whole sky reflected there; it is the mind which may jump to the mistaken conclusion that the depth of the puddle is as great as the sky is high. Lucretius describes an everyday vignette in language more typically used in cosmological descriptions and he humorously pictures the simple person who is amazed to see his body already down in what he supposes to be the underworld, which, to add to his confusion, looks like sky. Even if in truth no one would be fooled into thinking that a world does lie beneath the puddle, the reader will understand optical illusion better from such an extreme case. Porter (p. 169) remarks that by situating the grandeur of the cosmos in a puddle, Lucretius once again deflates a reader's potential awe at the majesty of the universe, awe which might lead to the acceptance of the idea that the universe was created by gods and is directed by them.

pushing it urgently upstream the next in this series of optical illusions, all of which are designed to reinforce the point that the eyes see what they see and it is the mind which then introduces a false interpretation. When the horse stops, it seems to be moving upstream, owing to the current's flowing so fast downstream. In addition, when the rider looks back up from the horse in the fast-moving current at objects on the river bank, everything up there seems to be flowing along too.

seems to be borne on and flowing along just like us. Again, although a **colonnade** 425
runs in a straight line and stands supported on columns of equal height the whole
way along, yet when one looks down its whole length from the top end, it gradually
contracts to the narrow tip of a cone, closing in roof to floor and entire right side to 430
left, until it has joined them all up into the cone's **vanishing apex.**

To sailors out at sea the sun seems to rise from the waves and to hide its light
in them as it sets – naturally, since they stare at nothing but water and sky – but
you should not rush to the conclusion that the senses are being undermined all 435
over the place. To those who are not familiar with the sea, ships in a harbour
seem to sit in the water crippled with their stern damaged. All the part of the oar
that protrudes from the salty spray is straight and the upper part of the rudder is
straight too, but the part which disappears down in the water **looks broken** and 440
bent back up at an angle, seeming to be warped and to float on the surface. When
winds carry scattered clouds across the sky during the night, then the shining
stars on high seem to be gliding the other way past the clouds and to travel in 445
quite the opposite direction to their actual course. If you bring a hand up to
one eye and press, it will affect your sense of sight so that you seem to see two of
everything that you are looking at: the lights of two lamps with their flames in full 450
bloom, two sets of furniture in pairs all over the house and people with two faces
and two bodies. Then again, when sleep has bound our limbs in sweet repose and
our whole body lies utterly quiet, even so we seem to ourselves to be awake and to 455
be moving our limbs all the while. In the blind and murky night we think we see
the sun and the light of day; we seem to exchange the room that encloses us for
sky, sea, rivers and mountains, to be walking through fields and to hear sounds, 460
though the grim silence of the night surrounds us, and to make answer, though
we are silent.

colonnade   a common feature of Roman towns. Public spaces, such as market squares
and exercise areas, had a colonnade running round the sides to provide shelter from the
Mediterranean sun (or, less frequently, rain) for those wanting to take a stroll, meet with
friends or business acquaintances, or watch what was happening. In Rome large private
houses often had a garden at their rear, around which ran a colonnade to allow their
owners to be outside and yet under shelter: this area was called the *peristylium*.

vanishing apex   such an effect occurs when one looks down a real colonnade, but
Lucretius may have observed how a colonnade was painted on a wall as part of a fresco
in a new style of decoration (known today as the Second or Architectural style) which was
becoming fashionable around the time he was writing; in this style walls were painted
with architectural motifs and landscapes to give an illusion of depth. Many of the houses
excavated at Pompeii contain rooms decorated in this style.

looks broken   Lucretius picks yet another illusion familiar to his readers, for not only did
Romans who wanted to travel any great distance usually do so by sea since it was quicker
and cheaper than land travel, but also many wealthy Romans owned seaside properties
and enjoyed pleasure-boating. The optical illusion described here occurs because light
travels more slowly in water than in air.

A fresco of an architectural landscape, from a villa excavated at Boscoreale, near Vesuvius (probably first century AD); there was a fashion for such decoration featuring a use of perspective.

We see a miraculous number of other things of this kind, all of which would seek to undermine our trust in the senses: in vain, since the majority of them succeed in their tricks only because our minds have preconceptions which we ourselves 465 then interpose, so that things which have not been perceived by the senses are taken for things that have. For nothing is harder than to distinguish between what is plain to see and what is doubtful, since the mind readily introduces doubt of its own accord. Then again, if anyone thinks that one cannot be certain of anything, then he is not certain of whether one can be certain of that either, since he admits 470 that he is not certain of anything. So I will refrain from arguing against a person who is standing upside-down on his head. Nevertheless, if I were to grant him that certainty, I would put this question: since he has never previously seen any truth anywhere, how can he be certain of what certainty is and by extension 475 what doubt is, of what created the distinction between truth and falsehood, of what proves that doubt is any different from certainty? You will find that the **concept of truth** is born from the senses first of all and the senses cannot be contradicted. For something would have to be found to be more reliable, something which by itself could 480

---

concept of truth Lucretius turns to a question central to any philosophical system: is knowledge possible? Some Atomists had expressed doubt that it was and some had gone so far as to deny it completely: such an approach is known as Scepticism. However, Epicurus thought knowledge was possible and he held that it can be obtained only through the senses, which cannot be wrong and which cannot contradict themselves or each other, though it is interesting to note that while all his reasoning depends on the senses, the atom, the basic component of his universe, is imperceptible. The question of knowledge interested philosophers of the ancient world and epistemology (theory of knowledge or 'how and what we can know') has continued to be an important branch of philosophy ever since.

disprove the false by means of the true – but then, in what are we to place greater trust than the senses? Will reason, which is the product of deceitful senses, have the authority to speak against them, when it is entirely derived from those senses? 485 For if the senses are not true, then all reason becomes false as well. Or will the ears fault the eyes or touch fault the ears? Will taste in turn disprove touch, will the nose plead otherwise or the eyes prove it false? I think not. For each has a distinct and separate power, each its particular capability; consequently we must perceive 490 what is soft or cold or hot by one means of sensing, but by another the different colours and **whatever is conjoined with colour**. Likewise, the power of taste is quite separate; smell comes about separately, sound separately. Consequently 495 there is no possibility that one sense could prove another wrong.

Nor then will it be possible for any sense to prove itself mistaken, since each must be considered consistently reliable at all times. It follows, therefore, that **what is perceived by them at any time is true**. If reason cannot untangle why it is 500 that things which were square from up close look round from a distance, then in explaining either shape it is preferable even to give a wrong explanation through a lack of understanding than to let something clearly seen slip from your grasp, and thereby to undermine what is trusted most and to tear up the entire foundations 505 on which life and health rest. For not only will all reason collapse, but also life itself will quickly collapse, if you do not have the confidence to trust your senses,

---

whatever is conjoined with colour   Lucretius' meaning is not always clear and this is one such occasion. These attributes which are 'conjoined with colour' have not been identified for certain. It has been suggested that Lucretius means that colour is connected to conditions of light or the shape of an object, or perhaps to how we perceive a particular object: we can at least be sure that the attributes are visual.

what is perceived by them at any time is true   Democritus held that sensation was not a reliable guide to truth – for example, what tastes sweet to one person may taste bitter to another – but was relative rather than absolute. He explained that this was so because everything depends on the arrangement of atoms of the sense-organ which senses the impact of the atoms on it, i.e. the atomic arrangement of one person's eyes will be different from that of another's. Plato too held that sense-perception afforded an uncertain sort of truth. The notion that there is no absolute truth but that all is relative was applied to moral philosophy by Archelaus (fifth century BC), a pupil of Anaxagoras. He argued that such concepts as justice and injustice are equally subjective, for what seems just to one person may seem unjust to another. The sophists, itinerant Greek teachers of the second half of the fifth century BC who offered instruction on questions of philosophy and science, developed this idea: for example, the sophist Gorgias wrote a treatise *On nature or the non-existent*, in which he attempted to prove that nothing exists, but if it does, we cannot know it, and even if we could know it, we could not explain it to anyone else. The sophist Protagoras wrote that 'man is the measure of all things', by which he meant that knowledge is relative to the knower.

to shy away from places with sharp drops and other such things to be avoided, 510
and to head for their opposites. So those were all a lot of **empty words**, be sure,
drawn up and deployed against the senses. Just as with a building, if the original
rule is crooked, if the square is untrue and out of line, if the level tilts at all at any 515
point, the whole building will necessarily be uneven, askew and off-centre, it will
sag, lean forwards or back and be out of harmony, with the result that some parts
look **ready to collapse** or do in fact collapse, utterly betrayed by mistakes in the
original calculations. Just so must your understanding of things be mistaken and 520
wrong – like anything based on 'deceived' senses.

---

1   How many of the examples of optical illusion chosen by Lucretius have you
    experienced? What others can you think of?

2   Is Lucretius correct in supposing that each sense is independent of the other?
    Or does one sense influence the other – for example, does the sense of taste
    affect the sense of smell?

3   Is Epicurus correct or can you think of examples where the senses themselves,
    and not the mind's interpretation of them, are mistaken?

4   Do you think Lucretius has successfully countered the sceptics' claim that
    nothing can be known?

5   What ways might there be to 'know' something other than through
    sensation?

6   Do you think that the senses are the ultimate arbiter of truth? If not, what is?

7   Is Lucretius right in saying that reason is the product of the senses?

---

to shy away this may seem far-fetched, but the biographer Diogenes Laertius
(*c.* third century AD) writes that the fourth-century BC philosopher Pyrrho refused to
rely on the evidence of his senses and would confront wagons, precipices and dogs with
equal scepticism, and that his friends were therefore always having to look out for his
welfare.

empty words Lucretius wishes to convince the reader of a principle central to
Epicureanism, that the senses are the only way to find truth, and so he makes use of a
number of rhetorical devices. He uses rhetorical questions inviting readers to suggest
their own answers, which they will therefore believe more readily. He addresses readers
directly, to attract their attention and keep it. He includes the sustained analogy of the
crooked house to make his point more accessible. He adds a touch of humour, as we
picture the sceptic refusing to admit that a precipice is dangerous and by ridiculing the
arguments of his philosophical opponents.

ready to collapse from the third century BC onwards, tall apartment blocks began
to spring up in Rome to cater for the growing population. These were often shoddily
constructed by unscrupulous landlords and so liable to subside or collapse, especially since
some rose higher than five storeys. These collapses were frequent enough for the first
Roman emperor Augustus (31 BC–AD 14) to impose a limit of five storeys (approximately
20 metres, 60 feet) on such buildings.

Sounds are composed of atoms

4.524–62   First of all, all sounds and speech are heard when they have worked their way into the ear and their matter has **struck the sense-organ**. For you must admit that 525 sound and speech are corporeal too, since they are able to strike against the senses. Moreover, speaking often scratches the throat and shouting makes the windpipe sore on its way out. Indeed, when the speech particles have gathered along the 530 windpipe in too big a crowd and then begin to head for the exit, assuredly they scratch the portal of the mouth too, when the throat is over-full. So, since they can cause pain, there is no doubt that spoken words consist of atoms. Likewise, it will not have escaped you how much is taken out of the body by **speaking** 535 **continually** from the gleam of sunrise to the gloam of nightfall, and how much is drained from a person's very muscles and strength, especially if the words are delivered at the top of the voice. So speech must necessarily be corporeal in 540 nature, since while speaking at length, a person loses some bodily matter. Now, a voice will sound rough owing to the **roughness of its particles** and similarly a smooth sound is caused by smooth ones. Nor are the particles which enter the ear arranged the same way when the trumpet bellows its low, muffled bass and there 545 reverberate back alien sounds in a hoarse drone, as they are when the swans of Helicon's winding valleys raise their mournful song with plaintive voice.

So when we force up some speech particles from inside our body and expel them 550 straight out through the mouth, our supple tongue, crafter of words, divides them up and our lips give them arrangement and shape. Then, when what we said arrives, if it has travelled no great distance from its starting-point, the actual

---

struck the sense-organ   the Atomists and Epicurus were close to the correct explanation of the process of hearing. In fact, when we speak, our vocal cords vibrate, causing the air around them to vibrate and producing sound waves in the air. It is these waves that strike our ears and cause us to hear; it is not because atoms are expelled from our mouths and fly across the intervening space. However, waves do carry energy and when they strike the eardrum, they cause it to vibrate.

speaking continually   ancient traders selling their wares presumably had to shout for much of the day, as did the town crier, a man whose job it was to make announcements. Likewise, a senator might speak at great length in the Senate in order that there should not be enough time for a vote on the proposed motion, a trick known in modern times as filibustering. Most probably, though, Lucretius is thinking of someone speaking in court, for speeches there often lasted at least several hours; in addition, trials might take place in the Forum, when participants would have to speak 'at the top of the voice' to be heard over the background noise of the general bustle of the city. Cicero writes how physically exhausting he found speaking in the courts at *Brutus* 313.

roughness of its particles   when listing the permanent properties of an atom, one of which is its shape, Lucretius explained at 2.410–43 that each atom has a particular shape, which can be rough or smooth.

words are heard clearly and distinguished syllable by syllable, for they have kept 555
their arrangement and shape. However, if the **intervening space** is too great, the
words are jumbled up across all that air and what we said is confounded as it
wings its way along the breeze. Consequently you can sense the sounds but not 560
pick out the meaning of the individual words, so completely confounded and
disrupted is what we said by the time it arrives.

> 1 Which jobs nowadays require one to speak for most of the day? Do you
>   think it is as tiring to do so as Lucretius claims?
>
> 2 What accounts for the difference in tone between different sounds? Is his
>   explanation close to being correct or is he fundamentally misguided?

4.563–672

Lucretius continues to treat the nature of sound, explaining how it may strike
an object and bounce back. For example, a shout will echo in the mountains,
but he is at pains to point out that the echo is not caused by nymphs and
satyrs returning one's shouts, as popular superstition would have it. He
finishes with an explanation of why sound will travel through closed doors
but an image will not: sound splits into numerous smaller versions of itself
and can travel through the void within objects, whereas visual likenesses
travel in straight lines and are broken up when they dash against an object.
Lucretius now turns to taste. He observes that the tongue, not the throat
or stomach, is the organ with which we sense taste, for it comes into direct
contact with food. Some foods taste sweet because their atoms are smooth,
others bitter because their atoms are rough. Different beings can or cannot
endure different foodstuffs according to whether the atoms of that food are
more or less compatible with the atoms of their tongues.

The nature of smell

4.673–705   Well then, I will explain how the impact of a smell touches the nostrils. First,
there must be many objects from which a stream of different smells flow out and
roll along; we must think of these as being emitted and flowing out, and scattering 675

---

intervening space once again the Atomists and Epicurus were close to the correct
explanation. We now know that sound is made up of waves which leave the source of
the sound and travel at a particular speed known as the 'wavespeed'. Sound is more
difficult to hear over greater distances because the waves lose their energy as they travel
and therefore strike the ear-drum with less force when they arrive.

in all directions. However, some smells are more suited to some animals because of differences in atomic shape. This is why **bees** are drawn towards the scent of honey on the breeze, however far away, and vultures towards corpses. Then, powerful **hunting-dogs** sent on ahead will lead hunters urgently in whichever direction a wild animal has set its cloven hooves; the white goose, meanwhile, **saviour of the citadel** of Romulus' sons, perceives the smell of humans from far away. Thus different creatures have been allocated different smells to guide each to its own food and to make each recoil from a poison which would harm it; in this way are species of wild animals preserved. 680

685

It is possible, then, that one particular smell which strikes the nose has travelled much further than another, but even so, no single smell carries as far as a sound or as far as the voice – not to mention the images which strike the pupil of the eye and stimulate sight. For a smell wanders off, arrives late and fades early: delicate as it is, it gradually falls apart among the airy breezes, first, because it barely manages to emerge from deep within an object – all objects seem to smell more when broken open or crushed or melted on a fire, which indicates that a smell flows up from deep inside before it leaves. Then, one can see that a smell is made up of larger particles than the voice, since it will not pass through stone walls, while a voice or a sound generally will. That is why you will notice that it is not so easy to track down where an object giving off a smell is located. For the impact grows 690

695

700

---

bees honey was the sugar of the ancient world and Romans were keen bee-keepers, so that Lucretius' reader would have been more likely to have witnessed bees' behaviour than many of us today; Virgil even makes bee-keeping the subject-matter of Book 4 of his *Georgics*. The same is true of Lucretius' second example: because the first half of the first century BC witnessed much bloodshed (the Social War of 90–89, the revolt of the gladiator Spartacus of 73–71 and the civil wars between Marius and Sulla), his readers might well have witnessed vultures drawn to the site of a battlefield.

hunting-dogs hunting was a popular pursuit amongst wealthy landowners and their poorer tenants alike. In a grander hunt, men might ride horses behind or run alongside dogs, which would pick up the scent of the quarry – perhaps a deer or boar – and chase it, often directing it towards nets held by men who had been stationed in a suitable place.

saviour of the citadel in 387 BC the Gauls crossed the Alps, marched down through northern Italy and arrived in Rome. Many Romans fled the city, but others took refuge inside the fortifications on the Capitoline hill, in part from a desire to protect the temples on its summit. When after a lengthy siege the Gauls discovered a hidden path by which they might ascend unnoticed to enter the citadel, they climbed up at night and would have captured it, had not the geese, sacred to Juno, sensed the arrival of the Gauls and cackled loudly, alerting the Roman watchmen, who successfully beat off the attack. Livy tells the story at *Histories* 5.47.

cool while lingering through the air and its **messengers** do not charge hotfoot at the senses – thus the hunting-dogs often go wrong and then search around for any trace of it. 705

1   What is different about the nature of smell (and sound in the previous passage) which led the Atomists and Epicurus to be closer to a correct understanding than they were in the case of sight?

2   In your experience, will animals respond more quickly to the sight of food or the smell of it?

4.706–876

Lucretius turns to new subject-matter: the mind. He explains that images are constantly flying about and these are so slender that they make no impact on our senses but do so on our minds, which themselves have a more slender atomic composition. In sleep, when our senses are numbed and so cannot distract the mind, the mind is able to perceive all manner of images and believe them to be real, for the senses are not awake to contradict it. Lucretius then addresses a new question: how is it that no sooner do we choose to think of something than its image appears to the mind? There must be many images always to hand and the mind is more receptive to the one which it seeks. Lucretius then proceeds to warn us against assuming that we have eyes in order that we may see; on the contrary, we see because we have eyes in the same way that we speak because we have a tongue. We put to use the senses and limbs with which we are endowed; it is not the case that these were given to us for a particular use. Lucretius then moves to a new topic: why we eat. He explains that living creatures lose more atoms, because they sweat, exhale and so on, than inanimate objects; it is therefore no surprise that they need food to replace those lost atoms. They are prompted to replace this matter by the body, which stirs a craving to eat.

messengers   Lucretius picks up the metaphor of a few lines earlier: there the smell reaching the nostrils slowly was like someone who 'wanders off' and 'arrives late'. Here, just as the smell travels slowly to the nostrils and loses some of its immediacy on its journey, so the messenger carrying his news takes his time and 'grows cool' instead of arriving 'hotfoot'.

How it is that we move

4.877–906 Now, how it comes about that we are able to take steps forward when we wish, how we come to have the gift of moving in a variety of ways and what force is in the habit of shoving our body's sizeable bulk forwards, I will explain: so listen 880 carefully to my words. I say that first of all **likenesses of walking** appear before the mind and strike against the mind, as I have mentioned before. Then the will arises, for no one starts to do anything unless the mind has previously visualized what it wants to do, and this visualization derives from the likeness. Therefore, when 885 the mind stirs in itself a desire to move and go forwards, it immediately knocks against the power of the spirit which is distributed throughout the body along the limbs and frame. This is easily done too, since mind and spirit are bound closely together. Thereafter, the spirit then knocks against the body and in this way the 890 entire mass is gradually given a shove forwards and set in motion. Moreover, at the same time the body also opens up and air comes in through the **openings** – as air assuredly must, since it is by nature always on the move – and penetrates down the passages in copious quantities, subsequently spreading out to all the 895 smallest parts of the body. So this process has two separate causes and accordingly our body is borne along as a ship is by both sail and wind. Nor is there anything amazing in such tiny, minuscule bodies being able to turn such a large body round 900 or shift our whole weight. For in truth the wind, though slight and composed of subtle particles, will drive and push a mighty ship of mighty size, while a single hand will steer it, whatever the speed it travels at, and will turn its single rudder

---

likenesses of walking Epicurus claimed that all sorts of images are constantly flying through the air. These strike the mind, but the mind does not choose to accept them all. When it does accept an image, it stirs its own atoms, which in turn set in motion the atoms of the spirit, which in turn stimulate the atoms of the limbs; the question remains, however, why the mind accepts one image and not another, and this is not properly answered. This question of the origin of our thoughts raises the issue of free will, for if the mind has no choice whether to accept an image or not, then we are not truly free but rather mechanical beings that only react to external stimuli. In the 1970s the scientist Benjamin Libet, working at the University of California in San Francisco, investigated the process of wishing to perform an action; he showed that even before the conscious wish arises, electrical processes in the brain have set that act in motion, and thus it is our subconscious – or an unconscious neuronal process – which in some way anticipates our conscious wish. This seems remarkably similar to the process as Lucretius describes it: on the subconscious level the mind is more receptive to one image rather than another, but once the image has struck the mind, the desire to act becomes apparent.

openings Lucretius has explained at 4.860–6 that our body regularly loses atoms when we breathe, sweat and so on, and that consequently our body can become less dense and more rarefied. Now he suggests that it is easy for air to enter and travel down a body which is less dense, with the result that the body, now containing even more air, accordingly moves with greater ease.

wherever it wants, and a **crane** too will move many objects of great weight by 905
means of pulleys and tread-wheels and lift them up at the slightest push.

1　In the light of the explanation of images striking the mind in this passage,
　how far do you think Lucretius makes us responsible for our actions?

2　Do you believe that you are free to choose your actions? What factors might
　limit your freedom to choose them?

3　Do you think Lucretius' analogy of the ship and the forces which power it is
　successful? Is there an equivalent to the hand which so effortlessly steers the
　rudder in his analogy?

4　What function(s) do analogies such as this play apart from painting a vivid
　mental picture?

4.907–1057

Lucretius turns to explain why we sleep: we do so because our spirit has been
weakened through loss of its atoms from the body. We lose atoms because
we are constantly buffeted by atoms driving against our body on the outside
and by atoms we inhale bumping against our body on the inside. Our spirit
is also weakened by the process of distributing down our limbs the food we
have eaten; sleep comes more easily then too. Then, whatever we have been
preoccupied with or recently doing while awake, we seem to be doing those
same things while asleep: this is also true of animals. Some people dream they
are urinating or having intercourse: in both cases they produce the actual
fluids as if their dreams were real. This latter observation leads Lucretius on
to discuss desire, sexual intercourse and procreation.

---

crane Roman feats of engineering such as amphitheatres, aqueducts and temples
remain impressive even by today's standards and the crane played a pivotal role in their
construction. Roman cranes varied in size and design: a simple crane consisted of a jib, a
winch, a rope and three pulleys and could be operated by one man to lift approximately
150 kilograms (330 lb). Bigger cranes with a tread-wheel instead of pulleys could lift
approximately 6,000 kg (13,000 lb), even though they could be operated by just two
men, thanks to the mechanical advantage which was gained from the diameter of the
tread-wheel.

The disturbance caused by desire

4.1058–1148   **This is our Venus**: from here comes **our word for love**, from here first the drop of Venus' allure dripped into our heart, followed quickly by the chill of anxiety. 1060 For even if the object of your love is not present, **their image is ever to hand** and their sweet name presents itself to your ears. But you ought properly to run from that image and scare away whatever might feed your love; you should turn your attentions elsewhere and eject your accumulated fluid **into any given body**, not 1065 keep it in as you focus your love on one person exclusively and thereby store

---

This is our Venus   Lucretius ended his treatment of dreams by observing that sexual desire stirs in us first while we are asleep, and this leads him on to a discussion of love. Though Epicurus argued that sex is not physically necessary and is therefore not a true need of the body, he admitted that humans have a natural desire for it, which demands an outlet. Lucretius accepted this, but his view of love – which is more like what we might call 'passion' or even 'obsession' – is wholly negative. The vehemence of his stance against love is striking, since the subject of love was not even included in his primary source, Epicurus' *On Nature*, and since most ancient literature sings the praises of *erōs* (the Greek word for love) – most famous, perhaps, is Plato's *Symposium*, in which banqueters take turns giving a speech in praise of love. Lucretius uses a number of literary devices in the course of the passage, such as this *tricolon crescendo* (three words or phrases of increasing length and/or importance) with which he begins it.

our word for love   Venus' son is Cupid and one of the Latin words for love is *cupido*, though its meaning is closer to our notion of desire rather than spiritual love.

their image is ever to hand   at this point Lucretius is referring to both heterosexual and homosexual love. Before the start of this passage he has explained that desire can be roused by a woman or by a 'boy with womanish limbs' (4.1053). Pederasty was acceptable in first-century Rome, whether solely for pleasure or also for romantic love, and all the love poets wrote about it: for example, Catullus poems 48 and 99, Tibullus 1.9, Propertius 1.20 (though he writes about another's love for a boy, not his own), Virgil *Eclogue* 2.

into any given body   the sexual impulse is a physical longing and so can be satisfied like any other: Lucretius advocates doing so in a way which will cause no disturbance to one's *ataraxia*. In ancient Rome, young women were expected to retain their virginity until marriage, but it was common for young men to have their first sexual experiences before marriage, whether with household slaves, professional prostitutes or even free-born women. Many of the last were sophisticated and financially independent, and their charm and wit were as appealing as their physical attractions; some even came from noble families or married into them, but were not happy in a marriage which may have been arranged for social or political reasons, or were simply lonely because their husbands were away on military service or administering a country under Roman control. Cicero paints a memorable picture of Clodia as one such loose woman in his speech *In Defence of Caelius* (14.33–15.36).

up anxiety and certain pain for yourself. For the **ulcer** gains strength and turns chronic if fed, and the madness grows daily worse and the affliction it causes grows more severe, unless you confound the original injury with fresh wounds 1070 and then treat these while they are raw by roaming off after some roving romance – or you can direct your mind's activity elsewhere. Yet the person who avoids love does not miss out on the fruits of Venus, but rather he takes the good parts that come at no cost. For certainly the pleasure gained from these things is less tainted 1075 for the healthy than for the love-sick. For in the very moment of possession the lovers' fire wavers in hesitant indecision and they are not sure what to enjoy first with their hands or eyes. They clutch tightly what they have won and they cause their bodies pain: often their teeth clamp down on one another's lips as their 1080 mouths collide, for their pleasure is tainted and under its surface there are goads which incite them to hurt the very thing, whatever it is, from which these shoots of madness spring up.

But Venus gently breaks off the punishment in the midst of their love and mixes in some soothing pleasure to rein in those teeth; here lies the hope that the flames 1085 can be extinguished by the same body that is the source of their fire. Yet Nature militates against this ever happening; this is the one thing that, however much we have of it, our hearts only become more inflamed by terrible desire. Our 1090 body will take in food and drink: our desire for bread and water is easy to satisfy, because it can only lay siege to particular areas. However, someone's face and beautiful complexion supply nothing for our body to enjoy except slender images 1095 – and even that pathetic expectation is often snatched away in the wind. Just as in a dream a thirsty man tries to drink, but is given no water to douse the fire in his limbs – instead he makes for the image of water and his efforts are futile, for though he finds himself drinking amidst a rushing river, he remains thirsty 1100 – so it is with love: Venus teases lovers with images, lovers can never be satisfied with just gazing at another's body, nor can they rub off any part of those tender limbs with their hands as they wander uncontrollably over the whole of the body. Finally, when their limbs are intertwined and they are enjoying the flower of their 1105 youth, when the body already anticipates its joy and Venus is on the point of sowing the woman's fields, they eagerly clasp their bodies, they share saliva and exchange breath as their teeth clamp round each other's mouths. All in vain, since they cannot rub off one little piece nor can they enter each other's body and 1110 merge with it completely, which they sometimes seem to want and make every effort to do – such is their desire as they are caught in Venus' snare, while their limbs quiver and melt with the force of the pleasure. At last, when their pent-up

ulcer desire is a physical sensation and Lucretius likens it to a disease, for it can do violence to the body and to the mind too; imagery of disease and violence runs through this passage.

passion has burst out of their sinews, for a brief while there is a short break in the 1115
intensity of their fire. Then that same madness returns, the frenzy revisits them,
as they seek what they desire to get hold of, but they cannot find any device to
overcome this sickness: such is the extent to which they restlessly fester from their 1120
invisible wound.

See too how they sap their strength and are undone by their efforts; see too how
their life is spent **at the beck of another**. Meanwhile their **wealth slips away** to
become **Babylonian** silk, their responsibilities are neglected, their reputation
falters and falls sick. Perfumes and elegant Sicyonian slippers smile on her feet, 1125
she is sure to sport enormous shiny green emeralds set in gold, her **sea-purple**
dress is threadbare from constant wearing and it drinks in Venus' sweat during a

---

at the beck of another   common in ancient love poetry is the notion of slavery to love
(Latin *servitium amoris*), when the lover becomes the metaphorical slave of his beloved,
thereby overturning the usual balance of power, for the rich nobleman is now turned
slave.

wealth slips away   Lucretius' description fits a stock scene from Roman comedy: in plays
such as Terence's *Brothers* we typically find a son passionately in love with an unsuitable
girl and spending large sums of money on entertainment and presents to woo and keep
her, much to his father's despair. We also find in the love poetry of Catullus (poem 8.15–
18 and poems 68–70), Propertius and Tibullus that the poet is obsessed with his lover
and admits to losing all powers of judgement because of his obsession. Gale (*CCL* pp.
68–70) remarks that Lucretius uses the vocabulary and imagery of such love poetry in
order to pour scorn on love, and she mentions that Cupid's dart, the fire of passion,
and love as madness are all examples of conventional poetic imagery which are 'brutally
deromanticized' (p. 68). She also notes how the clichéd image of one lover wounding
another here becomes a reality. It is typical of Lucretius that he echoes the style of an
author or genre but at the same time pointedly rejects its content.

Babylonian   during the first few centuries of the Republic Romans prided themselves
on their frugal habits and austere lifestyle. As Rome gradually increased her territories,
however, wealth flowed into the city from the conquered lands and some Romans began
to live more extravagantly, buying imported and exotic goods; the East in particular was
thought to set the standard for luxury and decadence. Lucretius here lists a variety of
expensive fashions: silks from Babylon, footwear from Sicyon (a city in the Peloponnese
near Corinth), clothes from Malta and the Greek island of Cos, the latter being famous
for its transparent silks. The poet Horace frequently satirized the Roman taste for
extravagant living (*Satires* 2.3, for example).

sea-purple   Lucretius writes *thalassina* or 'of the sea', by which he probably means that
the dress has been coloured with a purple dye made from shellfish (Latin *murex*), making
it expensive, since these shellfish were difficult to harvest from the seabed and a great
many were needed to dye just one dress. The lover likes her dress so much that she
even wears it during her sexual 'workout' and it may be that by making it the colour of
her dress, Lucretius subtly demeans the significance of the political office which purple
represents (see note on p. 60).

workout; the hard-won legacy of his ancestors turns into headbands or scarves, or is sometimes converted into some gown or garment from Malta or Cos. There are 1130 parties with decor and refreshments of the highest quality, there is gaming and an abundance of wine, there are fragrances, garlands and flowers: in vain, since at the centre of this fountain of delights a certain bitterness springs up, choking him amongst all those flowers. Perhaps his guilty conscience gnaws at him that he is 1135 frittering his life fruitlessly away and going to ruin in dens of vice; perhaps she left with an ambiguous parting shot, which fixes itself in his hungry heart and takes hold like a flame; perhaps he thinks she casts her glances too freely or is looking at another man and he sees a hint of a smile on her face. Such doubts will be found 1140 in a love which is true and very happy; but when love is troubled and doomed, countless are the problems you can find even with your eyes shut. So it is better to be on your guard beforehand in the way I have explained, and to take care that 1145 you are not lured in. For it is not as difficult to avoid falling into love's snares as it is to get out of those nets once caught, and to break through Venus' tight knots.

1   In first-century Rome adolescent boys had more sexual freedom than their female peers, though as girls became women, society became a little more willing to overlook infidelity in some cases. Do you think the sexes have equal freedom today? If not, what prevents them?

2   Does Lucretius treat love solely from a male perspective or do we learn anything of the woman's desires?

3   This passage contains several examples of medical imagery. Is Lucretius justified in describing passion as a disease or a sort of madness?

4   The Romans saw places to the east such as Sicyon, Cos and Babylon as decadent. Do you consider the East more exotic than the West? If so, why?

5   'Decor and refreshments of the highest quality' – do you think Lucretius is criticizing what the lover is spending the money on or the fact that the money is being spent in the first place?

6   'At the centre of this fountain of delights a certain bitterness springs up' – do you agree that sometimes in the midst of pleasure some concern will come to mind and so spoil it?

7   Why does Lucretius write in such detail about passion when he is arguing against it? Likewise, why might he lavish so much attention on describing the luxuries which lovers indulge in?

8   Do you think Lucretius' account of love is far-fetched? Or too narrow? Why does he say nothing about the emotional and spiritual rewards of love?

9   Do you think the sexual urge is a positive or negative force?

10   Some readers believe that the vehemence of this passage supports the ancient story, told by St Jerome (fourth century AD) but unconfirmed, that Lucretius was himself driven mad by some sort of love-potion: do you think this passage provides any support for this story?

4.1149–1217

Lucretius advises us that we can escape from the obsession of love once caught, if we are willing to notice and admit the faults of a lover. For he observes that desire blinds one lover to the faults of the other (faults that are obvious to all impartial observers), and that women will use make-up to alter their appearance and thereby deceive men. If lovers were less obsessive, they would realize how foolish their behaviour was. He then explains that intercourse is pleasurable to male and female alike, something we see also to be true of the animal kingdom. Finally he suggests that there is a male and a female seed, and a child will resemble whichever parent's seed has prevailed during intercourse.

Conception and the sex of the child

4.1218–56   It happens too that frequently children can look like their grandparents, or sometimes their features recall those of great-grandparents: this is because often the bodies of the parents conceal many seeds mingled in many ways, which father 1220 has passed on to father since the line began. Venus will chance to arrange these seeds in ways which recall the looks, the voice, the hair of an ancestor, since it is no more fixed that the seeds of those attributes will take hold than the seeds of the 1225 face or physique or any part of the body. Next, I say that a female may spring from the father's seed and the mother's body may cause males to be born. For offspring are always made from **twofold seed**: whichever of the two the child born resembles 1230 more, that is the seed it has more than an equal share of – as you can see, whether the child be a male offspring or a female birth.

There is no divine power which frightens off a man's fertile seed, so that he is never called 'father' by sweet children but passes his life under a sterile Venus. Yet most 1235 men think there is: **in their sadness** they splash the altars with blood and set light to

---

twofold seed   without the benefit of modern technology the Greeks were forced to make reasoned guesses about the process of reproduction. The Atomists held that male and female seed combines to form the beginnings of a child (what we call the zygote) and Epicurus agreed with this explanation, but this was not the only theory suggested in the ancient world. Others held that the father is the true parent as he provides the seed and the mother is merely a receptacle in which the father's seed is incubated, an explanation mentioned in Aeschylus' play *Eumenides* (fifth century BC) and in Plato's *Timaeus*.

in their sadness   there is no reason not to think that privately Roman men wanted to become fathers just as much as men do today. However, many Romans additionally held the belief that it was their civic duty to have children for the good of Rome, to produce future political and military leaders and so ensure her prosperity, and that it was their familial duty to produce an heir to continue their family line and name.

offerings at the shrines, in the hope that they may make their wives pregnant with
their plentiful seed, but they tire out the gods and the **lots** in vain. For some men
are barren because their seed is too thick or alternatively it is abnormally thin and 1240
runny. Since thin seed cannot latch on and stick anywhere, it quickly seeps away,
withdrawing to return in failure. However, with other men the seed comes out
unusually thick and viscous and either it does not fly out with such far-reaching 1245
force or it cannot penetrate to the right places so well, or the seed does penetrate
but fails to mingle with the woman's seed. For the couplings of Venus can be seen
to vary widely. Some men are more likely to make some women pregnant, some
women receive their burden more readily from some men and become heavy 1250
with child. Many women prove barren in several **previous marriages** but then
find someone by whom they can conceive children and grow rich with sweet
offspring. Also, when a wife, fertile in a previous marriage, is unable to bear
children in her present one, often her husband moves on to find a natural match 1255
so that together they can **make their old age secure** with children.

lots   at Praeneste near Rome there was a huge temple, possibly the largest sanctuary
in Italy, to the Roman goddess of Fortune (Latin *Fortuna*), and this was home to the
'lots'. These were wooden tablets which were inscribed with ancient lettering. They were
shaken together and the person hoping for information about the future would draw
one out and hope to be able to interpret what was written on it. The ancient world
contained a number of such oracles: in the grove at Dodona in northern Greece, for
example, priests of Zeus (Jupiter) would listen to leaves rustling on sacred oak trees and
interpret the sounds to discover the god's will.

previous marriages   it was quite common for Roman men to marry and divorce more
than once in their lifetime. A Roman might marry to make a political alliance with his
bride's family – before the civil war Pompey married Julius Caesar's daughter, for example
– but might divorce his wife when that alliance was no longer wanted. There was no
equivalent in the Roman marriage ceremony, which was itself flexible in wording and
importance, of the vow to stay married 'till death do us part'. Failure to produce children
might also lead to divorce; it was more common for husband to divorce wife than vice
versa.

make their old age secure   the average life expectancy was lower in ancient times than it
is today and many people would not have reached even the age of 50. However, Romans
who lived to be too old to work to provide for themselves might look to their children to
be a source of income and protection.

1   Epicurus claimed that procreation always involves a twofold seed. How does his theory compare to a modern understanding of the formation of the zygote? How do the theories about heredity that Lucretius sets out in this passage square with what we know about the role of X and Y chromosomes in the determination of sex and the role of DNA in genetic heritage?

2   Modern science can explain why a person cannot have children, but can it explain why that particular individual happens to be afflicted? Where might someone experiencing difficulty nowadays in having children turn for help beyond medicine?

3   Lucretius states that a man who has been barren with one partner may prove fertile with a different one. Does modern science accept that?

4   In ancient Rome a main reason to marry was to have children. Is this still the case today? Why might a couple today not want to have children? Is childlessness a legal grounds for divorce nowadays?

5   In which countries does the state set a limit to procreation rather than encourage it? What are the reasons for doing so?

6   Do you think that children make parents' old age more secure nowadays? If so, in what ways? Or is it more likely that they are a drain on parents' resources?

4.1257–87

Lucretius adds that diet and the manner of intercourse can affect the chances of conception. He ends by conceding that love need not rely solely on sexual attraction: a person's manner, behaviour and character can all engender love, as can simply spending time with another, just as over time the steady drip of water will succeed in boring through rock.

5 The origins of our world, and of life and civilization

Epicurus is the supreme benefactor of mankind

5.1–54   Whose mind is great enough to compose a poem worthy of the majesty of the truth and these discoveries? Who has sufficient skill with words to shape a **eulogy** befitting that man who has bequeathed us such gifts, sought out and produced by 5 his own mind? No such person, I believe, will ever be born of mortal body. For if my words are to befit the majesty of the truth which he made known, that man was a god, a god, **noble Memmius**, who **first** discovered that principle of living which 10 is now called a philosophy and who by his skill **rescued** life from the tall waves and deep darkness and placed it in such utter calm and such shining radiance.

---

eulogy   for the third time in the poem Lucretius opens a book with praise of Epicurus (see **1.63–79**, **3.1–30** and later **6.1–42**). This one goes further than the previous two in that Lucretius awards Epicurus divine status and makes the radical claim that his teachings are of greater benefit to mankind than any of the famous heroic exploits. Farrell remarks (p. 79) that each book begins with a formal prelude which is 'a brilliant epideictic performance, rhetorically charged, imagistically rich and often informed by mythology in a way that seems incompatible with the poem's rationalistic view'. In his will Epicurus did make provision for annual commemoration of his death (Diogenes Laertius, *Life of Epicurus* 10.18) and we hear from Cicero (*On the Nature of the Gods* 1.43) that contemporary Epicureans did indeed worship Epicurus as a god.

noble Memmius   not mentioned by name since Book 2 (see note on p. 63). Lucretius here uses Latin *inclute* for 'noble', an epithet he has previously reserved for Venus (**1.40**) and Epicurus himself (**3.10**). He may want Memmius to bask in the reflected glory of being mentioned here in the context of this exaltation of Epicurus.

first   Epicurus was not the first to espouse atomic theory, but, in the mind of Lucretius, he may be the first person who put this knowledge to practical use in teaching people how to live happier lives.

rescued   as in the opening lines of Book 2, the imagery contrasts the swirling maelstrom below with the serenity of the heights. Here, the picture is of the Epicurean as a shipwrecked sailor pulled to safety out of the stormy sea of life, with its swell of care and anxiety which prevents *ataraxia*, and out of the darkness, with its fear of the gods and of death, and the ignorance of the truth.

Hercules wrestles the Nemean lion: vase by the Kleophrades painter, 490 BC.

Just compare the divine discoveries of others in the past. For **Ceres** is said to have introduced grain to mankind and **Liber** the drink of the vine-born juice; yet 15 life could have continued without those things, just as **some races** are reported to live even now. No – life is only lived well if the mind is untainted. So all the more deservedly do we view him as a god: his are the sweet consolations for life 20 which now soothe the mind and which have spread across powerful nations too.

Ceres goddess of grain (giving us our word 'cereal'), known to the Greeks as Demeter.

Liber (meaning 'liberator') god of wine, the Roman name for the Greek god Dionysus/ Bacchus.

some races the Romans considered the drinking of wine, which was prevalent in Mediterranean countries, to be a mark of culture over the customs of barbaric northerners like the Germans, who drank beer (Caesar, *Gallic War* 6.22.1). The Romans fought a number of engagements against the Germans, and with mixed success. Towards the end of Lucretius' life, Julius Caesar bridged the supposedly unbridgeable River Rhine (55 BC) and advanced a little way into the German interior; but Augustus subsequently suggested maintaining the Rhine as the border between Roman and German territories. Four centuries later, German tribes crossed into Roman territory, marched on Rome and sacked it, and so fell the Roman Empire.

What is more, if you are thinking that **the deeds of Hercules** surpass his, you are being carried ever further away from true reasoning. For how could that old **Nemean lion** with its mighty jaws or the bristly Arcadian pig hurt us now? Again, 25 what could the bull of Crete do or the irksome Lernaean hydra, that fence of poisonous snakes? What of the threefold Geryon with his triple-chested strength? Could the birds which dwelt in the Stymphalian marshes have done us much harm or the horses of Thracian Diomedes, breathing fire from their noses beside 30 the beaches of Bistonia and Ismara? The dragon guarding the shiny golden apples of the Hesperides, a rough type with a rancid stare, his huge bulk wrapped round the tree-trunk – in the end what harm could he have done on the beaches of 35 the Atlantic and the wild ocean, where none of us dares to go and no barbarian either? All other monsters of this kind which have been slain: had they not been

---

the deeds of Hercules   (Greek Herakles) the son of Jupiter by the mortal woman Alcmene. When Juno discovered this affair, in her anger she decided to persecute Hercules by making him perform a series of challenging tasks at the orders of King Eurystheus. He succeeded in these tasks, most of which involved killing a dangerous monster: hence he came to be regarded as the epitome of a hero whose deeds benefited mankind. Lucretius' sarcastic dismissal of Hercules' achievements is in part an aspersion against the philosophy of the Stoics, who cited Hercules as the example *par excellence* of noble endurance in the face of great suffering. Among the great leaders who looked up to Hercules and traced their ancestry to him were Alexander the Great and Mark Antony.

Nemean lion   Hercules was ordered to kill the lion living in Nemea (near modern Corinth), but the lion's skin could not be pierced by any weapon made by a mortal. Hercules therefore used a club to stun the lion before strangling it. He then used the lion's own claw to skin it to provide himself with the impenetrable armour which he is usually pictured wearing in Greek and Roman art. As for the other labours to which Lucretius refers, the Arcadian pig was a violent boar which was ravaging the countryside around Arcadia; Hercules chased and captured it. He also had to capture the wild bull of Crete; once he had shown it to Eurystheus, he let it go free on the plain of Marathon. The Lernaean hydra was a many-headed serpent which lived in the swamps around Lake Lerna in the Peloponnese. Each time Hercules cut off a head, two more grew back in its place until he hit upon the idea of singeing each fresh, bloody stump with fire, and thus was able to kill the Hydra. He dipped some arrows in its poisonous blood so that each successful bowshot would prove fatal. The threefold Geryon was a giant with three bodies and three heads, which Hercules killed in order to steal his cattle. The birds were cranes which lived in the marshes around the Stymphalian lake in the Peloponnese and ate human flesh; he killed them all with arrows. The horses which fed on human flesh belonged to the cruel Diomedes, king of Thrace in northern Greece (where Bistonia and Ismara are situated). Hercules fought the king, defeated him and fed him to the horses, which were then cured of their need to eat human flesh. The shiny golden apples grew in the garden of the Hesperides, the daughters of Hesperus, situated at the western edge of the world, and were guarded by a fierce dragon. Hercules subdued the dragon and brought the apples back. Lucretius muddles the traditional order of the labours, perhaps in an attempt to trivialize them.

Hercules shoots at the Stymphalian birds (in this version with a sling): Attic black-figure vase, mid-sixth century BC.

vanquished, in the end what harm would they have done if they were alive? None, I think. Even today the earth abounds with a plethora of wild beasts, and the forests and mighty mountains and dense woods are filled with terrors to tremble 40 at, but for the most part it is within our power to avoid such places.

But if our hearts are not cleansed, what battles or dangers are we to be caught up in against our will? What sharp pangs of desire will then tear at the man who 45 is troubled, what fears too? What of arrogance, indecency and insolence? What trouble do they cause? What of self-indulgence or idleness? So the man who has conquered all these, who has driven them from the mind by his teachings, not by 50 arms – will this man not rightly be held worthy to rank among the gods? Even more so, since he used to speak many **inspired words about the immortal gods** themselves and reveal the entire nature of things through his teachings.

---

inspired words about the immortal gods   Epicurus wrote works entitled *On the Gods* and *On Holiness*.

1 Why do you think Lucretius does not mention Epicurus by name in this passage?

2 Is the eulogy too extreme for modern tastes? Do you think it is justified from what you have read of the poem so far?

3 Does Lucretius present Epicurus as a scientist, a philosopher or both? Do some people nowadays believe that science and philosophy have brought more happiness to mankind than religion? Which scientists in recent times might be considered to have bestowed great benefit on mankind?

4 Do you think that the anthropomorphic nature of the Roman gods meant that deification was a more likely feature in Roman times than it might be today? Are there cultures today in which certain individuals are revered as gods?

5 Do you think it is significant that Lucretius has not mentioned Memmius in Books 3 and 4 (see p. 63)? If so, do you agree that we must assume Book 5 was composed next after Book 2? Or can you think of another explanation?

6 From what you know of Epicureanism, why does Lucretius choose the particular inventions of Ceres and Liber to compare with the discoveries of Epicurus?

7 'Life is only lived well if the mind is untainted' – from your reading of Lucretius so far, what do you think he would say taints the mind?

8 In lines 43–8 Lucretius gives a list of dangers which threaten one's serenity: would the same ones feature on a modern list? What others might you add?

5.55–145

Lucretius sums up the contents of the first four books before giving a summary of this one. He promises to explain how the world is mortal, how the earth, sea, sky, stars, sun and moon were all born and how life on earth began. It is Nature and her laws which govern the movements of the planets, though it is easy to gaze in awe at the heavens and so fall back into traditional beliefs that the world is under divine control. Lucretius warns Memmius that the world will die, just as it was born; such a claim is not impiety but simply the truth. The planets are neither immortal nor sentient, for Nature only permits mind and spirit to exist inside beings of flesh and blood.

The world was not created for the benefit of mankind

5.146–234   Likewise, you should not believe that anywhere in any world there exist sacred abodes of the gods. For our minds can scarcely comprehend the **slender nature** of the gods, which is far beyond the reach of our senses; since their nature eschews   150
any touch or blow, it cannot touch anything that can be touched by us. For nothing has the ability to touch if it may not be touched itself. That is why their abodes too must be different from ours and be slender like their bodies, as I will prove to you later through extensive argument.   155

Moreover, to say that the gods wanted to produce a world so magnificent in nature **for the sake of mankind** and that consequently we must praise this praiseworthy achievement and must think it will never perish but will last for ever; to argue that it is **blasphemy** ever to do anything which might undermine the foundations of   160
what was established for the human race for all time by the ancient wisdom of the gods; or to launch a verbal attack or to turn it quite upside-down – to add other arguments of this sort or to elaborate upon them, Memmius, is madness. For

---

slender nature the gods themselves have bodies composed of slender atoms which none of our senses can perceive, and only our mind is capable of perceiving the slender images which they emit. Since the gods are of such slender atomic composition, they do not have the ability to affect anything in our world, for they 'cannot touch anything that can be touched by us' and thus there is no need either to fear their intervention or to placate them with sacrifice and prayer. However, the gods do still have physical form, for according to Epicureanism nothing exists that is not either atoms or void. The only benefit we can take from their existence – and it is accidental, not intentional – is that if we accept their images into our minds, we can learn from their serenity and come closer to attaining it.

for the sake of mankind Roman religion espoused the existence of providential gods who intervened in the universe on behalf of their devotees; the Stoics believed more particularly that the gods created the world to benefit mankind and that it was guided by a benevolent Providence.

blasphemy ever since philosophers started to consider the gods, they have been accused of undermining religion if their teachings have called even the nature – let alone the existence – of the gods into question: the clearest example of this is Socrates, who was charged with introducing new gods into Athens and put to death. Whatever criticism Epicurus himself experienced, however, he was not persecuted for his teachings. In comparison with other ancient and modern cultures, the Romans were more tolerant of other religions: when they conquered a nation, they tried to link local gods to Roman ones and thereby to assimilate them into Roman state religion in the hope that Roman rule would be more readily accepted. Thus Rome was content to allow people to worship gods of their choice, provided that they accepted the existence of the Roman gods: hence Jews and later Christians angered the Romans, for they would not accept the existence of any gods other than their own.

what could our gratitude profit the immortal and blessed gods that they should 165
set to doing anything for our sakes? What new circumstance could have tempted
them, previously at peace for so long, to desire to make a change to their former
life?

For clearly those whose former situation was unhappy would rejoice at a changed 170
one, but if nothing bad happened in times gone by, when they led happy lives,
what could have sparked in them a desire for novelty? How would it have hurt us
not to have been created? Or am I to suppose that life lay prostrate in darkness 175
and despair, until the initial creation of our world brought light? For anyone
born must wish to remain alive, so long as the allure of pleasure retains its hold.
However, for the one who has never tasted a passion for life or been counted
in its ranks, what harm is it never to have been born? Furthermore, how was 180
a model for creation or the very idea of mankind implanted in the gods, so that
they saw it in their minds and knew what they wished to do? How was the power
of atoms ever realized or what they could become, when rearranged with each 185
other, if nature herself did not provide the pattern for creation? For so many
atoms, continually moving in so many ways from the start of time and propelled
by their own weight, have been driven on, have bonded in every combination and
have tried everything they might be able to create by coming together, that it is no 190
wonder if they also have fallen into those combinations and have come to those
movements through which the universe currently operates by renewing itself.

But even if I did not know what atoms are, I would still be bold enough to make 195
the following claim from what happens in the sky and to prove it from many
other occurrences too: not to the least degree has the world been produced for
us by the gods. The flaws it is furnished with as it stands are too great. To begin
with, of all that the vast sweep of sky covers, the mountains and forests of wild 200
animals have taken a greedy share; it is possessed by rocks, by desolate marshes
and the sea, which keeps the shores of land far apart. Then, almost **two-thirds** of

---

a model for creation a reference to a notion peculiar to Epicureanism, that of
'acquaintance' (Latin *notities*). Epicurus held that we perceive images of objects, for
example a chair. Over time we build up a picture of the general idea of a chair from all
the examples we have seen and so we could make a chair ourselves from this picture
without having an actual chair in front of us. That image of the chair is not perceived at
the time but is based on a series of previous perceptions.

two-thirds the Romans divided the earth into zones according to temperature: they
understood that the centre zone along the equator was extremely hot, while the two
zones at the two poles were very cold. Gale remarks (*CCL* p. 65) that these lines recall the
description in Hesiod's poem *Works and Days* of the world as arranged by Zeus (Jupiter),
but, as ever, Lucretius radically changes their content, for he cites the difficulties faced by
farmers to argue against the existence of the gods.

it are swelteringly hot or stolen from mortals by unremitting falls of frost. As for 205
the arable land that remains, nature in her power would yet cover it over with
thorns if she were not resisted by the power of man, which is quite accustomed to
groaning over the sturdy mattock to survive, or to cleaving the ground by pressing
hard on the plough. If we did not turn the fertile clods with the ploughshare and 210
summon the crops to appear by subduing the soil of the land, they would be
unable to emerge into the clear air of their own accord. Even so, when after being
grown with great effort they put out their leaves and are flowering throughout the
land, sometimes either the sun in its heaven parches them with extreme heat or 215
sudden rainstorms or icy frosts destroy them, or blasts of wind flatten them with
their wild whirlwind.

Furthermore, why does nature maintain and multiply the frightening tribe of
wild beasts which harm the human race on land and at sea? Why do the seasons 220
bring diseases each year? Why does death roam the land prematurely? Moreover,
like a sailor cast up by the savage waves, a baby boy lies naked on the ground,
unable to speak, lacking everything he needs to survive, from the very moment
nature has pushed him from his mother's womb by sheer effort into daylight's 225
realms, and he fills the area with melancholy wailing, as is right for one who has
still to experience **life's many misfortunes**. On the other hand, the various flocks
and herds and wild beasts grow up without the need for rattles or for the soft
and incoherent prattle of a wet-nurse, nor do they seek different clothes for each 230
season; nor indeed do they need weapons or high walls to protect their own, since
the earth herself generously produces all things for them all, together with the
great artisan Nature.

---

life's many misfortunes Lucretius may mean the misery life has in store for the non-
Epicurean, but this still seems a more pessimistic view of life than Epicurus held, for in
his *Letter to Menoecus* (126) Epicurus specifically rejects a view expressed by the Greek
poet Theognis (sixth century BC) that it is better not to be born, but once born, to die as
soon as possible. The Greek historian Herodotus (fifth century BC) has the great Athenian
statesman Solon (sixth century) tell the following tale (*Histories* 1.31), which reflects a
common Greek approach to the tribulations of life. Two sons, Kleobis and Biton, dragged
a heavy ox-cart, in which their mother sat, five miles (8 km) to Argos so that she could
participate in Hera's festival. Their mother was so delighted at their piety and proud of
their achievement that she asked Hera to give them whatever is best for men: they went
to sleep in the temple and during their sleep they died.

1 'As I will prove to you later through extensive argument' – Lucretius never makes good this promise, which leads Costa, for example, to remark (p. 63): 'This line [155] offers us the clearest proof that Lucretius did not complete his poem.' Do you think that is a fair conclusion?

2 Do religions nowadays think of their god as having physical form?

3 Do all religions hold that the world was created by their god?

4 Which religions hold that the world was created for mankind's benefit and ultimately is ordered by a benevolent power? Do any hold that god benefits from the existence of mankind?

5 Do you think Epicurus' argument that the gods cannot have created earth without a model is valid?

5.235–533

Lucretius returns to his argument that the earth had a beginning and will have an end, and that it must be mortal because we see how all its constituents are mortal. Soil will dry out to become dust and blow away, or turn to mud and be washed away; the sea evaporates or seeps underground to nourish the springs. The air receives a constant supply of atoms which have come off all beings and it returns atoms to them when they inhale. The sun emits light continually, as we observe when it is blocked and a shadow is instantly formed; mountains crack and send down huge boulders. Finally Lucretius asks why there are no accounts of history before the wars at Thebes and Troy, if the earth has been in existence for ever: he insists that only atoms or void are indestructible and that therefore the earth is mortal, and warns that the sun's fire and the ocean's water are permanently at war and at some time in the future one of the two will win. The imbalance created by this victory will lead to the destruction of our world. He then turns to explain how our world – the earth and the heavens – was formed and how this did not happen by design but by chance. First there was chaos, a storm of atoms colliding but unable to combine. Thereafter atoms gradually found suitable ones with which to bond and there emerged earth, water, air and fire. Lucretius then explains the order in which the world was created: the earth formed first and sank to where it sits now, then the ether formed and rose to the outer reaches of our world. In between lies the air, lighter than earth but heavier than ether and therefore more turbulent. The mass of the planets broke away from the earth because they were lighter but not so light that they could ascend to the ether, so they remained in the air. Lucretius then gives various explanations of how the stars move, arguing that all the explanations are possible and therefore whichever is not true of our world will be true of another world elsewhere.

How the earth remains in place in our world

5.534–63   For the earth to rest motionless in the **middle part of the world**, it is natural that
its bulk gradually **lessens and thins out** and that its underneath is of a different   535
nature; from the start of the earth's existence, its underneath was conjoined to and
integrated with the airy part of the world in which earth is placed and lives. For this
reason the earth is no burden and does not press down on the air, just as a man's
own limbs are no weight to him and the head is no burden to the neck and we do   540
not notice that the whole weight of our body is on the feet, whereas any weight
that arrives from elsewhere and is loaded onto us will hurt, though often it is very
much smaller than us – so great a difference does it make what each thing can do.   545
So the earth was not suddenly brought in like some foreign body, imposed from
elsewhere onto air that is foreign to it, but was conceived together with the air at
the very beginning of the world and is a definite part of it, as our limbs clearly are of
us. Furthermore, when the ground is suddenly struck by an immense thunderclap,   550
as it shakes it rocks everything above: there is no possible way for it to do this,
unless it is bound up with the sky and the airy part of the world. For they cling to
one another with **shared roots**, conjoined and integrated from the start of their   555
existence. Do you not see too how the power of the spirit, extremely slender though
it be, sustains the sizeable bulk of our bodies because they are so conjoined and
integrated? Furthermore, what has the ability to propel the body in a nimble jump,
if not the power of the spirit which steers our limbs? Now do you see how strong   560
a slender nature can be, when it is conjoined with a heavy body, just as the air is
conjoined with the earth and the power of the mind is with us?

- Why is it that one feels the weight of an object one is carrying more than
  that of one's own body?

---

middle part of the world   Epicurus followed the Atomists in likening our world to a
hollow sphere with the earth at its centre, surrounded by the air in which the planets
moved, which was in turn surrounded by the ether in the outermost reaches of the
sphere. However, neither he nor they suggested that the earth itself was a sphere.

lessens and thins out   the Atomists suggested that the body of the earth was round and
flat and rested stationary on the air below it; Leucippus described its shape as being 'like
a tambourine'. Though nothing he wrote has survived to confirm it, Epicurus seems to
have accepted that the earth had such a shape; nevertheless, he was concerned to explain
how the earth could rest on air.

shared roots   Lucretius uses this same phrase at **3.325** when describing the integration
of spirit and body. Here he likens the conjoining of the earth and the air strong enough
to support it, to that of the human body and the spirit strong enough to move it. It is
another of the tools in his didactic workbox to repeat a word or phrase later but in
a different context, in order to compare the two things and draw attention to their
similarity.

5.564–704

Lucretius argues that the sun's fire and shape must be what we sense them to be. The outlines of sun and moon are so clear that there cannot be any further part to them that we cannot see because of their distance. We should not be astounded that the sun can send out so much light, for we see how a small spring can flood the whole of a plain; however, it may also be that the sun seems so hot because its rays kindle seeds of heat already in the air. He discusses the movements of the sun and moon, admitting numerous possible explanations for why the sun takes a year to complete its cycle while the moon takes only a month, for why the sun descends below the horizon and for why the days are of different lengths according to the season.

How the moon shines

5.705–50   **The moon is able to shine** because it is struck by the sun's rays and day by day it directs more of the sun's light into view as it moves away from the sun's orb, until it is opposite the sun and has shone with full light and, soaring high as it rises, has seen the sun set. Then little by little the moon must return and hide its light, so to   710 speak, the nearer to the sun's fire it glides from the opposite region through the circuit of the zodiac. **Such is the claim** of those who picture the moon to be like

---

The moon is able to shine   Epicurus relied on the senses for evidence of the world; thus when we have a near view of an object, we can be sure that what we see is the truth. However, there are things in the world which are too remote to allow us a near view, for example the moon. Epicurus argued that in such cases we are to proceed in accordance with what our senses perceive, but that we must accept that we will not be able to obtain confirmation – though we may at least be able to state that nothing contradicts our perceptions.

Such is the claim   as part of their investigations of the cosmos, many ancient philosophers attempted to answer the question of how it is that the moon shines, and Lucretius cites several theories. The first is that the moon reflects the sun's light, a theory put forward by some of the earliest philosophers such as Thales (seventh–sixth century BC) and Pythagoras (sixth century); this relationship between sun and moon is also found in Greek mythology, where Apollo (the sun god) and Artemis (the moon goddess) were siblings. The second theory Lucretius offers is that the moon gives out its own light, and he gives two alternative ways it might do this: the first is a theory expounded by Anaximander and Xenophanes (both sixth century); the second, a theory put forward by the Chaldaean astronomer Berosus (fourth–third century). The final theory that Lucretius puts forward is that a moon is born and then perishes every day, which is most likely based on the ideas of Heraclitus (sixth century).

---

a ball and to hold the path of its course below the sun. **It is also possible** that the
moon revolves with its own light but still shows various phases of brightness. For 715
it is feasible that there is another body which glides alongside the moon as it goes
and which blocks and covers it in various ways, but which itself cannot be seen,
since it is devoid of any light as it moves. Or possibly the moon may turn like a 720
sphere, one half awash with its shining light, and by turning its sphere produce
its changing phases, until it meets our gaze and staring eyes with that face which
is furnished with fire. Then little by little the moon turns back again and removes 725
the side of its round ball which gives off light. That is what the teachings of the
Chaldaeans from Babylon strive to prove, in opposition to the science of the
astronomers, which they deny – as if what each side fights for may not be equally
possible or there were any reason why you should be bold enough to embrace one 730
rather than the other.

Or again, it is difficult to demonstrate by reasoning or prove with words why
a new moon could not be created repeatedly, with a fixed sequence of phases
and with fixed shapes, and then each day each moon created would perish and 735
another would be supplied to take its place in the same position, since we already
see so many things having a fixed cycle. **Spring arrives** together with Venus, but
before them walks Venus' winged herald, while on Zephyr's heels mother Flora
fills all the path ahead of them as she sprinkles her glorious scent and colour. Then 740
arid heat takes up its station, with dusty Ceres for a companion and Aquilo's

---

It is also possible   when several explanations of a phenomenon are possible and none
is contradicted by our senses, any one could be true, and those which are not true of a
phenomenon in this world will be true of one in another. However, as we have seen,
when Lucretius offers alternative explanations (at **4.314–17**, for example) he probably
puts first the one he thinks most likely.

Chaldaeans   a people from southern Mesopotamia famed in the ancient world for their
practising of astrology. They may be the 'wise men' who followed the star to Bethlehem
in the account in the Christian gospels of Matthew and Luke.

Spring arrives   to demonstrate that fixed cycles exist in our world, Lucretius now paints
a beautiful and evocative picture of the cycle of seasons. He devotes the longest part of
his description to the arrival of spring: the west wind personified as Zephyrus arrives first,
then the flowers start to bloom, helped by Flora, an early Italian goddess of flowers, and
according to myth loved by Zephyrus. Following these two comes Cupid, Venus' son and
her 'winged herald', then Spring itself and finally as a climax of the procession, Venus,
whom Lucretius has already associated with spring at **1.1–28**.

arid heat   next comes summer, described in similar but less appealing terms to spring.
Ceres, goddess of the harvest, arrives without any attendants; she is 'dusty' because the
earth is parched by heat at harvest time in summer. She is accompanied by Aquilo, the
north wind, which blows in from the Mediterranean each year at the height of summer
and brings relief from the heat.

annual gusts. Then **autumn** draws near, and Euhius Euan walks alongside. Then   745
the other seasons and winds follow, Volturnus thundering on high and Auster
powerful with lightning. Eventually the solstice brings snow and fixes the frost
fast; there follows winter, teeth chattering with cold. For this reason it is not so
astonishing if the moon is born at a fixed time and at a fixed time is destroyed
again, since so many things occur at a fixed time.   750

---

1   Does it undermine or reinforce Lucretius' credibility that he is willing to
    offer alternative explanations for a phenomenon such as the light of the
    moon?

2   What elements of Lucretius' explanation of the moon's light strike you as
    especially Lucretian – both in the explanation of the phenomenon itself (i.e.
    the content) and in the way it is presented (i.e. style and structure)?

3   Why do you think Lucretius gives such a detailed description of the seasons?
    Does it conflict with his dismissal of conventional Roman religion that he
    describes this cycle of the seasons in mythological terms?

5.751–82

Lucretius offers various explanations for lunar and solar eclipses. After
summarizing the topics he has discussed in Book 5 so far, he explains that he
will now turn to the earth itself and how life here began.

The emergence of life on earth

5.783–836   **First of all** the earth sent up the grasses and the bright greenery to cover the hills
and all the plains, and the meadows shone green in their bloom; after that, trees   785
of all different kinds were given free rein to shoot upwards through the air in a
great competition. Just as feathers and hair and bristles are first to grow on the
limbs of four-footed creatures and the bodies of winged birds, so at that time the

---

autumn   accompanied by Dionysus and by two winds: the south wind, Auster, and the
south-east wind, Volturnus, which is more usually found as another name for the river
Tiber in Rome, whose festival was held in August. Euhius Euan derives from 'Euios', a
Greek title for Dionysus, whose ecstatic followers used to cry *euoi*: as god of wine, he is
associated with autumn as the time of the grape harvest.

First of all   Lucretius follows the established order of the ancient accounts of the formation
of our world: he has described the separation of matter and void, then the separation of
the world into its constituent elements (the planets, the sky and so on), and now he turns
to the emergence of life on earth itself, a question which had been answered in different
ways by Greek philosophers, though most agreed that vegetation appeared first and animal
life afterwards. Some (e.g. Anaxagoras, Democritus) suggested that animals emerged from
the ground itself, others (e.g. Epicurus) that animals emerged from cocoon-like wombs
which lay on the surface of the ground and that the animals were then nourished by milk
from the earth, others still (e.g. Anaximander) that animals emerged from the sea.

---

newborn earth quickly sprouted grasses and shrubs, then spawned the animals next, 790
many types born in many ways by different methods. For animals **cannot have
fallen from the sky** nor can those living on land have emerged from salt waters.
Consequently the earth has deservedly gained the name mother, since all things 795
grew out of the earth. Even today many creatures **emerge from the earth**, formed
by the sun's warmth and the rain, and so it is less surprising if at that time more
creatures were born and larger ones, reaching full growth while earth and air were 800
still new. First of all, the species of birds and various fowl hatched in springtime and
left their eggs, just as now in summer the cicadas voluntarily abandon their smooth
skins in a search for survival and sustenance. It was then, you see, that the earth first
produced the creatures which live on land. For there was a great deal of moisture 805
and heat in the fields, so that wherever a spot or location presented itself, there
grew up wombs, attached to the earth by roots. When in the fullness of time the age
of the infants inside caused them to open, and the infants fled from the moisture 810
and strove for air, nature would direct the earth's pores to those spots and make
them pour out a sap very like milk from her opened veins, just as now every woman
is filled with sweet milk after she has given birth, because all her urge to nourish 815
is channelled into her breasts. The earth provided food for her children, the warm
air their clothing, the grass a bed with a wealth of abundant soft down. However,
the newness of the world precluded harsh frosts or excessive heat or winds of great
force, for all things grow and reach full strength at an equal rate. 820

So it bears repeating: the earth deserves to keep the name of mother she has won,
since it was she who gave birth to the human race and who shortly afterwards
poured forth all the animals which dance wildly across the mighty mountains, and

---

cannot have fallen from the sky   the Stoics believed that the spirits of animals and the
fibre of plants were filled with the same mixture of fire and air that permeated the
universe itself and gave it life. Lucretius employs *reductio ad absurdum* by pursuing that
belief to its logical conclusion, to suggest that animals are therefore in effect creatures
of, or even born from, the air or the sky.

emerge from the earth   in more traditional accounts, such as that of Hesiod's *Theogony*,
creation is described in genealogical terms whereby the elements, described as divinities,
give birth to many descendants and are clearly part of the process of generation. Thus,
Lucretius' representation of Earth as a personified being would have seemed quite natural
to the ancients, and part of a long tradition of Great Goddesses or Creator Goddesses
(divinities such as Ishtar in Babylonian myth, Gaia and Demeter in Greek myth, Ceres
and Terra Mater in Roman myth) whose fertility was spontaneous and achieved through
parthenogenesis. Some Greek philosophers, Aristotle among them, asserted that worms
and insects appeared spontaneously out of mud. At 2.871–3 Lucretius remarks that he
has observed how worms can be born from dung or mud; thus it is not so absurd for him
to accept Epicurus' belief that creatures were once born from the earth itself. Though in
Graeco-Roman cultures the earth was worshipped as the mother goddess responsible for
life (Gaia, Terra Mater, etc.), Lucretius denies that the earth is divine, claiming it is neither
sentient (**2.652**) nor immortal (**2.1144**).

also the birds of the air with their different shapes. But because there must be some 825
limit to her giving birth, she has stopped, like a woman tired out by the length of
her years. For time is changing the nature of the entire world, and first one state
and then another must take possession of all things, nor does anything stay the 830
same as it was: all things change, nature transforms all things and forces them to
alter. One thing rots away as it grows weak and feeble with age, only for another to
grow up and emerge from its lowly beginnings. So in this way time is changing the 835
nature of the whole world, and first one state and then another takes possession of
the earth, so that what gave birth before cannot do so now and what did not before
now can.

> • Does there seem to be any logic to the order in which Lucretius suggests life
> on earth emerged?

5.837–54

Lucretius explains that in the early stages of the earth's history nature brought
forth many strange creatures, imperfect versions of creatures alive today, but
these did not survive because they did not have the means to obtain food or
to reproduce.

Why a species survives

5.855–77   At that time many species of creature must have perished and not been able to
forge their line by reproduction. For every animal that you see sustained nowadays
by the life-giving air, either their cunning or their bravery or their agility has
protected and **preserved their species** since the moment it was born; in addition,
there are many animals whose **usefulness** recommended them to us and so they 860

---

preserved their species   Epicurus suggested that when life on earth began to emerge, a
much wider range of creatures existed, though not infinitely wide, for at **2.700–10** Lucretius
explains that not all atomic combinations are possible. Of the variety of animals which
emerged by chance, some happened to be endowed with qualities needed for survival,
others with qualities useful to humans.

usefulness   that humans can make use of animals is a notion which appears in the
earliest extant didactic poem we have, Hesiod's *Works and Days*. Hesiod, a probable
contemporary of Homer, is yet another poet whose style and the content of whose poem
Lucretius echoes, while at the same time sending out a very different message. In his
poem giving out instructions on how to run a farm, Hesiod digresses from practical advice
to preach against idleness and dishonesty, reminding the addressee, one Perses, of the
threat of divine anger at such conduct.

survive, relying on our care. First of all, the species of **fierce lions**, a brutal race, is protected by its fearlessness, foxes by their cunning and deer by speed of flight. On the other hand, dogs, with their **light-sleeping** faculties and loyal hearts, and the entire race born of the seed of pack-animals, the woolly sheep and the ox-horned 865 cattle – these all rely on man's care, Memmius. For such animals were eager to run from wild beasts; they sought a peaceful life and food aplenty, gained by no effort of their own, which we give them as a reward for being of use. In contrast, 870 the animals to which nature assigned none of these qualities, which could neither survive independently themselves nor provide any service to us so that we would allow their species to feed under our protection and stay safe – such animals assuredly fell prey to others as spoil, each of them bound by **the shackles of their** 875 **lot**, until nature reduced their species to extinction.

---

1 Does Epicurus' idea that mankind is responsible for ensuring the survival of certain species seem possible? Is it acceptable to modern science?

2 Does domestication remove an animal's ability to survive independently?

3 Can you think of a species which has been wiped out by humans, or one other than the dinosaurs which has been wiped out by a natural disaster?

---

fierce lions though there were no native lions in Italy, many Romans would have seen lions at the Circus, where they were primed to be especially aggressive so that they would put up a good fight in the animal hunts, spectacles in which criminals or prisoners of war, or sometimes professional animal-fighters known as *bestiarii*, were armed and made to fight against wild animals which had been imported from Rome's various subject-nations. The Roman scholar Pliny the Elder (AD 23–79) gives a long description of the character traits and behaviour of the lion in his *Natural History* 8.16.

light-sleeping a Lucretian coinage not found anywhere else in surviving Latin literature. This coining of words is part of the richness of the poem and reveals 'Lucretius' inventiveness and his scrupulous care in choosing exactly the right word to express his meaning' (Bailey, p. 138). Some of the words which Lucretius invents are found nowhere else in any extant Latin text (e.g. fruit-bearing **1.3**, dire-sounding **1.103**), others were absorbed into the language and used by later authors, yet others are only found in works where the authors (e.g. Apuleius in the second century AD) wished to make explicit reference to the *De Rerum Natura*.

the shackles of their lot Epicurus stated that the formation of a species was a matter of chance and that, once born, a race was stuck with its characteristics and could not develop. In this he differs from Darwin, who showed that a species will adapt to survive, arguing that each species developed the means to get its own food and avoid becoming another's; within each species those unable to do this would die out and thus only the 'fittest' would survive to breed; in doing so they would ensure that their species comprised those able to survive. Modern science has concluded that a species can be wiped out by a natural disaster, as the dinosaurs seem to have been, or – much more likely in our times – by mankind encroaching on its habitat and destroying its food source.

Lucretius explains that there could not have been hybrid creatures such as centaurs or chimaeras, for the fixed laws of nature do not allow certain species to interbreed. Moreover, we know that old age arrives sooner for a horse than a human, so a centaur might have the legs of an old horse but the torso of a man in the prime of life, not to mention that humans and horses eat different food. Lucretius moves on to explain that the earliest humans were much hardier than his contemporaries: they had no fire to warm them, no plough with which to produce their own food; they lived on whatever nature produced and roamed the hills thinking only of themselves. They lived naked and slept under leaves, but they did not cower in superstitious fear of the dark, for they had witnessed the cycle of day and night since they were born. Only the arrival of a dangerous animal would scare them from their resting-place during the night.

Times were no more dangerous then than now

5.988–1010   Nor did mortals depart life's sweet light with tears in much greater numbers then than now. For then one of them would quite likely be snatched up by wild beasts 990 and supply them with food that was still alive and be chewed up by their teeth, and fill the groves, woods and mountains with his shrieks as he watched his entrails being buried alive in a living tomb. But those who rescued their half-eaten body and escaped, would afterwards press shaking palms to their festering lacerations 995 and summon **Orcus** with horrific screams, until the savagery of their stabbing pain robbed them of life, utterly helpless and unaware of what was needed for their injuries. On the other hand, **a single day** did not send to their deaths many

---

Orcus   an early Italian god of death whose name is also used of the underworld itself. Lucretius' use of it here is an anachronism: at this point in human development there was no religion.

a single day   for example, Livy reports (*Histories* 22.49) that at the battle of Cannae 45,000 Romans were killed by Hannibal's forces in a single day (see note on p. 72). In the civil war between Marius and Sulla during Lucretius' own lifetime, 20,000 men were killed or captured in a single day at the battle of Praeneste in 82 BC, while at the battle of the Colline Gate (at Rome) shortly afterwards, Sulla's men killed all 6,000 surviving Samnite troops; in 53 BC at the battle of Carrhae in Parthia (south-east Turkey) 20,000 legionaries were killed under their general Marcus Licinius Crassus.

thousands of men lined up behind the standards, nor did the stormy waters of the   1000
sea dash men and ships against the rocks; but the sea would still swell and seethe,
without purpose, absurdly, in vain, and then gently put aside its empty threats: the
treacherous allure of a tranquil sea could not tempt anyone by its smiling waters   1005
into its trap. The **wicked art of navigation** lay undiscovered then. It was lack of
food that would condemn their weakening bodies to death then, whereas now they
sink under a glut of food. Often in their ignorance men used to pour poison into
themselves; **now** they administer it all too skilfully to others.   1010

---

1   What is Lucretius comparing: rates of mortality or total numbers killed? Or is
    the distinction between the two types of statistics not important to him?

2   Do you think Lucretius wants the reader to feel any pity for the primitive man
    or those killed in battle? If so, which deserves the greater pity?

3   Is one more likely nowadays to die prematurely from one's own actions than
    from a natural cause?

4   How common is it nowadays for a large number of people to be killed all at
    once? What might cause that to happen?

5   Just as sea-travel was considered dangerous in the ancient world, so some
    people nowadays refuse to fly: is that solely because they consider it
    dangerous or do they feel that it is 'wrong' in some way?

6   To judge from the tone of the last three sentences, what is Lucretius' attitude
    towards contemporary Rome?

7   Lucretius lived through turbulent times: do you think that violent eras are
    particularly productive of great art?

---

wicked art of navigation   although the Romans built sturdy seagoing vessels, captains
nevertheless preferred to sail along the coast where possible rather than to venture
across the open sea. For if a storm struck a ship sailing near the coast, it could quickly
make for shore, and if the ship were sunk, the sailors could probably swim to safety.
In the literary tradition the invention of sea-travel marked the end of an innocent era
when men did not attempt activities for which nature had not equipped them, and so
sea-travel was often portrayed as an arrogant act (Greek *hubris*) which invited disaster. In
Odes 1.3 Horace asks Virgil not to travel by sea on the grounds that men were not meant
to do so. Lucretius contrasts the dangers of prehistoric times, which could not be avoided,
with those of his own day, which he observes are undergone voluntarily.

now   this passage is unusual for the poem in that there exists no Epicurean parallel nor
any ancient reference to one. This may be because here, as at **3.59–86**, Lucretius is thinking
specifically of his own troubled times.

5.1011–1160

Lucretius begins to describe the origins and growth of civilization. Men began to construct huts, to make clothing from animal skins, to build fires and to live with a single mate, all of which changes caused them to grow soft. Neighbours formed friendships and made pacts for mutual protection instead of looking solely to their own individual interests. Then people learned to speak: language was not the invention of one person alone but arose naturally, just as animals and birds make different sounds according to their mood. Likewise fire was not discovered by a single person but was a natural consequence of a lightning strike or branches rubbing together in the wind. Next men built cities, which were ruled by kings. First the strong and handsome were honoured, later the wealthy. Men became ambitious for fame and power but others' envy brought them low. The kings were overthrown: people appointed magistrates instead and devised laws.

The emergence of religion

5.1161–1240   Now, what gained **the gods' powers** their reputation amongst great nations, filling the cities with altars and teaching men to institute solemn rituals, rituals which continue to flourish at the great sites of great empires; what causes that fear   1165
still ingrained in mortals today, which puts up new shrines across the world and makes them so busy on holy days – it is quite easy to find the words to explain all this. For even then people already saw **the magnificent forms of the gods** while   1170
their minds were awake and in their sleep their size was all the more astonishing. People granted the gods sensation, because the gods were seen to move their limbs and to make proud utterances suited to their noble features and abundant strength. People gave the gods eternal life, since their images arrived in continual   1175
supply and their form remained the same, and above all because people thought that those possessed of such great strength could not readily be defeated by any force. They thought that the gods were unsurpassed in good fortune because the

---

the gods' powers   though a primary aim of the poem is to dispel our fear of the gods, this passage is one of a very few in which Lucretius addresses the nature of religion and worship. Greek philosophers before Epicurus had suggested explanations as to why men started to worship gods: the politician Critias (fifth century BC) claimed that early rulers invented religion to keep control over their people; the sophist Protagoras (also fifth century) argued that worship of gods was an instinctive urge which had its foundation in man's share of the divine nature; the sophist Prodicus (also fifth century) asserted that early man deified the sun, the moon, the rivers and so on and later additionally invented figures who gave humans gifts such as bread and fire.

the magnificent forms of the gods   according to Epicurus the gods must exist because we perceive the images they emit, which strike the human mind both when awake and asleep. This was his only evidence that the gods existed and therefore Lucretius puts it first.

fear of death never troubled any of them and also because in their dreams they 1180
saw the gods accomplish many astonishing feats and yet undergo no exertion
themselves while doing so.

Furthermore, people observed the workings of the heavens in their fixed order and
the different seasons coming round and they were unable to establish **the reasons** 1185
why this happened. Therefore they took refuge in attributing everything to the
gods and holding that all things were guided by their will. People positioned the
abodes and haunts of the gods in the sky, because it is across the sky that night and
the moon are seen to roll – moon, day and night, and night's solemn stars and **the** 1190
night-wandering torches of the sky and its hurtling fires, the clouds, sunshine
and showers, the snow and winds, the lightning, the hail, the sudden crashes and
ominously loud rumbles.

O unhappy race of men, who have attributed such acts to the gods and added bitter 1195
anger too! What torment for themselves they created then, what injuries for us, what
tears for our children! It is **not piety** at all to be often seen, **head veiled**, turning

---

the reasons why this happened   this second cause of the emergence of belief in gods,
that primitive man was awestruck at the workings of the heavens, is the one which
Lucretius tries to counter in his poem, which argues that Epicurus has since given us a 'true
understanding' and that therefore the feeling of awe is no longer a valid justification for
believing in gods.

the night-wandering torches of the sky and its hurtling fires   respectively shooting stars
(small meteors which enter the earth's atmosphere and rapidly burn up) and meteors
(bodies of matter which become incandescent because of friction with the earth's
atmosphere and which appear as a streak of light).

O unhappy race of men   the power of such an emotional direct address is increased by
the rarity with which Lucretius uses it; he reserves it for moments (such as **2.14**) at which he
expresses pity for the ignorance of the human race of the truth revealed by Epicurus. The
'O' here is an exclamation of despair rather than an invocation (**3.1**); such exclamations
are commonly found in Greek tragedy and when used in narrative or didactic verse add
a dramatic intensity to the passage.

not piety   at issue here is the nature of worship. Epicurus was himself devout and advised
worshippers to approach an altar in a calm state, which would allow their minds more
easily to receive the images of the gods which are flying through the air. This notion
would be quite alien to most Romans, who viewed worship as a contract between gods
and mortals: mortals made offerings to the gods at their altars and it was hoped that the
gods, if pleased, would grant mortals their prayers (see note on p. 43).

head veiled   this is how Romans ritually prayed; Greeks did so with head bared. In
addition, Romans were supposed to approach a god's statue keeping it on their right and
might also prostrate themselves before it. Correct observance of ritual was important: if a
mistake were made, the entire religious act (the sacrifice, the offering, etc.) would have
to be restarted. Such superstitious slavery to ritual procedure is the sort of oppression
from which Lucretius hopes to liberate his readers.

towards **a stone** or to approach every altar, nor to lie prostrate on the ground or **to** 1200
face one's open palms towards the shrines of the gods, nor to drench the altars
with plenty of animal blood, nor to pile vow upon vow, but rather to be able to
contemplate all things with a calm mind. For when we look up at the celestial
realms of our great world and the air above dotted with sparkling stars, and we set 1205
to thinking about the course of the sun and moon, then in hearts already weighed
down with other troubles this worry awakens and begins to raise its head: that we
may be subject to the immeasurable power of the gods, which keeps the bright 1210
stars turning in their various motions. For a lack of understanding assails our
minds in their uncertainty: did the world have a beginning or birth, and likewise
is there to be an end, until which the walls of our world will be able to stand
the effort of their fretful movement? Or have these things been granted eternal 1215
existence by the gods and so will be able to glide down the endless sweep of time
and disregard the mighty power of the immensity of time?

Besides, whose mind does not shrink with fear of the gods, whose limbs do not
crawl with terror, when the scorched earth shudders under a dread lightning bolt 1220
and a rumble races across the broad sky? Do not nations and peoples tremble and
proud kings shiver as they are struck with fear of the gods, afraid that the time is
at hand to pay the penalty for some terrible crime or arrogant decree? Or when 1225
on the seas the power of a **violent squall** at its height sweeps the commander of

---

a stone   perhaps a derisive reference to the god's statue, or it may refer to the marker at
a crossroads or by the roadside, which often had religious significance by association with
the goddess of magic and witchcraft, Hecate. There was also a stone (the *manalis lapis*)
kept in the temple of Mars in Rome and brought out in times of drought, when water
would be ceremonially poured over it and ritual prayers offered.

to face one's open palms   Romans prayed in a fixed way: standing up, reaching up with
their hands and speaking aloud. It was important to refer to the deity by the proper titles
and use the correct prayer formula; after praying one might prostrate oneself on the
ground. Roman altars were positioned outside, in front of a temple or at the top of its
steps, since the smoke from offerings was thought to rise up to the heavens for the gods
to appreciate; the altar's position outside also prevented the temple from being sullied
with the blood from a sacrifice.

violent squall   De Lacy (p. 153) notes that in Lucretius' poem the sea is almost always
turbulent and dangerous. He argues that this is an implicit but deliberate rejection of
the philosophical commonplace that the world is like an orderly ship sailing before a
favourable wind with divine providence at the helm, and he adds that it was typical of
the Epicureans not just to reject opposing views but if possible to subvert them.

a fleet across the waters with mighty legions and **elephants** alike, does he not seek **peace with the gods** through **vows** and request in frightened entreaty peace between winds and a favouring breeze? In vain, since often he is snatched away by the violence of the whirlwind and swept onto the shoals of death nevertheless. So much does some **secret power** trample on human affairs and kick away the noble *fasces* and merciless axes, and thereby amuse itself. Lastly, when all the ground reels underfoot and cities are toppled and fall, or threaten to as they totter, why the astonishment if men belittle themselves and make a place in their world for the mighty power and astonishing strength of the gods to govern all things?

1230
1235
1240

---

1 Why might dreams about the divine be less common nowadays?

2 The religions of ancient Greece and Rome ascribed destructive acts to their gods: do any religions nowadays do the same?

3 How do religions define piety today? Is it in terms of thought or of action – or a mixture of both?

4 Do you think Lucretius is scornful of people's fear of the elements (lines 1218–40) or is his tone sympathetic?

---

elephants they appear rather suddenly in this passage. Perhaps Lucretius has in mind the commander Pyrrhus, who sailed across from Greece (bringing elephants with his army) to assist fellow Greeks living in southern Italy against the Romans' attempt to gain control of the whole of Italy. He defeated a Roman army at Asculum in 279 BC, but lost so many men that he complained when he was congratulated on his victory: 'One more such victory and the Romans will destroy us completely!' (Plutarch, *Life of Pyrrhus* 21); hence our phrase 'Pyrrhic victory' to describe a military success which cost almost as much as it gained.

peace with the gods (Latin *pax deorum*) a much-used phrase in Roman religious ritual and an important concept. Prosperous times implied that there was peace between Rome and the gods and such a relationship had to be maintained through proper enactment of prescribed rituals; disasters were held to be an indication that the *pax deorum* had been disturbed, either through a sin of commission, an act which angered the gods, or of omission, an act which should have been performed but was not or which was not performed correctly.

vows on the eve of a battle a commander might vow to a god that he would fulfil a certain promise, such as to build a temple to that god, in return for victory in battle. The situation here is quite different from the commander's usual position of strength: gone are his sense of control, his preparations and his plans – he is completely at the mercy of the arbitrary nature of the elements.

secret power comprises both the element of chance and the fixed laws of nature. The power is 'secret' because the former is unpredictable and the latter are unknowable to non-Epicureans.

fasces sticks bundled together with an axe at their centre (see note on p. 79). Here the combined force of chance and nature is personified: it metaphorically kicks the symbols of power out of the hands of those who hold it.

5.1241–1378

Having given an explanation for the origins of religion in his account of the development of civilization, Lucretius moves on to treat the discovery of metals, first bronze and then iron, and how they were used in making weapons; this leads into a brief description of the use of horses, lions and elephants in warfare. He then turns to agriculture: when men observed that berries dropped off trees and took root, they copied nature and began to sow and plant, so that cultivation of the land became widespread.

The pleasure of music; with progress comes dissatisfaction

5.1379–1435   Men **imitated the liquid sounds of the birds** with their mouths long before they could pursue smooth melodies in song and delight the ear. The whistling of the 1380 zephyr down hollow reeds first taught country-folk to blow down **hollow hemlock stalks**. Then little by little they learned the sweet lament that courses from the pipe when stopped by the player's fingers – the pipe invented in the pathless woods 1385 and forests and glades, among the forsaken haunts of the shepherds and the sunny places of their leisure. **So gradually** time brings each individual thing out into the open and our reasoning guides it into the realms of daylight. These melodies would 1390 soothe their minds and delight them after a full meal: for that is the time when everything pleases the heart. **So people often used to spread themselves** out in the

---

imitated the liquid sounds of the birds   an explanation suggested in Aristophanes' *Birds* and probably put forward by the Atomists. Democritus thought that primitive man learnt a great deal from the animals: by observing spiders, how to weave; by copying swallows, how to build a house; and by imitating birds, how to sing.

hollow hemlock stalks   what we call the pan-pipes (since tradition had it that they were invented by Pan, god of the countryside), several reeds of different length and thickness tied together in order and played by running the 'curled' upper lip along the level end, in contrast to the single-reed pipe, which was played using stops.

So gradually   these two lines also occur at 5.1454–5 and some editors argue that they are better located there; such repetitions often lead to debate (see note on p. 61) about whether lines are deliberately repeated by Lucretius or whether they have been inserted later by an interpolator. Once an ancient text was written down, readers or scholars often made emendations, thinking that the original scribe had made an error; when a subsequent copy was made, these emendations were often copied too. In addition, ancient scholars often made notes in the margins, which occasionally found their way into the text itself when another copy was made.

So people often used to spread themselves   these lines too occur elsewhere (at **2.29–33**), but this time Lucretius has made minor alterations of tense or vocabulary. These changes make it almost certain that he wrote both passages and they provide helpful evidence that he will deliberately repeat himself on occasion; thus they serve as a warning to us not to assume that every instance of repetition needs revision.

---

soft grass in groups under the boughs of a lofty tree near a flowing stream and
refresh themselves pleasantly at no great cost, all the more so if the weather smiled 1395
and it was the time of year when the luxuriant grass was painted with flowers.
Then they would make jokes and they would chat and laugh happily. For then **the
country muse** was at her peak; then their merry spirits would lead them to ring
their heads and shoulders with garlands woven from flowers and foliage, and to 1400
dance out of time as they clumsily moved their limbs and **trod on mother earth**
with clumsy feet, which led to smiles and happy laughter, since all these things
had the power of novelty and wonder then. It became a comfort to those who
could not sleep to maintain a song through different notes, to follow its twists 1405
and to run their curling lips over the reeds; thus today too watchmen uphold this
tradition and have learned to keep the rhythm of a song, even though they take
not one jot more enjoyment from its sweetness than did the woodland race of 1410
earthborn men.

For things which are ready to hand – unless we have experienced something
nicer before – afford very great pleasure and seem excellent, but when something
better is subsequently found, it generally spells their end by changing our feelings 1415
towards all our former favourites. Thus men started to hate acorns, thus they
abandoned beds strewn with grass and piled up with leaves. Likewise they began
to despise their clothing of wild animal skin, which had been so envied when
it was invented, I imagine, that the man who first wore it met his death in an 1420
ambush – and yet it was ripped apart among his assailants and spoiled by a lot
of blood, and so could yield no profit. So in those days it was skins, today it is
gold and purple which confound men's lives with cares and wear them out with 1425
war – and the greater blame falls on us, I would say. For the cold was torture for

---

the country muse Lucretius' description of this rural scene owes much to the Greek
tradition of pastoral poetry, which celebrated life in the countryside. However, those who
wrote such poetry were educated and articulate and they often painted a stylized and
idealized picture of country life; shepherds, who were likely to be quite unsophisticated
in real life, in these poems tend to sing rather sophisticated and contrived songs. Lucretius
copies the motifs of the pastoral genre but his country-folk are genuinely simple and
primitive.

trod on mother earth   it is not hard to believe that early man danced rather wildly; the
poet Horace (first century BC) tells us at *Odes* 3.18.15–16 that peasants enjoyed stamping
on the ground with their feet while dancing, and at *Odes* 1.37.1 he enjoins his friends to
do the same (to celebrate the defeat of Cleopatra at the battle of Actium in 31).

the earthborn, who were naked without skins; but it does us no harm at all not to have **purple** robes embellished with great figures of gold, so long as we have something cheap to protect us at least. So the human race toil perpetually without 1430 purpose and waste their lives in futile worry – without doubt because they have not learned that possessions have their limits, nor do they have any idea whether **true pleasure** can be increased. Little by little this has swept our lives out to sea 1435 and stirred up from the deep a great surge of war.

---

1 Do you agree that an improved version of a thing generally means the end of an earlier one? What might lead one to retain the older version?

2 Is it true that the modern capitalist system requires us to be regularly making new purchases in order for the economy to prosper? If so, is this likely to allow us to reach contentment?

3 Do you think one can ever be satisfied with the possessions one has?

4 To judge from this passage, do you think Lucretius has a positive view of the march of civilization?

5.1436–57

Lucretius ends Book 5 with a brief overview of assorted further developments in the history of civilization: ownership of land, sea-travel, treaties between nations, the emergence of poetry and writing. He explains that necessity brought about certain discoveries, but that others were a product of the inventiveness of men's minds and the application of their reason.

---

purple the colour of status, for the togas of senators or *equites* were bordered by a purple stripe; it was also the colour of wealth, because the dye needed to create it was difficult to obtain (see note on p. 104) and therefore very expensive. Romans had an inconsistent attitude towards ostentation: they were proud of the modesty of their ancestors but liked to flaunt their own wealth, as Horace makes clear at *Satires* 2.8, for example, where Nasidienus serves up an extravagant dinner to impress his guests.

true pleasure Epicurus argued that pleasure cannot be increased but only varied (see note on p. 30).

6 Phenomena of our world explained

Epicurus' achievement; the nature of worship

6.1–95   The first to give **corn-bearing crops** to struggling mortals in time gone by was the
city whose name is renowned – Athens. She gave them new life, **she enacted laws**
and it was she that first provided sweet consolations for life, when **she gave birth**
to a man of such intelligence, who poured forth all knowledge from his truthful   5
lips in time past. Though his light is extinguished, the glory he won long ago for
his divine discoveries has spread far and wide and now reaches up to the heavens.
For he saw how almost everything demanded and required by mortals to survive
was already provided for them and so their lives were safe, as far as was in their   10
control. He saw that men gained an abundance of power through wealth and
honour and fame, and were supreme in the fine reputation of their sons – and
that even so not one of them had a heart less troubled at home, that they made
their lives unceasingly miserable despite themselves and were driven to fury in   15

---

corn-bearing crops   in mythology the Athenian king Triptolemus was credited with the
discovery of agriculture, but in Lucretius' eyes neither this nor the gift of law to mankind
can be compared to the greatest blessing of all – that Athens raised Epicurus. Tatum
notes (p. 135) that Lucretius appears to have been 'remarkable in his exclusive veneration
of Epicurus', for by the first century BC the majority of Epicureans revered the other three
founding members of the Epicurean school (Metrodorus, Hermarchus and Polyaenus) as
much as they did Epicurus.

she enacted laws   although Athens was and still is rightly seen as the cradle of democracy,
that she is also thought to have invented constitutional law is in large part due to her
dominance in the literary tradition. Other city-states in Greece had law codes at around
the same time Athens did: for example, the city of Gortyn on Crete, whose inscribed laws
have survived on tablets of stone.

she gave birth   Epicurus was in fact born on the Greek island of Samos, off the western
coast of Turkey; his parents were Athenian and he moved back to Athens as a young
man. Although Epicurus lived just two centuries earlier, Lucretius mythologizes his life
story in these lines, using a heroic vocabulary that seems to set Epicurus in the distant
and heroic past.

Marble bust of Epicurus: Roman copy of a Greek original (third–second century BC).

angry frustration. Then he understood that **the vessel itself** caused the corruption, corruption which then contaminated all things within it which were introduced from outside, even those which arrived as blessings, in part because he saw that the vessel was so full of holes and leaky that there could never be any way of filling it, in part because he saw it infect with a sour taste whatever it took in. 20

So he cleansed their hearts with the truth of his words and set a limit to desire and fear. He set out **the highest good** which we are all striving for and he pointed out the path by which we might make for that goal by a direct route down a narrow track. 25

---

the vessel itself   the mind (Latin *animus*), as becomes apparent later in the passage. At **3.1003–10** Lucretius compared the mind to jars riddled with holes, which were used in myth by the daughters of Danaus: just as they can never fill those jars, so no quantity of good things will ever satisfy the human mind. Lucretius treats two kindred conditions: one is the problem of leakiness, that humans do not understand what their true needs are and so are never satisfied, and the other the problem of corruption, that the blessings that we do receive are tainted by our ever-present fear (of death and of the gods). There is a contrast between the things which should satisfy us (food, safety, etc. mentioned at lines 9–11) and those to which people aspire (riches, honour, fame: lines 12–13) but which do not offer satisfaction.

the highest good   that is, the absence of pain. Epicurus held that all creatures by nature seek this end and therefore for them that must be the highest good; in this he follows an idea suggested by Aristotle, namely that there is a supreme good for humans, a primary goal for life, which he called mankind's *telos* or 'end'. Other philosophers preferred to suggest some more virtuous purpose for human existence, but in a material world where all consists of atoms or void, the purpose to life must be explicable in atomic terms.

He revealed what pain there is in all aspects of human life, pain which emerges and flies out in various forms through **natural chance or necessity**, because nature had 30 arranged it so. He showed us the gates from which we are to sally out to face each of these troubles and he proved that for the most part human beings stir up these waves of care in their breasts to no purpose. For just as children tremble in blind 35 darkness and are afraid of everything, so even in the light we too are sometimes afraid of things which are absolutely no more to be feared than those which the children are afraid of in the darkness and imagine will happen. So what we need to scatter the terrifying darkness of the mind are not the sun's rays or the day's bright 40 light but an understanding of nature's outward form and inner workings. For this reason **I shall continue to weave** with words what I have started.

Now, since I have shown that the regions of our world are mortal and that the heavens consist of matter which itself came into being, since I have dissected almost everything which does happen there and which must happen, keep listening to 45 what remains. Given that I have already ventured **to mount the glorious chariot** [...] I will explain how winds get up and drop, so that everything changes back to what it was before, once such fury is appeased. I will also explain everything else which mortals observe taking place on earth and in the sky, with the result 50 that their frightened minds often waver and they lower their spirits in fear of the gods, keeping them crushed to the ground. For it is ignorance of the causes that

---

natural chance or necessity some pain is inflicted by chance events, such as disease or injury, and some arises of necessity, such as old age and death: both kinds of pain are part of the natural order of the world and are therefore quite different from the pain which the human race inflicts upon itself.

I shall continue to weave in Book 6 Lucretius will treat phenomena such as storms, earthquakes and disease, which cause mortals fear and pain but which have purely natural causes. This metaphor of weaving a tapestry demonstrates his awareness of the artistry of writing poetry.

to mount the glorious chariot an image previously used by Parmenides in the fifth century BC in the opening to his poem *On Nature*. A chariot is a heroic mode of transport (in the ancient world most people travelled by foot, in a cart or on horseback) and has a fanciful sound to it: heroes ride chariots, as do gods as they fly through the air. The chariot imagery occurs again at the end of the passage. The text is uncertain at this point and it may be that several lines are missing: Godwin hypothesizes (comm. 6.123) that a whole page may have fallen out, in which Lucretius may have 'extended the image of a poet riding the Muses' car into another "poetic preface" such as we read in 1.921–50 and 4.1–25'.

forces them to attribute such things to the **authority** of the gods and to grant 55
them absolute power. Some have successfully understood that the gods live their
lives free from care, yet if they wonder now and again how it is that everything
takes place, especially the things which they observe overhead in the realms of 60
the sky, they are whisked back again to **the old beliefs** and they **welcome stern
masters** whom in their misery they believe omnipotent, since they are ignorant of
what can be and what cannot, and indeed of the system by which there is a limit 65
to what each thing can do, a boundary-stone which cannot be moved. Thus they
lose their way even more and are carried along by reasoning that is blind.

Unless your mind spews this back up and you banish far away these thoughts
which are unworthy of the gods and quite at odds with their peaceful state, you
erode the gods' sacred powers and they will often do you harm – not that the 70
supreme power of the gods can be weakened, so that in their anger they would
thirstily seek bitter retribution, but because you yourself will have beings who are
tranquil and in serene peace stirring up a great swell of anger. Then you will not
approach the gods' shrines with a peaceful heart; you will not have the strength 75

---

authority   (Latin *imperium*) the term for power legitimately bestowed by the Senate;
'absolute power' (Latin *regnum*) was the power held by a king and so was an abhorrent
notion to the independent-minded Roman nobility. Livy (*Histories* 1.58–60) tells how
Sextus, the son of Tarquinius (the last king of Rome), was banished in 509 BC because
he raped the noblewoman Lucretia; Rome had been a republic ever since. Through the
Latin word-order Lucretius thus builds his sentence up to finish climactically with a word
(*regnum*) denoting hated and rejected authority.

the old beliefs   these compare unfavourably with Epicureanism. To the Roman way of
thinking, antiquity conferred distinction and extra weight on a religion: because Judaism
was so ancient, the Romans regarded it highly and gave it special treatment (at least
until the Jews rebelled). Likewise, a mysterious ancient black stone (the *lapis niger*) of
unknown origin sat in the Forum in Rome and was venerated more for its antiquity than
any definite religious significance.

welcome stern masters   this touches on an important theme of Epicurean philosophy,
namely freedom. Epicureans believed that while they themselves lived a life of freedom,
the uninitiated unwittingly took on a life of bondage and oppression; hence Lucretius
talks here of human spirits being 'crushed to the ground' and speaks in very similar terms
elsewhere (**1.63**, **1.69**, **5.1200**). He pities those who choose to adopt such harsh gods as
their masters – an inversion of the normal process whereby a master would choose to
acquire a slave.

erode the gods' sacred powers   it may seem a contradiction that humans cannot affect
the gods themselves but can erode their power, yet it becomes clear that it is not the
gods' power to control us which is eroded, for they cannot touch us, but the power they
unwittingly have to help us attain *ataraxia* if we accept their images into our peaceful
hearts (see note on p. 128).

to receive **in peace and tranquillity of mind** those images which pass out of their blessed being and into the minds of men as heralds of their divine form. It is easy to see then what sort of life will ensue. Indeed, so that the truest reasoning may hurl such a life far away from us – even though I have already sent many words on their way, many still remain to be adorned by my **polished verses**. I must tackle the workings of earth and sky, I must sing of storms and bright lightning, how they behave and why it is each occurs, so you do not **divide the sky into sections** and worry in your madness where the flying fire arrived from or where it went on to from here or how it could infiltrate enclosed spaces, take control and then complete a withdrawal. Show me the way ahead as I race on towards **the finish line chalked out in white**, Muse, cultured **Calliope**, relaxation of men and pleasure of gods, so that with you as my guide I may win both wreath and eminent praise.

80
85
90
95

in peace and tranquillity of mind these lines constitute the clearest and fullest account found in Lucretius' poem of what we can assume are Epicurus' beliefs about worship. We learn from accounts of his life that Epicurus visited the gods' shrines and participated in their worship, and he taught that piety is to approach the gods' altars peacefully and to accept their images into one's tranquil heart, and thereby move closer to the attainment of *ataraxia*. We have heard (**4.26–109**) that all things continuously issue images of themselves and at **5.1169–78** Lucretius discusses the gods' images in particular.

polished verses although we have no idea how quickly Lucretius composed, Virgil is supposed to have been laboriously slow in writing the *Aeneid*: on average two or three lines per day.

divide the sky into sections Roman soothsayers known as 'augurs' divided the sky into 16 parts and accordingly interpreted any occurrence, such as lightning or the appearance of an eagle or a vulture, in a particular part as an indication of the gods' wishes. This division originated with the Etruscans, an older civilization north of Rome from whom the Romans derived many of their religious practices. Even sophisticated Romans such as Cicero wrote on these phenomena (*On Divination, On the Responses of Soothsayers*) despite their scepticism towards popular religion. Barbour comments (p. 150): 'In the first century BC any Roman would have known that when Lucretius rejected augury, with its division of the sky into *templa* (regions), he was flouting something far greater: the power of Roman magistracy, law and empire.'

the finish line chalked out in white this continues the chariot metaphor from earlier in the passage. Chariot racing took place in the Circus Maximus at Rome and was the city's most popular spectator sport, in part because the Circus could hold so many (approximately 250,000 spectators) and there were so many races. While it was a literary convention that the poet would be 'crowned by the Muses', just as the winner of a real race might be crowned, there is no extant literary precedent for the image of a Muse urging the poet to arrive at the finish-line first. Lucretius may mean by this metaphor that he will be the first poet to have rendered Epicurean philosophy into Latin verse.

Calliope the Muse (see note on p. 7) who inspired poets to write epic. Lucretius plays on the name Calliope by describing her as *callida*, the Latin word for clever. In the opening lines of the poem he invoked Venus, so this conventional appeal to a traditional deity has precedent; it also echoes the language of that first invocation, for Calliope is the 'relaxation of men and pleasure of gods' while Venus was 'pleasure of men and gods' (**1.1**).

1. If you had to sum up what Epicurus' greatest contribution to humanity is according to Lucretius, what would it be?

2. What obstacles might prevent us from obtaining everything which mortal needs demand for us to survive (**6.9–10**)? Did the same obstacles also exist for Epicurus or Lucretius?

3. What would you say are people's most pressing needs in the modern world? Do those needs incur the greatest financial outlay? If not, what things do people choose to spend the most money on, and why do they want them?

4. Are people nowadays unhappy even if they are physically and materially comfortable? If so, why? Who or what could help relieve their troubles?

5. 'He saw it [the mind] infect with a sour taste whatever it took in' – do you agree with Lucretius that we cannot truly enjoy the blessings we have because we are always conscious of our mortality?

6. Does it help to be in a peaceful state when making a prayer? Is one not more likely to pray in times of despair or joy when one's mind is agitated?

7. Do you think any religion practised today has anything in common with Epicurean beliefs about the nature and purpose of worship?

8. What wreath do you think Lucretius wishes to win? Who does he think will give him eminent praise?

6.96–245

Lucretius begins his account of celestial phenomena by offering several possible causes of thunder, such as the collision of the clouds or the sudden escape of wind from clouds like a balloon bursting. He then turns to the causes of lightning and again offers several, such as the rapid movement of wind inside a cloud making it hot so that it then scatters seeds of fire, or sparks being caused by the friction of clouds colliding. Now he considers the causes of thunderbolts.

The formation of thunderbolts

6.246–94 We must suppose that **thunderbolts** are born from a dense mass of thick cloud, for none is ever dispatched in a clear sky or when cloud is packed together loosely. Indeed, observation of events proves this beyond doubt; across the sky so much 250 cloud accumulates that we imagine all the darkness has come out from every

---

thunderbolts more properly called bolts of lightning, which descend to earth to vent their charge by striking solid objects; flashes of lightning are visible in the clouds but do not strike the ground.

part of **Acheron** and filled the vast caves of the heavens, and faces of black fear loom large overhead, when the hideous night of the thunderstorm has arisen and 255 the storm begins to cast its thunderbolts. Furthermore, quite commonly out at sea too a black cloud, brimming with darkness from afar, falls upon the waves like **a river of pitch** poured down from the heavens; itself bursting at the seams with wind and with fire, the cloud drags with it a black storm pregnant with 260 thunderbolts and squalls, so that on land too people shudder and seek shelter. So we must suppose that the storm-cloud up above rises to a great height, for the land would not be buried in such total darkness unless many clouds built up high on top of many more and so blocked out the sun. Nor could they come and 265 inundate us with rains so heavy that they make the rivers overflow and the fields swim, if the upper air were not thick with clouds piled high.

So in this case everything teems with fire and with wind, and consequently there are roars and flashes in all directions. For I explained earlier that the hollow clouds 270 contain abundant seeds of heat, which they must absorb in great numbers from

---

Acheron   again we find Lucretius using conventional mythological terms when it suits his purpose, which is here to embellish his description of the storm and to conjure up the fear that such awesome natural phenomena inspire, especially in the minds of those who do not understand their causes (as Lucretius has already mentioned at **6.58–67**). Compare Lucretius' dramatic account, with its language of power and violence, to Epicurus' explanation of how the thunderbolt forms:

> Thunderbolts can occur as a result of repeated gatherings of winds, and their compression and powerful conflagration, and the fracture of one part and its very powerful expulsion towards the areas below, the breakage occurring because the places adjacent to it are more dense owing to the thickening of the clouds; and [it may occur] just as thunder too can occur, simply because of the expulsion of the fire, when a great deal of it is confined and very powerfully struck by the wind and has broken the cloud because it cannot escape to the adjacent areas since they are always compacting together. And thunderbolts can be produced in several different ways – just be sure that myths are kept out of it! And they will be kept out of it if one follows rightly the appearances and takes them as signs of what is unobservable.

> *(Letter to Pythocles* 103)

a river of pitch   Lucretius' description echoes a simile from *Iliad* 4.275–9, where densely packed clouds of a thunderstorm, falling black as pitch and causing a goatherd grazing his flock to take shelter, are compared to the dark form of a dense-packed battalion of soldiers. He extends the simile, adding the grim image of a river of pitch poured down from the heavens onto the sea, and increasing the number of spectators from Homer's single goatherd to all those on land seeking shelter, to emphasize the terrifying power of the storm. Many Romans memorized large portions of the works of great poets as part of their education and would therefore have recognized Lucretius' adaptations of lines from earlier poets such as Homer.

the fire of the sun's rays. When the same wind which is driving them together to any one place has squeezed out these many particles of heat, and has at the same time mixed itself in with their fire, then a whirlwind works its way into the cloud and spins in the narrow space, and thereby **sharpens a thunderbolt** in the hot furnace inside. For the wind is set alight in two ways: it grows hot both **from its own movement** and from contact with the seeds of fire. Then, when the wind's energy has reached its hottest and the fire has launched its heavy attack, the thunderbolt – now ripe, as it were – suddenly rips through the cloud and, stoked to blazing, it shoots out to illuminate the entire region with flashes of light. There immediately follows a loud crash and the realms of the sky above seem suddenly to burst open and crush us. Then the ground is seized by a violent shaking and rumblings race across the high heavens; for in that moment well nigh the whole storm is smashed open and shakes and roars. Once the blow has struck, a torrential downpour ensues so that the whole sky seems to turn to a deluge and pour down as if to summon us back to **the flood**. Such is the quantity of rain produced by the rip in the cloud and storm of the gale, when the thunderclap flies out with a fiery bang.

275

280

285

290

---

1 How much of Lucretius' explanation of the formation of a thunderbolt is given over to scientific explanation and how much is poetic embellishment?

2 How does Lucretius make the description of the thunderstorm both vivid and dramatic?

3 Do you think Lucretius' explanation of the cause of a thunderbolt would be enough to stop any of his readers being afraid of it?

---

sharpens a thunderbolt   the phrase may well have conjured up before the ancient reader the familiar picture (such as those found at Apollonius Rhodius' *Argonautica* 1.730–4 and Callimachus' *Hymn to Artemis* 46–79) of a monstrous Cyclops imprisoned under Mount Etna in Sicily and forging a thunderbolt to be used by the sky-god Jupiter. Lucretius here and elsewhere deliberately uses language which echoes traditional mythology in order to remind his reader of a myth while at the same time debunking it.

from its own movement   Lucretius has already explained at 6.177–8 that the wind can grow hot from its own movement. Anaxagoras and the early Atomists had suggested that objects became hot from travelling quickly through the air, a phenomenon with which space engineers have to contend in developing materials capable of resisting the high temperatures to which the outer surface of a space shuttle is subjected on re-entry into the earth's atmosphere.

the flood   in his epic poem *Metamorphoses* (1.318–415) the Roman poet Ovid (43 BC– AD 17) relates the myth that the gods sent a flood (to punish humans for their wickedness) which covered the earth and wiped out all of humankind, except for the virtuous Deucalion and his family. Lucretius describes the cataclysmic effect of the thunderstorm in similarly apocalyptic language.

Lucretius provides further possible explanations of how thunderbolts are formed: the wind itself may ignite, or wind and cloud clash like iron on stone to produce sparks. He then accounts for the speed and power of thunderbolts. They can move so quickly because they contain a large amount of energy which has built up in the clouds; in addition, they are made up of smooth atoms and therefore can fly through the air and through objects all the more quickly, and they are also borne down by their own weight and movement. Thunderbolts occur most frequently in autumn and spring, because those seasons involve a mingling of hot and cold, which results in the turmoil suited to the violent discharge of thunderbolts.

The nonsense of thunderbolt-wielding gods

6.379–422   This is to perceive the true nature of the fiery thunderbolt and to understand the force used in what it does, not by pointlessly **scrolling through Tyrrhenian** 380 **prophecies** to seek out signs of the gods' hidden intentions – where the flying fire arrived from or where it went on to from here; how it could **infiltrate** enclosed spaces, take control and then complete a withdrawal; or what damage a 385 thunderbolt strike from the heavens can do. But if Jupiter or **the other gods** do rock the sky's shining realms with a frightful bang and hurl their fire wherever

---

scrolling through Tyrrhenian prophecies   ancient texts were usually written on scrolls, which were unrolled to be read (see note on p. 26). The Etruscans, also called Tyrrhenians after their legendary king Tyrrhenus, were experts on divination and the interpretation of omens, and the Romans often looked to their expertise in such matters. Prophecies in the ancient world were often expressed in obscure riddles and set to verse, adding to their mystique.

infiltrate   as he mentions the ability of the lightning-bolt to penetrate interior spaces, Lucretius uses military vocabulary, likening it to a combat operation in which an attacking force breaches a fortification, captures it and then executes a successful withdrawal of its troops. Lines 383–5 repeat **6.87–9**.

the other gods   Etruscan lore held that there were nine gods who had the power to wield the thunderbolt, while in Greek and Roman mythology Zeus/Jupiter sometimes lent his thunderbolt to other Olympians to use: for example, Athene threw it at the ship of Ajax (son of Oileus) as he was returning from Troy, in anger at his rape of Cassandra in her temple (Apollodorus, *The Library* E5.22–6).

they want, **why do they not ensure** that the man who has brazenly committed a   390
shocking crime is struck down, exhaling lightning fire from his punctured chest
– to be a sharp lesson to mortals – rather than **an innocent man**, guilty of no base
deed, who is engulfed in the flames, embroiled in a sudden whirlwind from the sky   395
and snatched off in a blaze? Why do they also attack uninhabited places too and
expend pointless effort? Is it to exercise their arms and build up their muscles? Why
do they allow **their father's weapon** to be blunted against the ground? Why does he
himself permit this and not reserve it for his enemies? Or again, why does Jupiter   400
never launch a thunderbolt or make a racket when the sky is completely clear? Does
he himself, as soon as the clouds have assembled, then lower himself down into
them so that he may direct the impact of his weapon from up close?

What is more, why does he hurl his bolts into the sea? What charge does he lay
against the waves, the **mass of water** and the swimming plains? Besides, if he wishes   405

---

why do they not ensure   Lucretius launches a diatribe against the traditional Roman
view of the gods. Godwin comments (p. 120): 'The purpose of these diatribes is partly
to afford light relief after the scientific theory and the complex ideas, partly to promote
Epicurean ideas by ridiculing the opposition, partly also to remind the reader of the sort
of rationalist arguments that had been advanced against "theological" interpretations
of nature for centuries before.'

an innocent man   the question of why lightning strikes the innocent person is one
manifestation of the more general question of why bad things happen to good people:
those who believe that a benign Providence governs the world must find an answer to
this question. In Aristophanes' comedy *Clouds* (398–402) Socrates asks why Zeus does
not aim his bolts at guilty men but instead blasts trees or his own temple; some Greeks
thought that if a man was struck by lightning, he must have some guilty secret. Lucretius'
phrasing here echoes the description in Hesiod's *Theogony* (854–69) of the monstrous
giant Typhoeus being blasted by the thunderbolt of Zeus. However, while Hesiod narrates
a traditional story of Zeus' wrath, Lucretius repudiates both the story and the existence
of Zeus himself.

their father's weapon   Godwin detects innuendo in this phrase, suggesting (p. 123) that
the Latin word for 'blunted' has sexual connotations and that therefore Lucretius' words
conjure up a picture of Father Sky trying frustratedly to force himself on Mother Earth.
He adds that there may be similar innuendo a little later when Jupiter 'lowers himself
down into' the clouds, especially since in classical literature clouds are occasionally
used to represent women (Euripides, *Helen* 705, 750, 1219; Pindar, *Pythian Odes* 2.36;
Aristophanes, *Clouds* 341).

mass of water   Lucretius deliberately employs mock-heroic language to conjure up
an absurd visual image of Jupiter taking on not his usual adversaries but the formless
expanse of the seas. Grand expressions such as 'swimming plains' make Jupiter's actions
seem all the more ridiculous.

us to beware the thunderbolt's strike, why does he hesitate to let us see his throw? On the other hand, if he wants to wipe us out with his fire without warning, why does he thunder from exactly that region so that we may take evasive action, why does he first round up some bellowing, rumbling and darkness? Can you accept 410 that he can let loose in many directions at once? Or do you dare argue that it has never happened that there were different strikes at the same moment? No, it does happen – and must do so frequently – that, just as it may be raining or showers may be falling in many different places at once, so too many thunderbolts can 415 shoot out at the same moment. Finally, why does he shake the holy shrines of the gods and his own **magnificent homes** with destructive thunderbolts? Why does he smash finely worked images of the gods and **rob his statues of their glory** by 420 doing them violent injury? Why does he typically target high ground, why do we see the traces of his fire for the most part high up in the mountains?

---

1   We know that the guilty often get away with their actions. How do different religions address this problem? How does society address it?

2   Are we less afraid of our gods today solely because for the most part we live secure and predictable lives? Or because we do not believe our god could ever mean us harm?

3   Do any believers of today's religions fear their gods in the way that the Romans feared theirs?

4   What might be the reaction to such lampooning of any of today's religions? Would it make a difference whether the satirist was of that religion or not?

---

magnificent homes   temples, given their size, their height and frequent location on hilltops, must have often been struck by lightning. For example, Juno's temple on the Aventine hill was struck by lightning in 207 BC (Livy, *Histories* 27.7). The wooden beams of early temples would have been highly flammable and many of the famous temples of Rome were destroyed by fire caused by lightning at least once in the early part of their history.

rob his statues of their glory   in 63 BC (around the time Lucretius was writing his poem) lightning destroyed a statue of Jupiter in the Capitoline temple of Jupiter Optimus Maximus ('the best and the greatest') in Rome, which was a key site of Roman religious and political ritual. For example, it was there that Roman consuls made their vows upon accepting office and to there that generals marched in triumph.

6.423–607

Lucretius returns to his account of meteorological phenomena. He explains that clouds both contain moisture of their own and absorb moisture off the sea; then it rains, either because the wind presses on the clouds and forces the water out or because the sun's heat thins the clouds, which allows the moisture to fall. Lucretius then turns to underground phenomena, treating earthquakes first. The earth contains caverns, cliffs, lakes and rocks beneath its surface, just as it does up above. When those rocks fall, the earth's surface above is shaken; when powerful winds force their way through the caverns, the earth trembles. Then people fear the collapse of buildings overhead and the appearance of chasms beneath, and on such occasions are more ready to believe that the earth itself may one day perish.

Why the sea remains a constant size

6.608–38   In the first place, people marvel that **nature does not make the sea bigger**, since so much water runs down into it and since all the rivers come in from all directions. 610 Add the passing rains and the storms which fly in, showering and soaking all the seas and lands, add the sea's own springs too: yet compared to the sum total of the sea, all of these will scarcely be equal to the increase of a single drop. So it is less astonishing that the vast sea does not increase in size. Besides, the sun's heat 615 draws off a large portion, for we observe that the sun's burning rays will dry out

---

In the first place   this constitutes rather an abrupt transition from Lucretius' treatment of earthquakes. Given that at the end of this passage Lucretius moves straight to his treatment of volcanoes, which seems a natural progression from earthquakes, editors have suggested that this paragraph is out of place and that this is yet another indication that Lucretius had yet to revise his poem; on the other hand, it has also been suggested that the question of the increase in size of the sea is the first in a series of phenomena to be wondered at rather than feared and that therefore these lines are in their proper place, but that a few introductory lines are missing. Bailey argues (p. 165) that Lucretius often finishes one topic, digresses and then picks up the next topic as if there had been nothing in between, and he coins the phrase 'suspension of thought' to describe this habit.

nature does not make the sea bigger   this phenomenon had been observed by philosophers before Epicurus and is referred to by Socrates in Aristophanes' comedy *Clouds* (1290–2). In contrast to Epicurus, Anaxagoras held that the sea was in the process of drying out, while the Stoics suggested that the permanent fullness of the sea was evidence for divine intervention, and so it may be that Lucretius is once again implicitly attacking Stoic belief.

clothes which are dripping wet. We know that there are many seas and they are laid out over a wide area: therefore, although the amount of water which the sun sips from the sea's surface in any one place is small, nevertheless over such a large 620 expanse of water the sun will steal heavily from the waves. Furthermore, winds too can pick up a great deal of water as they sweep the plains of the sea, since we often see the roads dried out in a single night by the winds and the soft sludge 625 cake into crusts. Besides, I have explained that clouds too draw off and pick up a lot of water from the ocean's vast plain and sprinkle it all across the globe, when it is raining on land and winds carry the clouds along. Finally, since the land's 630 body is porous and since it is conjoined to the sea, **encircling the shores** all the way round, it must be the case that, just as the liquid water runs off the land and into the sea, so likewise it seeps out from the salty sea into the ground. For **the saltiness is sieved out** and the substance of water seeps back again and all of it 635 flows to converge at the sources of the rivers; then it returns overland in **sweet-tasting formation**, down a road it cut out previously and moved its waters along in liquid march.

clothes   the sun will still dry them out when they are not just wet, but dripping wet. Lucretius continues the clothing analogy by describing the seas as 'laid out', just as clothes might be put to dry in the sun. He also contrasts the sun's sipping a little from each part of the sea with its stealing heavily from the sea as a whole.

encircling the shores   a reference to the shores of the Mediterranean sea. According to the ancient conception of the world, the Mediterranean was surrounded by land, but the land itself was encircled by water known as Ocean.

the saltiness is sieved out   salt had a multitude of uses in the ancient world, most importantly to season or to preserve food. *Sal*, the Latin for salt, is the root of *salarium*, the word for 'a regular and official payment to the holder of a civil or military post' (*Oxford Latin Dictionary*) since this was originally paid in the form of salt (Pliny, *Natural History* 31): hence the English 'salary'. This may reflect the value placed on salt and its role in bartering in early times. Salt was gathered in salt-pans from man-made coastal lagoons; Lucretius could have observed first-hand how the water evaporated and the salt residue remained.

sweet-tasting formation   in Lucretius' lifetime the Aqua Marcia aqueduct (built in 144 BC) brought water to Rome from the source of the river Anio (about 50 miles (80 km) away), famed for the purity of its water. Lucretius typically adds some poetic 'honey' here: the water does not just flow along the river-bed back to the sea, it proceeds like an army on quick-march down a road carved into the countryside during an earlier campaign. When the legions conquered new territory, they set to building roads, for the primary purpose of facilitating the rapid deployment of troops, but they provided the secondary benefit of allowing trade to flourish (merchants could pay for the right to use the roads), which in turn helped to secure the newly acquired territory. The Romans understood that trade was the glue which allowed the different nations of the empire to gel, and that economic stability was a cornerstone of peace.

6.639–1229

Lucretius now treats the subject of volcanoes. He reminds us that we are not to wonder at eruptions, for volcanoes are an infinitely small part of the universe: just as things occasionally go wrong with the human body, so of necessity on a larger scale things will go wrong with the earth. He explains why volcanoes erupt, using Mount Etna as his model. He then moves on to address certain geographical phenomena: why the Nile floods in summer, why certain places are harmful to some birds or animals, why certain springs have unusual properties. He then begins a lengthy treatment of magnetism, explaining how it is that magnets repel or attract. He finishes Book 6 with an investigation into the cause of plagues, and this culminates in a description of the plague at Athens in 430 BC and the terrible agonies suffered by its victims.

The plague at Athens

6.1230–86   **The single most pitiable** and distressing feature of these times was that when individuals saw themselves ensnared by the disease and so sentenced to death, their courage failed them, they lay down with despair in their hearts, and as they gazed on all that death, they breathed their last there and then. For indeed at no time did the contagion of the ravenous disease cease to spread from one person   1235 to another, as though they were wool-bearing sheep or horned cattle, and it was mainly this which piled death upon death. For if people shunned visiting sick relatives out of too strong a craving for life and a fear of dying, soon afterwards   1240

The single most pitiable   Lucretius' account of the plague at Athens in 430 BC is based on that written by Thucydides (*c.* 460–*c.* 400) in *Peloponnesian War* 2.47–52 and this passage on 51–2 in particular, a text which we are fortunate to have in its entirety and which makes it possible to compare Lucretius' version with his source. Thucydides cites popular opinion that the plague originated in Ethiopia and spread through Egypt and Persian territory to Athens: as many as a third of those sheltering inside the walls of Athens died. Although Lucretius is following Thucydides' lead in exploring the psychological effects of the plague on people's attitudes to life and their moral choices, Thucydides, in keeping with the rest of his work, maintains an impersonal distance in his narrative, whereas Lucretius gives a more sympathetic account.

a murderous neglect would punish them with a shameful, horrible death –
abandoned and destitute. On the other hand, those who had given their services
would die from becoming infected or from the exertions which they had been
forced to undergo either from a sense of shame or by the cries of mourning,
blended with the plaintive moans of the exhausted. All the most virtuous people   1245
met this kind of death. After toiling to bury so many relatives, one on top of
another, they would come home exhausted by grief and their tears; then a good
number would take to their beds in mourning. Not a single person could be found   1250
whom neither disease nor death nor grief did not assail at such a time.

Furthermore, by now the shepherds, all the herdsmen and likewise those hardy
men who steer the curved plough had collapsed and their bodies lay crammed
together inside their huts, surrendered up to death by poverty and disease. There   1255
were times when you could see lifeless bodies of parents on top of their lifeless
children and conversely children giving up their lives on top of their mothers
and fathers. In no small measure did this misery flood in from the country to
the city, but a wilting throng of country-folk, in their sickness gathering from all   1260
directions, brought it in with them. They filled all the buildings and open spaces
and therefore – and all the more so from the heat – death heaped up piles of
them stacked together. Many bodies, laid low by thirst and curled up on the road,
lay scattered around the water-fountains, after choking on water which tasted all   1265
too sweet. Across all the public spaces and in the streets you would see many of
them exposed, weak-limbed and barely alive, disgustingly squalid and wrapped in
rags, dying amidst the filth of their bodies, mere skin and bone, well nigh buried   1270
already under hideous ulcers and muck.

a murderous neglect   those who are too cowardly to visit a dying relative themselves are
then neglected and die. Lucretius implies that the personified god 'Neglect' punishes them
for their cowardice, a notion quite at odds with the scientific explanations of Epicureanism.
Godwin notes (p. 182) that 'murderous' in Latin derives from the verb meaning to kill for a
sacrifice, so that here Neglect is killing the wicked in ritual sacrifice to himself.

the shepherds   herders and ploughmen work alone in the wide open spaces of the
countryside, but by way of grim contrast, they are now crammed up against other people
in the dark recesses of huts: this detail and that of the lifeless bodies of parents lying on
top of their children and vice versa are not in Thucydides' version – he does not describe
the effects of the plague in the countryside at all, because the majority of Athenian
country-folk had moved inside the city. Lucretius' account seems designed to evoke pity.

flood in from the country   unable to take the enemy city of Athens by force during the
Peloponnesian War (431–404 BC), the Spartans would make annual incursions into the
Attic countryside and destroy its farms and harvests. Their aim was to demoralize the
rural population both by this regular devastation and by the consequent overcrowding in
the city itself. It was this sudden increase in the population of the city which enabled the
disease to spread so quickly and to such devastating effect. In his account Lucretius gives
no reason why the country-folk of Attica should come to Athens: perhaps he thought his
readers would already know.

Death also filled up all the gods' sacred shrines with lifeless bodies, and across the city every temple to the heavenly gods remained heaped up with corpses, for the temple custodians had packed them with **guests**. For the worship of the gods 1275 and their majesty did not count for much any longer: the ongoing grief was too overpowering. The usual custom of burial was discontinued in the city – in the past its citizens had normally always been interred. For the entire population 1280 were panic-stricken and afraid, and each man in his grief buried his relative as time allowed – hastily. The suddenness of it and their poverty prompted many terrible deeds; for with loud shrieks they would place their blood relatives on top of pyres constructed for others and set their torches underneath, often coming to 1285 bloody blows rather than let the corpse be **abandoned**.

---

1 'Death by poverty and disease' – why would the poor be more likely to succumb to disease than the rich? Is illness a respecter of wealth?

2 What do you think Lucretius' purpose is when he offers such an emotive description of the scenes of death at Athens?

3 How expensive is it to bury someone nowadays? What costs are involved? What determines what happens at a modern funeral?

4 What comparisons can be made between this passage and the opening lines of the poem? Are such comparisons relevant when considering whether this passage is the intended conclusion to the poem?

5 Do you think that this is the ending Lucretius intended for his poem? If so, why might he have chosen to end the poem in such a way?

---

guests   since all the lodgings in the city were soon full, new arrivals had to find any shelter they could. Religious sanctuaries frequently fulfilled a variety of roles and some (e.g. at Epidaurus and Olympia) had extensive quarters for visiting guests, so that it was a natural extension of this practice for the temples themselves to be put to this use in times of disaster.

abandoned   it is horribly ironic that the living come to 'bloody blows' and so risk their lives for the sake of the dead, who according to Epicureanism are oblivious because their spirits cannot exist. In Thucydides' account the relatives throw a body on the pyre and walk away: Kenney (*CCL* p. 109) suggests that Lucretius adds the fighting to demonstrate the spiritual darkness from which Epicurus has rescued mankind. Many critics have been struck by the abruptness of this conclusion to the poem. Some have argued that it demonstrates that the poem is unrevised if not unfinished, others that the transition from the joyous invocation at the start of the poem to this grisly ending represents some sort of inclination in the poet towards depression. The modern critical trend has been to try to explain the ending as it stands rather than alter it because of difficulties of interpretation. Commager suggests that we can read the end of Book 6 with equanimity after understanding the Epicurean message of the poem, whereas Peta Fowler suggests (p. 232) that the ending is left open 'as a kind of test for the reader to see if she has absorbed the message of Epicureanism'.

Recommended reading

Translations

Three recent translations include *On the Nature of the Universe* by **Ronald Latham** in the Penguin Classics series (London, 1994) with an excellent general introduction by **John Godwin**; *On the Nature of the Universe* by **Ronald Melville** with notes by **Don Fowler** and **Peta Fowler** in the World's Classics series (Oxford, 1997); and *The Nature of Things* by **Alicia Stallings** in the Penguin Classics series (London, 2007), in rhyming verse and with an excellent introduction by **Richard Jenkyns**. There is also a volume in the Loeb series (Latin text with facing translation): *Lucretius: On the Nature of Things* with translation by **Martin Ferguson Smith** (Cambridge, Mass., 1924).

Texts and commentaries

Commentaries are available for each of the poem's six books. Each commentary has a useful introduction to the poem as a whole as well as to its particular book. In addition, the two volumes by **John Godwin** have translation facing the text and are designed for the reader without Latin as much as for Latinists. *Lucretius de rerum natura I*, edited with an introduction, commentary and vocabulary by **P. Michael Brown** (Bristol, 1984); *Lucretius on Atomic Motion: A Commentary on* De Rerum Natura *Book Two lines 1–332* by **Don Fowler and P. G. Fowler** (Oxford, 2002); *Lucretius de rerum natura III*, edited by **E. J. Kenney** (Cambridge, 1971); *Lucretius de rerum natura III*, edited with a translation and commentary by **Michael Brown** (Oxford, 1997); *Lucretius de rerum natura IV*, edited with a translation and commentary by **John Godwin** (Oxford, 1986); *Lucretius de rerum natura V*, edited by **C. D. N. Costa** (Oxford, 1984); *Lucretius de rerum natura V*, edited with a translation and commentary by **Monica R. Gale** (Oxford, 2008); *Lucretius on Creation and Evolution: A Commentary on* De Rerum Natura, *Book Five, Lines 772–1104* (Oxford Classical Monographs, 2004) by **Gordon Campbell**; *Lucretius de rerum natura VI*, edited with a translation and commentary by **John Godwin** (Oxford, 1991). The most complete and thorough single work on the poem is the translation and commentary in three volumes by **Cyril Bailey**, *Titi Lucreti Cari de rerum natura* (Oxford, 1947), though his commentary assumes familiarity with both Latin and Greek.

Authors referred to in the commentary of this volume

Two recent books contain a range of excellent articles about various aspects of the *De Rerum Natura*: *The Cambridge Companion to Lucretius* (*CCL*), eds. **S. Gillespie** and **P. Hardie** (Cambridge, 2007) contains a series of newly commissioned articles and includes helpful chapters by **Monica Gale**, 'Lucretius and previous poetic traditions'; **Joseph Farrell**, 'Lucretian architecture: the structure and argument of the *De rerum natura*'; **E. J. Kenney**, 'Lucretian texture: style, metre and rhetoric in the *De rerum natura*'; **Philip Hardie**, 'Lucretius and later Latin literature in antiquity'; **Reid Barbour**, 'Moral and political philosophy: readings of Lucretius from Virgil to Voltaire'; **James I. Porter**, 'Lucretius and the sublime'.

Oxford Readings in Classical Studies: Lucretius (*ORCSL*), ed. **Monica R. Gale** (Oxford, 2007), contains a range of important articles from the last 50 years, including: Monica R. Gale's own Introduction; **David Sedley** on 'The Empedoclean opening'; **W. J. Tatum**, 'The Presocratics in Book 1 of Lucretius' *De rerum natura*'; **Phillip De Lacy**, 'Distant Views: The Imagery of Lucretius 2'; **Peta Fowler**, 'Lucretian Conclusions'; **Robert D. Brown**, 'Lucretius and Callimachus'.

Also referred to in this volume is **H. S. Commager, Jr.**, 'Lucretius' interpretation of the plague', in *Harvard Studies in Classical Philology* 62: 105–18 (Harvard, 1957).

Also recommended:

On Lucretius

One easy and excellent read is **John Godwin**, *Lucretius*, in the 'Ancients in Action' series (Bristol, 2004). There are also two good books by **Monica Gale**: *Myth and Poetry in Lucretius* (Cambridge, 1994) and *Lucretius and the Didactic Epic* (London, 2001). **E. J. Kenney**'s short pamphlet *Lucretius* (Greece and Rome, New Surveys in the Classics, 1977) remains a good introduction; while **David West**'s book *The Imagery and Poetry of Lucretius* continues to be a seminal work (Edinburgh, 1969). An interesting and enjoyable take on Lucretius' influence is **W. R. Johnson**, *Lucretius and the Modern World* (Duckworth, 2000).

On the Roman world

For information about any aspect of the Roman or Greek world, *The Oxford Classical Dictionary* edited by **Simon Hornblower** and **Antony Spawforth** (3rd edition revised, Oxford, 2003) has an entry on most subjects. On the particular topic of religion, a helpful and clear guide is **Valerie M. Warrior**, *Roman Religion* (Cambridge, 2006).

On Epicurus

A good overall account of Epicureanism is **J. M. Rist**'s work *Epicurus: An Introduction* (Cambridge, 1972). A good place to start for the translated texts of Epicurus and a helpful introduction is *The Epicurus Reader* (selected writings and testimonia), translated and edited by **Brad Inwood** and **L. P. Gerson** (Indianapolis, 1994). More thorough is the work of **A. A. Long** and **D. N. Sedley**, *The Hellenistic Philosophers* (Cambridge, 1987) which contains the most important Epicurean texts whether in Latin or Greek, and includes a translation and commentary.

Glossary

Atomists a collective term for those philosophers, most of whom lived in the fifth or fourth centuries BC, who first advocated the indivisibility of the smallest elements of the universe and the existence of void. Prominent exponents of Atomism were Democritus and Leucippus: their teachings influenced Epicurus, but he developed their ideas and added to them, so that Lucretius can justifiably claim that Epicurean Atomism is an original system.

Callimachus (Cyrene, North Africa, third century BC) the archetypal example of an 'Alexandrian' poet, that is, a poet of the third century living in Egyptian Alexandria and taking advantage both of royal patronage of the arts and of the magnificent library there (Alexandrian poetry is full of learned reference). Callimachus wrote a large number of works in various genres, including the *Origins* (Greek *Aitia*) of Greek cults and festivals, hymns to the gods, epigrams and a narrative hexameter poem *Hecale* about an old woman who offers Theseus shelter in a storm. Lucretius shows an awareness of Callimachus' work, but imitates his style only to depart from his content.

Catullus (Rome, *c.* 84–54 BC) a poet writing at about the same time as Lucretius. He wrote various types of poetry, many of which were based on the works of previous Greek poets. A large number of his poems treat the pleasures and agonies of love and desire, sensations which can be contrasted with the serenity advocated by Epicurus and which Lucretius therefore often criticizes in his poem, most notably in his tirade against the destructive nature of desire at **4.1058–1148**.

Cicero (Rome, 106–43 BC) a contemporary of Lucretius: a political figure, an advocate in the courts and a philosopher. His writings are a helpful source for much Greek philosophy including Epicureanism, though he generally inclines toward Stoic ideas. He may have edited or revised Lucretius' poem in some way; in one of his letters (*To My Brother Quintus* 2.9.3), written in February 54, he comments on the *De Rerum Natura* that it is 'illuminated by much innate talent [Latin *ingenii*] as well as much poetic craftsmanship [Latin *multae artis*]'.

Democritus (Thrace, northern Greece, fifth century BC) one of the first exponents of Atomism, together with Leucippus. He advocated the existence of atoms and void, the infinity of the universe, the existence of other worlds and the lack of any ultimate purpose to the world. His theories influenced Epicurus heavily, and Lucretius mentions him by name at **3.1039** in a list of great achievers.

Empedocles (Acragas, Sicily, *c.* 492–432 BC) author of a philosophical poem *On Nature*. In it he argued for two alternating principles in the world, Love and Strife, which govern the behaviour of the four elements: earth, water, fire and air. He also advocated the existence of effluences as the basis for perception, an idea taken up by the Atomists. Lucretius follows Empedocles in writing about scientific subject-matter in poetry, though he devotes a section of Book 1 to refuting many of his theories (1.743–829).

Ennius (southern Italy, 239–169 BC) author of plays and theological and philosophical works, as well as an epic poem (*Annales*) on the history of Rome from the fall of Troy to his own times, from which Lucretius occasionally borrows a phrase or adapts one. Lucretius mentions him by name in the poem (**1.117**), acknowledging him as a founding father of Latin literature.

Hesiod (Boeotia, eighth century BC) author of two epic poems, one narrative and one didactic. *Theogony* tells of the origin and genealogies of the gods; *Works and Days* advocates the virtues of an honest life spent working the land and provides practical instruction on farming matters. Lucretius rejects both the mythological stories and the theological explanations of the world put forward in Hesiod's poems; on occasion he uses language which recalls Hesiod's poems and which therefore makes the contrast in content more noticeable.

Homer (Ionia? eighth century BC?) traditionally held to be the poet of the *Iliad* and *Odyssey*, which most subsequent ancient poets (both Greek and Roman) allude to or acknowledge in some way. Lucretius mentions him by name at **1.124** and **3.1037**, and in the poem we find various allusions to specific Homeric passages or to stories made famous by the Homeric epics.

Parmenides (Elea, southern Italy, fifth century BC) author of a philosophical poem, of which fragments survive. In it he focuses on the power of logic and argues that whatever we can conceive of must exist, since otherwise we could not conceive of it and there could not be a word for it. Therefore all philosophies which suggest that there are things which do not exist must be false, since what does not exist cannot be conceived. Lucretius borrows imagery and ideas from Parmenides' poem.

pre-Socratics a collective term for philosophers who lived before Socrates (469–399 BC) and who tried to answer the question 'What is the world made of?' or 'What is the ultimate cause of all things?'; in their number are Thales, Anaximander, Empedocles, Heracleitus and Anaxagoras. Socrates changed the focus of philosophy from such questions about the make-up of the world to ones such as 'What is our place in the world?' and 'How should we behave?' Thus Cicero could say that Socrates brought philosophy down from the heavens to earth (*Tusculan Disputations* 5.10).

Pythagoras (Samos and then southern Italy, sixth century BC) an important figure in terms of both religion and science. He is said to have introduced the doctrine of the transmigration of souls and accordingly to have suggested a special diet to avoid eating meat, and he became a cult figure at the head of an exclusive sect which lived according to his principles. He also propounded the geometric theorem named after him and in music made discoveries about the relation of octaves and harmonies to the length of the string. Lucretius rejects his beliefs about the transmigration of the soul at **3.741–83**.

Stoicism one of the two great philosophical schools which emerged in the fourth century, the other being Epicureanism, from which Stoicism differed in a number of key areas. The Stoics believed that virtue, not pleasure, is the basis for happiness and that everything happens in the world according to providence, not chance. During Lucretius' lifetime Stoicism was the rival philosophical school to Epicureanism in Rome and at times in his poem he refutes Stoic ideas, even on occasion to the point of ridiculing them. However, ultimately Stoicism won out and the popularity of Epicureanism fell away, only undergoing a revival a thousand years later.

Index